"You taste so sweet," he murmured against her hair.

He reached up and tugged off her veil, sinking his hands in the bounty of her hair and loosening it. The wind caught the long, dark strands, billowing them about, enveloping him in her scent of flowers and spice—of woman. He smoothed his fingers through the fragrant mass, the feel of its softness brushing against his skin sending shards of heat to stoke the fire of madness burning through him.

She stroked his scalp, his neck, before her hands caressed their way to his arms. "You've such strength," she whispered, closing her hands about his upper arms as she met his eyes. "Yet you are so gentle with me." She looked down for a moment, then met his eyes again, her own a smoldering blue. " 'Tis an exciting combination."

'Twas a miracle he didn't leap out of his skin…!

Dear Reader,

This month our exciting Medieval series KNIGHTS OF THE BLACK ROSE continues with *The Conqueror* by Shari Anton, when a prized knight returns from war to clam his promised reward—marriage to his liege lord's daughter—but finds she's betrothed to another.... *The Marrying Man* by bestselling author Millie Criswell is a darling marriage-of-convenience tale about a spunky mail-order bride who tames a rough coal mine owner and his tomboy daughter. Pat Tracy concludes THE GUARDSMEN series with *Hunter's Law,* in which a haunted rancher decides to take the law into his own hands and falls into the path of a beautiful Eastern miss on a "rescue" mission of her own. And don't miss *Lady of the Keep,* another terrific L'EAU CLAIRE book by Sharon Schulze. Here, a knight falls in love with the pregnant widow he is sent to protect.

For the next two months, we are going to be asking readers to let us know what you are looking for from Harlequin Historicals. We hope you'll participate by sending your ideas to us at:

Harlequin Historicals
300 E. 42nd St.
New York, NY 10017

Q. What types of stories do you like; i.e., marriage of convenience, single father, etc.? ______________________

____

Q. Are our books too sensual or not sensual enough? _______

____

Whatever your tastes in reading, you'll be sure to find a romantic journey back to the past between the covers of a Harlequin Historicals novel. We hope you'll join us next month, too!

Sincerely,

Tracy Farrell
Senior Editor

SHARON SCHULZE

LADY OF THE KEEP

HARLEQUIN®

TORONTO • NEW YORK • LONDON
AMSTERDAM • PARIS • SYDNEY • HAMBURG
STOCKHOLM • ATHENS • TOKYO • MILAN • MADRID
PRAGUE • WARSAW • BUDAPEST • AUCKLAND

ISBN 0-373-29110-8

LADY OF THE KEEP

This edition published by arrangement with Harlequin Books S.A.

Visit us at www.eHarlequin.com

Printed in U.S.A.

Available from Harlequin Historicals and SHARON SCHULZE

Harlequin Historicals

**Heart of the Dragon* #356
**To Tame a Warrior's Heart* #386
**The Shielded Heart* #442
**The Hidden Heart* #484
**Lady of the Keep* #510

*The L'Eau Clair Chronicles

To Patrick and Chrissy,
my two most wonderful creations.

Prologue

Ireland, 1215

Moira FitzGerald released her hold on her husband's callused hand and let it rest, flaccid and pale, against the heavy woolen coverlet. She lowered her palm and cupped it round the bulk of her belly, then, ignoring Father Thomas's offer of help, struggled up off her knees and stood. Forcing herself to look upon what remained of her lord and husband, she bent and kissed his grizzled cheek. ''Forgive me, milord,'' she murmured, too low for the priest to hear.

Straightening, she crossed herself. ''May God speed you on your way and give you ease.''

The babe chose that moment to kick hard beneath her ribs, the vigorous sign of life in this chamber of death piercing her heart with sorrow. *And may God have mercy on us both,* she thought, placing a soothing hand over her fatherless child.

The child stirred once more. Despite her burden, Moira stood tall and willed her face into an emotionless mask as she stared at the remains of the once-vital man she'd wed.

Life and death…all her sins come to fruition.

Her hands cupped her belly yet again. Never more, she vowed, would she permit another to pay the price of her misdeeds.

Chapter One

'Twas nothing like FitzClifford.

Connor FitzClifford stood atop the headland and stared down upon the fortress of Gerald's Keep. Nestled among the rolling hills, its massive bulk rose dark and brooding from the soft green Irish countryside, the tall tower a dagger thrust deep into the heart of the land.

Abandoned huts dotted the hillside below him, the simple stone and turf structures melting back into the earth that had spawned them. In time, they'd disappear with barely a trace.

'Twas ever the Norman way, he thought, scrambling over the rocky slope to his restless mount. Conquer, wreak vengeance, then sap the lifeblood of the people until they were gone from sight, if not from memory.

Just as his Irish mother had been crushed within his Norman father's keeping.

He turned from the scene below him, looked back to the churning sea and allowed its simple power to wash away the curious thoughts. His hand clenched hard about the well-worn hilt of his sword. His world lay outside the turbulent landscape of his mind, he reminded himself. Thinking had done nothing to ease his plight or that of those he loved, nor had it changed one whit the hellish reality of life at FitzClifford.

Deeds, not thoughts, had changed his world, brought light into the darkness of his existence, shown him another way to live.

That they'd been the deeds of another, and not his own, was a shame he would carry with him to the grave.

But he'd learned from past mistakes, and had no plans to repeat them. Never again could anyone call Connor FitzClifford weakling or coward.

Though fool he undoubtedly was, to permit the past to taint the present.

He shook off the lingering disquiet and strode back to his men. They'd paused along the winding road to rest the horses before completing the last, rugged stretch of the journey.

They stirred to motion when he drew near, packing away food and drink and preparing to leave.

"Here, milord," said Will. The former man-at-arms—now a knight newly made—had come from l'Eau Clair, the keep belonging to Connor's sister by marriage. He smiled and held out a squat pottery flask. "I've a new drink for you to try. This Irish brew is as fine—" he waved the bottle beneath his nose and rolled his eyes "—nay, 'tis better than anything we've got at home. 'Tis sure to burn the travel weariness from your bones."

Connor took the jug, raised it to his lips and let the smooth fire of usquebaugh warm its way to his belly. He grinned as Will's roguish look gave way to surprise. The young Norman had doubtless expected the potent drink to knock him on his arse. "Burn the flesh from your bones, more like," he said, sampling the brew again before returning the flask to Will. "'Tis a rare treat. I thank you."

Will tucked the flask away in his saddlebag. "Thought

I had you fooled again, milord.'' He shook his head and laughed. ''I'll have to try harder next time,'' he added, climbing into the saddle.

Connor took his stallion's reins from Padrig, his newly acquired squire, and mounted up, wondering all the while what bit of mischief Will might think of next. For the entire journey from the Marches, the Norman seemed to have made it his purpose in life to jolt Connor's hard-won air of composure with his japes and tricks.

Of course, Will had no notion that that composure was naught but a sham, an invisible cloak Connor drew about himself to conceal the weak, cowering fool he'd been.

Will was doomed to failure, however, for Connor had no intention of allowing that coward free rein ever again.

His men formed up into two columns behind him. ''Gerald's Keep sits over the next rise. We'll have a hot meal and dry beds tonight,'' he told them, nudging his horse into motion and preceding them down the road.

'Twas nearly dusk by the time they guided their mounts up the narrow, rocky track to Gerald's Keep. The road had dwindled to little more than a path scarce wide enough for a man to lead his horse, and the terrain grew more rugged the closer they drew to the castle.

Connor knew that once he stood within the walls of the place, he'd admire the ingenuity of the man who'd built atop this rocky crag, even as he cursed him for it now. But the journey had been long and hard, and he was eager to be done with it.

He shook his head. He'd once envied his brother Rannulf the freedom to travel from one end of the country to the other. Considering 'twas Rannulf who'd sent him here—while remaining at home with his wife and child—it seemed his twin still had the better bargain.

Connor halted at the edge of the spike-strewn dry moat, his men and their horses restless behind him. The raised drawbridge made an impenetrable barrier—a good sign, he thought, except for the fact that they stood on the wrong side of it. He could see no one atop the walls, nor were there any torches lit against the encroaching darkness. Yet he could hear people within.

Had they so few men they couldn't mount guards? "Open up, in Rannulf FitzClifford's name," he shouted.

After an interminable wait, light glowed through the shutters covering the tower windows, then appeared atop the battlements. "Who's there?" cried a voice too high in pitch to be that of a man grown.

Connor handed the reins to his squire and stepped closer to the edge of the moat. "I am Connor FitzClifford, sent by my brother Rannulf to bring you aid."

"Indeed? And have you proof of who you are?" 'Twas a woman speaking, no mistake. Mayhap the situation was worse than they'd thought, else why not send a man to answer his summons?

"I've a letter from my brother. Will you lower the drawbridge so I might give it to your master?"

"Not likely," the woman said, her tone harsh. "Do you think we're fools?"

"Nay. But how do you propose I hand over the letter, mistress? Shall I shoot it over the walls impaled on an arrow?"

"You needn't mock me. And a letter means little—it could be forged." Though she said the French words slowly, her accent bespoke nobility. One of the women who attended Lord Brien's lady, perhaps? Whoever she was, she sounded as though her patience was stretched to the limit.

So was his. In truth, his attention had been focused more on reaching the place; he'd scarce given a thought to how they'd gain entrance once they arrived. "Madam, I know of no other way to prove—" Someone jostled him, then stood beside him on the embankment. Connor glanced over and saw Will.

"Do they know Lord Rannulf?" Will asked. "If they do, they only need to look at you to know you for his brother."

"True." He felt a fool himself, not to have thought of that solution. "Madam, surely there is someone within who knows my brother?"

Though he could not see the woman clearly, he could tell that she'd turned away to speak with another shadowy person behind her. She nodded, then mounted the torch she held in a bracket on the outer wall of the tower. "I have met Lord Rannulf myself. Is the resemblance between you so great?"

"Aye, madam," he said with a laugh. "To see me is to see my brother's face." More or less, he added silently, the thought deadening his mirth nigh before it had begun.

"You alone may enter the bailey, sir," she said, "that I may judge for myself whether you're the man you claim to be."

"I thank you." He bowed, though he doubted she could see him in the deepening gloom. Her nodded response proved his assumption wrong, however, and made him glad he'd made the effort.

Her movements awkward, she turned away and left the wall without another word.

"Padrig, bring the letter from my pack," he ordered while he waited for the drawbridge to come down. He took the rolled parchment from the lanky lad and handed over his helm. "I won't need this."

"You'll be careful, milord?" his squire asked, though

he appeared more intent upon polishing the dust of travel from the helm with the tail of his tabard.

"Aye." Connor had yet to grow accustomed to having someone concerned for his well-being, but that seemed to be one of his squire's many obligations. "Though I doubt there's anyone within who's ready to risk their overlord's wrath by harming his brother," he added wryly.

Will gave a mirthless laugh. "You'd be surprised what some are capable of, milord." Eyes squinting in the dusky shadows, he peered at the keep. "Wouldn't hurt to have a care," he added, checking his sword in its sheath. "We'll be ready to come fetch you, should the need arise."

Nodding his thanks, Connor fought back a grin at Will's eagerness for battle. While he himself enjoyed a good fight as well as the next man, he'd just as soon not engage in one tonight.

Nor did he believe he'd have to.

The squeal of metal upon metal heralded the drawbridge's ponderous descent, and they backed out of the way. As soon as the platform hit the embankment, Connor gave Padrig an encouraging slap on the back and headed into the torchlit maw of Gerald's Keep.

Moira took her time as she made her way down the steep stairs of the gatehouse and entered the bailey to await FitzClifford's arrival. The uneven cobblestones felt slick beneath the soles of her boots, and her balance of late had become uncertain. Despite the circumstances of her child's creation, she'd do everything within her power to ensure the babe's well-being.

She reached beneath the enveloping folds of her mantle and smoothed her gown over the mound of her belly. The child grew apace, and now, with scarce six weeks left before her time, Moira couldn't help wondering whether 'twas possible for her body—and her patience—to stretch any further. Her back ached, her ankles swelled and she'd a shrew's temper most days.

Ah, Moira, you'll never again be vain about your looks after this, she thought with a quiet laugh.

A meager guard—a large portion of their able-bodied men—gathered near the gate as the drawbridge creaked downward. They stood ready to protect the keep should the party outside try to make its way within, ready to seize the man she'd spoken with if he proved a threat.

She prayed neither event occurred, for she had grave doubts about how well many of them could fight. 'Twas evidence of how desperately they needed the help she'd requested from Lord Brien's overlord.

Light footsteps echoed down the stairwell behind her. "I still say you shouldn't be here, milady," Sir Ivor, one of her husband's few remaining knights, said. He halted beside her, his thin face looking more stern than usual in the uncertain light. "What if 'tis another MacCarthy trick? They're capable of anything to gain what they want, as you know better than most, milady."

She forced herself to meet his gaze, to remain as placid as a milch cow beneath the censure he didn't bother to disguise. He alone of Lord Brien's men held her accountable for all that had happened since the MacCarthys decided to make Gerald's Keep their own. Though there were times his blame of her matched her own, she had no intention of making him aware of that fact. Her guilt was hard enough to face in the endless, lonely nights since her husband's injury and death. She'd not drag it out into the harsh light of public scrutiny. "The MacCarthys don't know we sent to Lord Rannulf for help." Nodding toward their men, she murmured, "Look at them—they'd give their lives to save us all, but there are so few of them left. We've been lucky till now, but how long can they prevail if the MacCarthys return?'' She shook her head. ''We must let FitzClifford in. 'Tis a risk we must take. We've no chance of withstanding another attack otherwise.''

Sir Ivor frowned, but nodded. ''You'll stay back until we've determined he's no threat, at least.''

''I will not. How am I to tell if he is who he claims he is, unless I'm close enough to see him?'' She gathered her skirts in her hand and started toward the men clustered by the gate, then paused and glanced back at him over her shoulder. ''I'll simply have to trust you to protect me.''

''I gave my word that I would, milady,'' he said, though his scowl deepened. His hand clutched tightly on his sword hilt, he strode past her and positioned himself at the head of the guards as FitzClifford—alone, she noted with relief—passed through the gate. She hastened forward in turn.

FitzClifford halted just inside the bailey, hands out at his sides to show he held no weapons. Moira drew a deep breath, smoothed her palms down the rough wool of her skirts and moved closer.

Despite his stance, he bowed, then glanced up at her as Sir Ivor stepped forward and reached out to take his sword. ''Nay, you need not disarm him,'' she cried. She lunged and caught Sir Ivor by the arm, holding on to him as much to steady herself as to halt his action. Shifting, she found her balance and released him at once.

''Milady, stay back,'' Sir Ivor protested as she moved closer still, staring at Lord FitzClifford in the flickering torchlight.

Moira looked FitzClifford full in the face and nodded. ''Aye, milord, 'tis true you've the look of your brother.''

So alike—and yet so very different.

His face appeared much the same as his brother's—his twin, she thought as she sank into an awkward curtsy and accepted his hand to steady her as she rose. They could not be so similar otherwise. Wavy auburn hair; dark eyes sharp with intelligence; his tanned, handsome face spattered with a redhead's freckles...

But this FitzClifford's hair fell loose and waving to his shoulders, a narrow scar slashed his left cheek from cheekbone to jaw, and he carried an untamed aura about him that she'd not observed in her admittedly brief contact with his more polished brother.

He did have the same air of courtesy, she noticed as he continued to clasp her hand within the callused strength of his. "Are you well, milady?"

"Aye, sir. 'Tis just that I'm a bit unsteady on my feet these days."

He nodded and released her. "You believe that I'm Rannulf's brother Connor, then?" he asked, his mouth curved in a faint smile.

"How could I not, milord?" She returned his smile, then fought back a grimace as the babe chose that moment to kick hard. She placed a comforting hand upon the mound of her belly, not that it ever did much to soothe the child. "I am Lady Moira FitzGerald, Lord Brien's widow. Welcome to Gerald's Keep, sir, and thank you for coming to help us."

"I am glad to be of service, milady. Will you send for my men now?"

"Of course." She gave the order before turning to present Sir Ivor. "Sir Ivor d'Athée, milord, my late husband's man—" Pain twisted through her belly, wrenching the air from her lungs and causing her legs to crumple beneath her.

Strong arms caught her, lifted her and cradled her against cool, rough mail. "By the Virgin, lady, is it your time?" FitzClifford shifted her so that her face rested on the soft wool of his tabard. ''Where shall I take her?'' he asked, his voice urgent.

Moira couldn't reply. She could only wrap her arms about her stomach and try to breathe as the pain continued to swell.

''This way, milord,'' she heard Sir Ivor say. She opened her eyes, raised her head, tried again to speak.

The world went black and she knew no more.

Chapter Two

With Lady Moira cradled in his arms, Connor followed d'Athée through the bailey to the keep and up a steep flight of stairs into a dim and smoky hall. Sir Ivor shouted for a maidservant before leading him to a narrow spiral staircase at the far end of the wide expanse. "The master's chamber is above, milord," he said, hesitating at the foot of the stairs.

Connor glanced down at the woman nestled limply against his chest. She'd not awakened yet, though a moan escaped her once again and her pale face contorted with pain as another spasm stiffened her entire body. Her veil had slipped aside, sending a long spill of straight dark hair cascading over her. Murmuring comfort, he tugged the cloth free and handed it to Sir Ivor, then brushed her hair away from her face. "If you'll not come with us, get out of my way." Not waiting for a reply, he shouldered the knight aside and mounted the first, uneven steps.

"We should wait for a maid, for someone," Sir Ivor protested. "'Tis not seemly to go up there with her alone."

Connor stopped and turned to look back at the smaller man. "Why? Is your lady such a threat?" He didn't bother to hide his disdain—nor his disgust. "Or if you're concerned I might harm her, I assure you I've never attacked *any* woman, let alone one in Lady Moira's condition.''

He ignored Sir Ivor's sputtered protests and climbed the rest of the way. Lady Moira had begun to stir, and he wanted to settle her someplace more comfortable than curled up in his arms. What if he caused her or her child some injury?

A short, door-lined corridor lay before him, lit by two torches at the top of the landing. He chose the sturdy, iron-bound door at the end as the most likely one and shifted the woman in his arms so he could reach for the latch.

She groaned. ''Why are you bringing me here?'' she asked, her voice scarce loud enough to hear. ''Set me down.''

Connor opened the door and carried her inside. ''Be easy, milady. Someone will be here soon to help you.'' Moving carefully in the dark room, he bumped against a bed frame, turned and bent to ease her onto the mattress.

''Nay,'' she whispered. When he would have straightened and stepped away, she clutched at his arm, pulling herself up to sit on the edge of the bed. ''Not here.''

He covered her hand with his own, turning it so she grasped his fingers rather than his hard, rough sleeve. ''Milady, you need attention. What does it matter where you rest?''

''I cannot stay in here.'' Her fingers tightening about his, she moaned and, though curled in on herself, tried to climb off the mattress.

Stubborn woman!

He scooped her up and strode into the corridor just as a maidservant reached the top of the stairs. ''Where should I take her?''

The woman, red faced and out of breath, gestured toward a door near the head of the stairs and, snatching a torch from the wall, hurried ahead of him to open it. "Here, milord." She stuck the light into a bracket near the door and went to push aside the bed curtains.

He settled Lady Moira against the mound of pillows at the head of the bed and moved back for the servant to attend her.

"Now then, milady, 'tis most discourteous to force Lord Connor to work so soon after he's arrived," the maid scolded. "You'll have him ready to turn round and head back to England."

Shocked by her words, Connor observed the woman more closely as she fussed with the bedclothes and loosened the ties at the neck of Lady Moira's gown. Though her voice and her age-seamed visage expressed naught but the good-humored nagging of a loyal servant, her eyes told of her worry and concern.

Footsteps sounded on the stairs, heralding a small army of servants bearing hot water, a basket of dried peat and a stand of candles. He moved toward the door, planning to leave and let them be about their business. They'd wish him elsewhere—as would he—once Lady Moira's labor progressed any further.

"Lord Connor," Lady Moira called, halting him before he could leave the chamber. Ignoring the bustle surrounding her, she held out her hand to him. The maidservant stepped aside so he could return to her mistress. He took Lady Moira's hand and cradled it in his. "Thank you for your kindness." She squeezed his fingers before slumping back against the pillows. "And for bringing your men to our aid. I fear we'll have need of them before much longer."

"Don't worry about that now," he told her. "You've more important concerns for the moment." He bowed. "Sir Ivor will be help enough, I'm sure."

A frown crossed her face, but she nodded. "Thank you, milord," she whispered, closing her eyes.

Connor left, grateful to be away when he heard her voice raised in a pain-filled cry as he descended the stairs. She'd likely been eager for him to go, to leave her to deal with her discomfort without a stranger's intrusion.

It didn't appear that Sir Ivor had moved since Connor carried Lady Moira upstairs, for he still stood at the bottom of the steps, her veil clutched in his hand. But he seemed unaware of the activity surrounding him, his attention focused instead upon the cloth. He continued to stare at it once Connor had reached him, his face twisted into an unmistakable expression of hatred.

"Sir Ivor, will you show me where my men are to be quartered?"

The knight started, then glanced up, his face shifting almost at once to a look of polite interest. "Milord?"

Connor repeated his request, adding, "And have someone show my squire where we're to lodge, if you will."

"Aye, milord." He stepped past Connor and shouted up the stairs for a manservant.

Connor pulled Sir Ivor back and called upstairs himself to overrule the order. "Are you mad, or simply a fool?" he demanded, noting the hatred glowing in Sir Ivor's eyes once again. "Your lady's need is greater than mine!"

"But you said—"

"If there aren't servants enough without taking one away from Lady Moira, then you may carry out my orders yourself." Connor turned his back on the other man and headed across the hall. His temper flared hotter with every step, so that by the time he heard d'Athée's light tread behind him, he'd gladly have picked up the other man and tossed him against the nearest wall. Damned arrogant fool! How dare he ignore his lady's distress, then act as though her needs meant nothing?

Connor tugged open the door and waited for Sir Ivor to catch up to him. He would make it a point to learn the reason for the man's behavior before much longer.

Moira smoothed her hands over the mound of her belly, pausing to stroke her fingers against the tiny protrusion where the babe pressed foot or elbow hard against her. *Soon, little one, soon I'll be able to touch you, to hold you.*

But not quite yet. According to Brigit, these last pains, strong though they'd been, were naught compared to true labor.

Moira only hoped she'd not disgrace herself completely when that time finally arrived. While she told herself again and again that she'd bear the pain gladly—that she *deserved* to feel pain after all that had happened—she feared she'd find herself unequal to the task.

Only look how she'd crumpled at Lord Connor's feet, how she'd clung to him like a weakling as the pain clutched its fist about her womb! 'Twould be a miracle if he didn't take his men and leave them—leave *her*—to face the MacCarthys alone.

She'd do whatever was necessary to keep him there, for 'twas clear Lord Connor was a warrior through and through. He'd carried her as though she weighed nothing; despite wearing mail from head to toe, he moved with a grace and ease that bespoke long familiarity with such cumbersome garments. He bore himself with confidence, wore an air of command that would surely weigh heavily against the MacCarthys the next time they threatened Gerald's Keep.

She could only trust that Lord Connor FitzClifford could

protect her child from the men who sought to take him from her.

If he would, once he heard the truth about their situation, and her part in it.

Connor rose as the sun began to tint the sky with color, drew on his chausses and shirt, took up his sword and crept past the sleeping servants whose pallets lined the floor of the great hall.

It seemed as though he'd just gone to bed, since he'd refused to seek his rest until he'd seen his men settled. After that he'd conferred briefly with Sir Ivor about the defenses and spoken with Brigit, Lady Moira's servant, to learn how she fared. 'Twas a relief to know 'twas not her time after all, especially since her child wasn't due for weeks yet. The poor woman had suffered much—lost much—these past months, from what the maid told him. Who could say what the sorrow of losing a child might do to her?

But according to Brigit, 'twas naught but false labor—no doubt caused by the recent loss of her husband, as well as concern for her home and people—that had dropped Lady Moira into his arms the night before. Perhaps now that he'd brought more men to defend her home, 'twould ease her mind and permit her to await her babe's arrival in peace.

If he were to successfully safeguard Gerald's Keep, Connor couldn't relax his vigilance, nor his training, one whit. He'd worked hard these last few years to mold himself into a warrior, and he refused to allow himself to fall into his old habits.

Besides, now that he was awake, he looked forward to the daily ritual with anticipation. The air still carried a trace of the night's chill and more than a hint of the damp his mother had claimed gave Irishwomen their beautiful skin.

There was a softness to the air here that he'd never noticed at FitzClifford, an almost otherworldly aura that enveloped everything in a mystical cloak.

The bailey stood empty, its solitude perfect for his needs. Finding a sheltered corner, grass-covered rather than muddy, around the far side of the keep, he set aside his sword and removed his shirt to stretch the kinks from his back.

Once his muscles had warmed, he took up the weapon and began the series of training drills that Walter, an ancient soldier left from his grandfather's days, had taught Connor when he'd decided to bolster his courage and become a warrior.

He'd been surprised to learn that the discipline and exertion also cleared his head and helped him to order his thoughts. They'd strengthened his mind as well as his body, enabling him to see the world in a much more adult manner than had been his wont for most of his life.

As he swung the sword, thrusting and parrying against an invisible enemy, his thoughts strayed back to those days a few years earlier. Back then he'd been a spineless weakling—the coward Rannulf had proclaimed him to be as their father lay dead at their feet.

The throbbing pain in Connor's face, where their father's dagger had traced a path along his left cheek, had been as nothing compared to the anguish he'd felt inside as Rannulf's words—his accusations—struck deadly and deep within his heart.

They'd added their weight to the guilt already echoing through him.

Guilt resolved nothing, could not bring their father back to life, God forfend, but it could force Connor to look within himself and vow to change.

He knew better than most just how empty words—vows

and promises—could be. He'd not allow himself to fall into that trap ever again.

His breathing short, sweat pouring down his face and chest, he stopped for a moment, focusing his attention on his surroundings. He lowered the sword and arched his neck, then paused in midmotion when he caught sight of the woman sitting just inside the open window above him.

He bowed. "Good morrow to you, milady," he called up to Lady Moira.

"Indeed it is, milord," she said. She held a brush in her hand, her hair falling in a smooth, shining swath of brown over her shoulder. Unlike her previous pallor, healthy color rode high along her cheekbones this morning, although the shadows beneath her eyes showed she'd not recovered completely from the past night's events.

From this angle, her condition wasn't apparent. All he saw now was a lovely young woman, not a widow great with another man's child. She drew the brush through her hair, reminding him of the women in the tales his mother had told to him and Rannulf when they were small, stories of beautiful, mysterious women who could enchant a man with naught but a glance or a smile.

Lord help him if she *did* smile at him. He'd not realized last night how lovely—and tempting—she was. He looked away for a moment, then felt a fool. He had strength enough to resist any temptation. He met her gaze fully. "How fare you this morn?"

"I am well, and have suffered no ill effects, so Brigit says. She'd best allow me out of my chamber, for it looks to be a fine day," she said, though her gaze appeared fixed upon him, not the brightening sky.

He glanced down, recalling only then his state of dress—or undress. Hoping she'd think the flush he felt climbing his face a result of his exertions, he set aside his weapon, picked up his shirt from the ground and slipped it over his head. "I beg your pardon."

She waved aside his apology and sat forward, leaning closer to the sill. The shutters were open wide, revealing her precarious position. His heart faltered at the sight. "Nay, 'tis I who must cry pardon, milord, for interrupting you. I didn't mean to—"

"Milady, please move back from the window," he said, his voice sounding much calmer than he felt, for he feared to startle her. "For your own sake, if not for that of my heart—" she looked down, gasped and moved away from the edge "—which I swear has ceased to beat." He drew in a shaky breath and nodded. "Thank you." Bending, he picked up his sword belt and sheathed the weapon. "You did not interrupt me," he added as he straightened and wound the belt about the scabbard. "I was nearly finished."

Lady Moira edged closer to the window, moving much more cautiously this time. "Would you be willing to track down Sir Ivor and bring him with you to my solar? I'm certain you have questions about our situation. Brigit will bring food," she offered. "I wouldn't want you to think that the poor greeting you received last night was an example of our hospitality."

Her invitation fit in well with his plans for the morning. The sooner he learned precisely what had happened at Gerald's Keep, the faster he could act to resolve the problem and go home.

Though that plan held scant appeal.

He tucked his sword under his arm and bowed. "I thank you, milady. Sir Ivor and I will join you as soon as I find him."

Her movements slow but surprisingly graceful, she stood and leaned against the window frame, causing his heart to falter again. This time, however, he couldn't be certain whether fear for her caused the reaction, or some other, less benign, reason.

For as she stood there with the morning sun shining full upon her, her hair gleaming, her body rounded with child, 'twas all too clear to him that Lady Moira FitzGerald was a very enticing woman.

The image of Lord Connor stripped to the waist, his skin gleaming with a healthy sheen of sweat from his labors, filled Moira's mind as she finished dressing and sat to braid her hair. His movements as he spun and feinted with the heavy sword had possessed a grace she'd never before associated with fighting. She'd witnessed swordplay aplenty over the years, for her three brothers were always practicing with each other—or fighting each other, she thought dryly. Lord knew, if they'd no enemy to battle, their tempers grew so fierce 'twould take a saint's own patience to live peacefully with them.

But neither her brothers nor her late husband, fit though he'd been, especially for a man of his years, had ever worn that look of intensity, of focus, that she'd seen in Lord Connor. What thoughts filled his mind? Would his skill at arms be that much greater than Lord Brien's or her brothers'?

If so, then mayhap the MacCarthys had finally—blessedly—met their match in Lord Connor FitzClifford.

Unable to sit for long with any comfort, she roamed the chamber, pausing yet again to rearrange the dishes and the platters of food on the table before giving up and easing her bulk onto a cushion-lined settle near the window. She took up her needlework, but the simple embroidery about the neck of the tiny gown required little attention, and her thoughts soon wandered back to the man Lord Rannulf had sent to help them.

Don't follow that path, she cautioned herself. What did she know of men, after all, save that they did as they wished—usually without giving much thought to any matter beforehand—and that she'd never been more than a powerless pawn beneath the thumb of one or another?

Just as her mother had been caught within her father's power, before she—and her babe with her—had succumbed to a difficult childbirth when Moira was ten years old. A chill ran down her spine as *that* possibility burrowed into her thoughts. But matters of life and death were in God's hands, not her own.

She fought back the sob threatening to fill her chest as she considered what *was* within her control. Could she be so easily tempted where men were concerned? Blessed Mary save her, all it took for one to lead her astray were a few kind words to her, and a friendly smile.

She must never forget where that path led. To death, and suffering, and guilt enough to weight her down for the rest of her life.

'Twas the litany she repeated each morn before she rose from her bed, every night before she closed her eyes.

Every time her child stirred beneath her heart.

Boots thumped against the stone steps outside her chamber, bringing her useless thoughts to a welcome end. The past was done and gone; all she could hope for was to do better in the future.

For her child's sake, if not for her own.

At the sharp rap against the door, she thought to rise, then decided against it. "Come in," she called.

Lord Connor opened the door and entered the room, Sir Ivor hesitating behind him. "D'Athée," Lord Connor urged as he held the door wide and waited. Sir Ivor, his face twisted in its habitual scowl, ambled in just far enough so that FitzClifford could swing the door closed.

After doing so, Lord Connor came to stand before Moira and bow politely, while her husband's man scarcely deigned to nod in her direction.

"Thank you for agreeing to join me here," she said, setting aside her sewing and making to rise.

Lord Connor reached out and took her by the hand before she could do so. "By your leave, milady." He released her, then caught her arm in a firm, gentle grip and eased her up from the settle. "I can't have you falling at my feet every time we meet," he said, his solemn tone at odds with the glint of humor in his dark eyes. "'Tis most unnecessary, and it cannot be comfortable for you."

"As you say, milord." Ruthlessly suppressing the urge to smile, she nodded and slipped past him toward the table. "Please, sirs, sit and be comfortable," she said, motioning toward chairs on opposite sides of the long, narrow board. Lord Connor pulled out the stool at the end for her, and remained standing until she'd seated herself. Sir Ivor followed his example, surprising her. Not since before her husband's mortal injury—when he was forced to take to his bed for his final, lingering illness—had his man honored her with the simplest of courtesies.

Considering that Sir Ivor d'Athée prided himself on his fine manners and knightly ways, that lack had shown as clearly as any words he might have tossed her way what he thought of her.

Perhaps he wasn't bold enough to slight her in Lord Connor's presence—not yet, at least.

She slid a platter of meat toward Lord Connor. "I thought you might want a substantial meal to break your fast, milord. You must be hungry after your exertions this morning, especially since I doubt anyone thought to feed you and your men last night. 'Tis my province, and I know the maids were busy with me as well." Her face heated with shame. "I trust that you were at least lodged comfortably."

She served them both and poured ale into their mugs, taking only a small portion of bread for herself. She'd eaten a hearty meal the night before—possibly too hearty. Perhaps she should blame the pains that had felled her on a surfeit of spiced frumenty, and not on the child.

Once he'd cleared his trencher, Lord Connor pushed it away and poured himself more ale. "I've scant knowledge of your situation here. Rannulf explained the terms under which your husband, God rest him, held Gerald's Keep for our family, but he could tell me little about the men who've caused you trouble."

Before Moira could answer, Sir Ivor made a sound of disgust and tossed a chicken bone onto his trencher. "The damned MacCarthys." His hand shook when he reached for his drink. "Bloody Irish bastards, just like all their kind. Think they can just come along and steal away what an honest man labored hard to hold. Too lazy to work for what they want." He looked at Moira, and it was a wonder the enmity in his gaze didn't slay her where she sat. "But they're not beyond using any weak slut they can find to get them what they're after." The hatred burning in his eyes held Moira motionless, stunned. "Isn't that the way of it, *milady?*"

Chapter Three

Moira, shocked already by Sir Ivor's words, gasped as Lord Connor rose and, reaching across the table, grabbed the knight by the front of his tunic with one hand and picked him up out of his chair. "How dare you?" he growled, holding the other man suspended with apparent ease. "You owe your lady an apology at once," he said in a more temperate voice, though he tightened his grip and raised Sir Ivor higher still. "Though it could scarce make up for the offense."

She'd never seen Sir Ivor so pale, nor his manner shift from arrogant to obsequious so swiftly. "P-p-pardon, milord." He squirmed, then stopped when it became clear that his efforts to free himself would accomplish naught. "My words were rash, ill-advised," he mumbled, eyes lowered. "Forgive me, milady, I pray you."

"'Tisn't much, but it's a start." Lord Connor opened his hand and let Sir Ivor drop into his chair with a thump. "What say you, Lady Moira?" he asked, straightening. "Is his apology—such as it was—acceptable to you?"

The sight of Sir Ivor so easily routed gave her great satisfaction, a pleasure difficult to suppress. But she tore her gaze from the man nigh cowering in his seat to focus on the warrior who had so swiftly and effectively subdued him. Lord Connor stood tall and relaxed by his chair, neither his stance or expression betraying the slightest hint of anger or impatience. He'd been angry—nay, more than that, he'd been enraged—scarce a moment before. How had he changed so swiftly, hidden his emotions with such ease?

She had never known a man who could do so. She turned her attention to picking up her cup, sipping at the ale while she considered this strange turn.

How would she manage herself in Lord Connor's presence if she had no notion how to read him, how to react according to his moods?

She'd worries enough already without having to contend with that as well.

"Milady?" Glancing up, she saw that he stood ready to reach for Sir Ivor again.

"I beg your pardon, milord. Aye, 'tis acceptable." She braced her hands on the edge of the table and levered herself up from her seat. "I should not have called for this meeting so soon. I know we must discuss our situation, but I fear I've not yet recovered from last night, and must seek my bed for a little longer," she told him, cringing inside at the thought of beating so cowardly a retreat—and lying in the bargain. But she simply could not face more problems, more questions—not now. "Please stay, finish your meal. Perhaps once I've rested..."

Though she kept her gaze lowered, she dared to peer at him through her lashes. He believed her falsehood, it seemed, for he nodded, the concern in his eyes making her feel more ashamed of her deception. "Shall I send for your maid?" he asked.

She shook her head. "Nay, milord. I can manage." She crossed to the door leading to her bedchamber.

"Lady Moira." Lord Connor's voice stopped her with

her hand on the latch. "Send for me as soon as you're feeling better. We've much left to resolve here, and we cannot delay for long."

She glanced back at him. He'd moved to stand at the head of the table; though his attention appeared fixed upon her, she could see that he'd not abandoned his vigilance over Sir Ivor, who still sat crumpled in his chair. "Of course, milord." His sympathetic gaze made her want to squirm with guilt. But when she looked past him and caught a glimpse of the hatred still burning in Sir Ivor's eyes, a chill skittered over her spine to lodge, heavy and frightening, deep within her belly.

Refusing to back down beneath the force of his rancor, she met his gaze until he looked away. But she knew his submission was only temporary. She dared not permit Sir Ivor to have his say before she had her own chance to tell Lord Connor the details of what had brought them to this position.

No matter how painful the telling.

One hand resting upon her child for reassurance, she slowly turned and made her way back to the table. "We've waited long enough already, though I know you came to us as quickly as you could," she said. Lord Connor took her hand to steady her as she lowered her bulk back onto the stool, gifting her with a nod of approval. "I'll not be responsible for delaying things any further now that you're here."

"I thank you." He resumed his place across from Sir Ivor, though he remained standing. "But first I must finish this 'discussion.'" He rested his hands on the table, leaning toward Sir Ivor. "Let me warn you now, d'Athée, you'd best guard your tongue in your lady's presence. Should you *ever* again choose to deride those with Irish blood flowing in their veins, within my presence or without, be certain I shall hear of it.

"And you *will* feel the bite of my anger yet again." Lord Connor picked up his goblet and drained it. "'Tis a wise man who keeps his silence when he's wandered into unfamiliar territory," he remarked. "It's a wonder you've survived here so long, given your opinion of your companions. Unfortunately for you, sirrah, you've exposed your ignorance one too many times in my presence." His even gaze appeared to weigh the other man and find him wanting. "You'll pay for your insolence soon enough."

"My lord?" Sir Ivor rose slowly to his feet, staring up at Lord Connor, his eyes stark with fear.

Lord Connor's smile held not a jot of humor that Moira could see. "Your error was greater than you intended, I'm sure. You not only cast grievous insult on your lord's wife, but also upon myself. My mother is Irish, Sir Ivor," he said smoothly. "Gerald's Keep was one of her dower lands." The scar on his cheek stood out, stark and pale, against his tanned skin. "I will permit *no one* to insult my mother, in any way. Ever."

Sir Ivor's mouth moved, but made no sound. Moira felt not a whit of pity for the man—indeed, the pleasure that filled her as she witnessed his well-deserved comeuppance did her no credit, but was enjoyable nonetheless. She'd suffered more than enough of his sly insinuations, his veiled comments outside her husband's presence.

And since Lord Brien's injury and lingering illness, Sir Ivor had become nigh unbearable.

Perhaps she'd gained a champion in Lord Connor....

Nay! She'd let no man stand between her and any threat. Never again.

Lord Connor rose, crossed the room and opened the door, calling to a maid sweeping the corridor. "Send a manservant to the barracks to bring my lieutenant, Will, to me at once,'' he told her. Bobbing a curtsy, she left to do as he bid.

Leaving the door ajar, he rejoined them at the table. ''I believe we'll accomplish more, milady, without d'Athée here to distract us.''

''Milord!'' Sir Ivor cried. Color flooding his face, he leaped to his feet and pounded his fist on the table. ''She knows nothing of our defenses, nor of what we've already done. Surely my assessment is necessary for you to determine your course of action.''

''When I want your advice, I'll ask for it,'' Lord Connor told him in a cold voice. ''For the nonce, you may go with Will when he arrives, and you'll do as he commands. You are no longer in charge of the defenses of this keep, nor have you any authority unless I choose to allow it.'' The sound of footsteps on the stairs was followed by a rapping at the door. ''Enter.''

A tall young man wearing a man-at-arm's rough garb—but the sword and spurs of a knight, as well—came in, closing the door behind him. ''Milord,'' he said, but he bowed to Moira.

''Milady, this is Sir William Bowman, one of my brother Rannulf's most trusted men,'' Lord Connor said. ''Will, this is Lady Moira, Lord Brien's widow, whom we have come here to serve.''

Sir William bowed again, deeper this time. ''My lady, I'm sorry for your loss.''

''Thank you.'' Moira nodded in acknowledgment and tried to observe him without being obvious about it. He neither sounded like nor had the look of a common soldier, and 'twas clear the FitzCliffords trusted him. His bearing held a confidence she hadn't expected to see, and something about his face, his eyes, made her think him a man used to laughing.

Lord Connor moved to stand behind Moira's chair, frustrating her efforts to watch both men, to study them. "Will, take Sir Ivor out with you to the bailey. He will help you drill the foot soldiers we brought from l'Eau Clair, along with those of Gerald's Keep. Mayhap a morning's hard labor will teach him something, though I doubt it."

Sir William eyed Sir Ivor, who was standing by the table, his face twisted into its usual near grimace, more closely. "'Twill be my pleasure," he said, smiling. "We'll whip our men into shape in no time, Sir Ivor, I have no doubt. I've already heard rum—" He cleared his throat, blue eyes bright with humor. "Beg pardon—tales of your training methods. Why, your name comes up in nearly every conversation with the men here. 'Twill be an education to watch you at work."

"Indeed." Sir Ivor looked as though he didn't know whether to be pleased or offended by what Sir William said, but he had no chance to mull it over.

"Well then, best get to it," Sir William said, his smile widening to a grin. He stood aside to allow Sir Ivor to precede him out the door. "By your leave, milady." He bowed to Moira again. "Milord."

"I'll expect a report from you at dinner, Will," Lord Connor said. "See that you've something positive to report—and that you make Sir Ivor work for his keep."

"'Twill be my pleasure, milord," Sir William said, laughing as he pulled the door shut behind him.

Connor watched Will leave and resisted the urge to join his laughter. As he'd learned almost as soon as Rannulf had put the new knight under his command, the rogue had an uncanny ability to understand exactly what Connor had in mind. Connor enjoyed outsmarting Will, for it happened so seldom.

But Lady Moira would likely think him a lunatic should he burst into laughter now. Not to mention the fact that, other than Will's japes, he'd heard nothing since his arrival at Gerald's Keep to inspire merriment.

She sat huddled on her seat, gaze lowered. He'd noticed that she seldom looked at him—or the other men, for that matter—directly. He'd felt her eyes upon him several times since he'd entered this chamber, but surreptitiously, as though she didn't want to be caught at it.

As he'd felt her watching him earlier, when he'd been immersed in his morning ritual.

"Lady Moira."

"Milord?" Her glance rose no higher than the middle of his chest, and the way she remained curled upon the low stool made him believe she'd be happy if she could escape him altogether.

Did she fear him?

The possibility hadn't occurred to him before now. He'd brought her the aid she'd asked for, had come to protect her, her unborn child and her people from their enemies. Last night she'd sounded glad of his arrival.

But his reaction to d'Athée might have frightened her. It had been swift—though not excessive, in his estimation. Indeed, given the provocation—the insult to *her*—he thought he'd kept his temper well in hand, though the fire of it still burned through his veins.

He returned to the table and pulled out his chair, watching Lady Moira as he did so. She turned toward him, but still did not really *look* at him. "Would you rather I call for your maid?" he asked. He pushed in the chair and rested his hands atop the high, carved back. "I don't wish to make you uncomfortable, and I can see that something about me does.''

She drew in a deep breath and released it in a sigh. ''It's not you, milord,'' she said, though as he watched her face—what he could see of it—he didn't believe her. '''Tis this place. I need to get outside, I think, away from these rooms.'' She looked up at him, surprising him. ''If you wouldn't mind?''

The turmoil and pain he saw in her deep blue eyes would have made him agree to far more than her simple request, had she asked for more. The power of his reaction, so foreign and unexpected, nigh stopped his mind from forming any reply at all.

She looked away, turning in upon herself. ''It matters naught,'' she said, her voice quiet, flat.

He reached out and covered her hand with his, gently holding hers captive when she tried to slide it free. ''Nay, milady. How can I deny so simple a request?'' He could see that his touch disturbed her, so he moved his hand away. ''We cannot leave the walls, but we could go outside, if you desire.''

Slowly, like a blossom opening, she faced him again and met his gaze, her cheeks faintly tinged with color. ''I would like that, milord. First, I could take you to the parapet, where I can show you how we've managed to cultivate the fields this year. Then afterward, if you wish, there's a place on the headland where we could go to talk. The wind there blows away all the cares of the world. I've not been there since...'' She closed her eyes for a moment, then sighed and opened them. ''In a very long time.''

''Agreed. You will show me the fields, and then we shall go to the cliffs.'' He hurried to help her as she pushed back her seat and rose. ''As long as it's not too far for you to walk.''

''If you don't mind helping me over the rough ground, I should have no trouble,'' she said, moving away from his touch as soon as she'd found her balance. Despite her words, he doubted she'd ask him for help unless the terrain proved impossible to traverse.

In which case they'd not chance it, for he had no intention of causing her child—Lord Brien's heir—the slightest risk.

Chapter Four

Connor scanned the area close to the castle's outer ward, where a small group of crofters, under the protection of several burly, well-armed guards, toiled in the fields. Many of the peasants had sought sanctuary within the walls of the keep in the months leading up to Lord Brien's death, having been the victims of fast, devastating raids on their meager holdings. The result had been that Gerald's Keep had more people to support, and scant means to do so. Lady Moira and the priest, Father Thomas, had worked with Sir Ivor to devise the present system, whereby some fields could be cultivated and the workers kept safe.

They mounted a guard over the fields at night, as well, though there had been no attempts to destroy them.

''We cannot risk losing the grain and foodstuffs planted there,'' Lady Moira explained. ''Our resources are stretched thin now. This way, we're doing everything possible to provide for everyone, while giving the crofters a chance to earn their keep.''

Connor couldn't help but be impressed. He'd expected to find a castle under siege, which evidently was not the case. But they'd apparently been under attack on occasion, enough so that they must remain alert and prepared for every eventuality.

Lady Moira led the way back through the keep itself and out a postern gate to what amounted to a rough swatch of pasture land. It rose away from the keep toward the sea, providing grazing for cattle and a small flock of sheep.

A maze of paths meandered through the coarse tussocks of grass, from the gate to where the land dropped away in a steep, rocky cliff. "'Tis dangerous to climb down the hillside," she told him as they followed a well-worn trail, moving slowly in deference to her condition. "It is nigh impossible to gauge where to go, for much of the rock is loose, and will fall away with the slightest touch."

"Yet 'tis clear that someone comes out here," he said, indicating the paths.

"Aye, the lads who tend the animals. And 'tis a popular place to escape the confines of the hall and bailey in safety." She slowed to negotiate a patch strewn with sharp stones, then stopped in the midst of it when her foot slipped. He grabbed her arm and steadied her. "I should have tried going around." She scanned the area. "Though I doubt it would have mattered."

She looked so forlorn, so pale and weary, that he scooped her into his arms and continued along the route before she could protest. "You allowed me to carry you last night," he said, halting the words she so clearly wished to voice. "I'll set you down as soon as we reach the end of the path, I promise you."

She fixed her gaze upon his face, measuring, judging him. What she sought he couldn't guess, but this close, he could see the honesty in her eyes. He thought her a woman without guile. Wary, of a certainty, but a woman in her position would be a fool not to be cautious.

Control over her future rested in her family's hands, if

she had one, or in her overlord's. Rannulf's judgment, should the decision fall to him, would depend upon Connor's report. 'Twas a great responsibility—greater than any he'd ever had thrust upon him. He welcomed it, relished the fact that his brother believed him competent to handle the situation.

Whatever the situation proved to be.

He set Lady Moira on her feet in the open area at the end of the path and stepped past her. The ground here was even, the grass a soft, verdant carpet. The dark gray bulk of Gerald's Keep loomed behind them, but in front of them, the ground sloped toward the sea and the sky.

Standing there with the wind whipping his hair about his face, he could almost imagine that nothing else existed in the world but this vastness spread out like a feast before his eyes.

Nothing save the woman whose presence he could feel with an awareness that owed nothing to sight, to sound—to any sense he knew of. But he *knew* Moira stood behind him, just as he could see her in his mind's eye—her back straight, her hands cupped protectively about her belly, her eyes closed as she savored the wind's power to chase away her cares.

Compelled to prove himself wrong, he turned, his eyes confirming what his mind already knew. 'Twas just as he'd imagined.

His heart beat faster in reaction to the picture she made—her face awash with pleasure, relaxed, beautiful—or mayhap in response to the eerie sense of rightness that struck him like a lance to see his thought made real.

The ends of her veil lifted on the wind and swirled about her. Her eyes snapped open and she reached up to capture the billowing fabric, catching it just as it flew off her head. Her laughter surprised him, as did her smile. "Didn't I tell you it was windy here, milord?'' She held the veiling up and let it stream around her like a pennon.

Her pleasure was an irresistible lure. ''Aye, that you did.'' He returned to her, noting how the gusty breeze tugged at her body as well. ''But perhaps we should find a place for you to sit and rest.''

She scanned the area, then motioned toward a large, smooth stone at the crest of the hill. ''The view from there is beyond imagining,'' she told him, already heading for it, her voice carrying back to him on the wind. '''Tis a good place for what we must discuss.''

He caught up to her as she settled onto the stone and sighed. Her smile, any hint of laughter, had disappeared in the time it took for her to cover the short distance. She held her veil in her lap, wound so tight in her hands that her knuckles looked nearly as pale as the soft white linen.

Her hair had come free of its bindings and hung loose past her waist, smooth and sleek as it had appeared when he'd watched her this morn, perched above him in the window. It blew away from her, allowing him a clear view of her face.

And of her anguish.

He sat down beside her on the rock, near, but not touching her. The pain had returned to her eyes, wound itself tight round her till he thought she'd shatter from its fierce grip.

But she faced him, reaching up to gather her hair in one hand and send it flying over her shoulder, away from him. ''What is it you wish to know, milord?''

''First off, exactly who is it that threatens Gerald's Keep?''

She gazed out over the water, though her eyes seemed focused elsewhere. '''Tis the MacCarthys, our neighbors to the south. They're an old Irish family. Perhaps your mother spoke of them?''

Connor shook his head. His mother had seldom mentioned anything of her life before she'd married his father.

''Their family lost this land long ago, when Lord Striguil—Strongbow—brought the Normans to Ireland. I believe your mother's family took control of it then. Was she an O'Connor?''

''Aye. Deirdre O'Connor.'' Perhaps he could learn more about his mother, something that might explain to him the woman he knew.

''My husband was her kin, then—distant, but related nonetheless. Some sort of cousin.'' Her expression had seemed to relax, but tension wrapped about her as he watched. ''According to Lord Brien, Liam MacCarthy—Hugh and Dermot's father—had wanted to wed your mother, but her family refused his offer and urged her to marry a Norman they preferred.''

''My father, I assume,'' Connor said, his voice flat.

''Evidently so,'' Lady Moira agreed. ''They left for England after they wed, and when her father was dying, he chose Lord Brien to hold Gerald's Keep for her heirs.''

Connor shifted his gaze to stare out at the sea. He'd learned more just now about the O'Connors than he'd heard in his entire life. He'd known he was named for his mother's family, but that was all.

Rannulf had been here before, had known Lord Brien. *He* had to have known more as well, not that he'd thought to share the information with his brother.

Of course, despite the fact that they'd done much to resolve the problems between them, they'd scarce spoken of their parents. 'Twas too painful to drag their childhood demons out, to expose them to the light of day.

Connor shook off his abstraction and glanced back at

Lady Moira's anxious face. "The MacCarthys never gave up their obsession with regaining this land, I take it?"

"'Twas quiet for many years. The O'Connors were powerful, in their day, as was my husband. Liam MacCarthy didn't dare to attack them, to risk drawing down the Normans' wrath upon his head. I believe he feared your father might come after him."

"I can understand that," Connor muttered.

"But he instilled his hatred in his sons. Once your father died, Liam had grown too old himself to do much save continue to foster the notion that his sons deserved to hold Gerald's Keep, not some absent Norman lord. After Liam died last year, Dermot and Hugh decided they'd not allow another old man—Lord Brien—to keep them from what they considered theirs."

"No doubt they believed 'twould be an easy victory," Connor said.

"Aye, especially since they had help from some of the other Irish families hereabouts. Fortunately for us, after everything that happened here, most of their allies refused to help them further. They feared retribution for their part in causing Lord Brien's death."

"And well they might," Connor said harshly. "You should have sent for reinforcements as soon as your husband was injured, or at least explained the situation in more detail when you sent word to Rannulf of Lord Brien's death. He'd have sent you assistance at once."

"My husband would not allow it," Lady Moira said quietly. "And after his death, I didn't know what to say, what to do." She glanced down at her fingers, knitted tight together in her lap. "I'm sorry, milord."

Connor sighed. "Nay, 'tis I who should apologize. 'Tis too late to change the past. There's no use blaming you for what is not your fault, milady." He stood and stared out at the sea, letting the wind cool his thoughts. ''The MacCarthys haven't abandoned their quest to gain Gerald's Keep, then?'' he asked, turning back to her.

''Nay. They simply waited until Lord Brien died to begin harassing us again. Hugh MacCarthy leads them now, though 'twas Dermot, his elder brother, who caused my husband's death.''

''From the letter you sent, we thought Lord Brien died of some sickness, since he...'' How should he put this, Connor wondered, without giving insult in some way? ''Rannulf told me your husband was some years older than you.''

''Aye—forty years, give or take a few. He was just past sixty when he died.''

She said the words so easily, as though 'twas the most natural thing in the world that her husband had been old enough to be her grandfather. The thought alone made him want to shudder, while the reality of this particular young woman, sweet and lovely, with a man so much older seemed beyond his comprehension.

'Twas certainly not a thought he wished to contemplate in any detail.

Yet his mind would not leave it alone.

He needed to know all the facts, he reminded himself, else how could he arrive at a proper evaluation of the situation here, and what to do about it?

The fact that he seemed to have developed a rapidly growing fascination with Lord Brien's beautiful widow was an unfortunate circumstance he'd do well to ignore.

''How long were you wed?'' he asked.

''Five years.''

She must have been a child, he thought with disgust. How had she come to—

''I was fifteen,'' she told him. ''Lord Brien wished for

a young bride. His first two wives had been older—in their twenties—when he wed them, and they never were able to…'' She gestured toward her stomach. ''So he thought they must have been too old to give him the heir he wanted. My family are minor Irish nobles. My brothers were pleased to forge a bond with so powerful a Norman lord as Lord Brien FitzGerald.''

Such bargains were not unusual—indeed, his own parents had been brought together in a similar fashion, though they had had but five years difference in their ages, not forty.

Aye, and look how their marriage turned out, a voice in his mind snarled.

Time to move on, he told himself, before the anger that dwelled deep within him stirred to life.

''If it wasn't age that sickened your husband, what did?''

She twisted the veil in her hands, pulling the material snug about her fingers. ''He was gravely wounded in battle,'' she said, her voice little more than a whisper.

''But he prevailed?''

''Aye.'' She drew in a deep breath, more of a sob, though her eyes remained dry. ''He killed Dermot MacCarthy in hand-to-hand combat, but his injuries were severe. He lingered for months before his body simply could not fight any longer.''

''MacCarthy was of an age with your husband, I take it, for Lord Brien to have beaten him?'' Connor couldn't imagine how he'd have overcome MacCarthy otherwise.

Lady Moira stared out at the sea, then shifted her attention to the twisted veil in her lap. Why did she hesitate to answer now, when she'd been so forthcoming with information before?

And why had her eyes filled with tears, when talk of her husband's death had left them dry?

He reached down and caught her hands in one of his. ‘‘Milady?’’

‘‘Dermot MacCarthy was a young man, no more than thirty, I would guess.’’ A tear traced its way down her cheek unchecked. ‘‘He was hale and strong, but Lord Brien's rage was so immense… He fought like a wolf—cunning, wily. He felt the stain on his honor could only be washed away with blood—either his enemy's or his own. I don't believe he cared which.’’ She released her grip on the veil and, pushing Connor's hand away, stood and faced him.

Grimacing, she clutched at her stomach.

‘‘'Tis enough, milady. I should not have insisted you speak of this now. I wish no harm to come to either you or Lord Brien's child.’’

Tears poured down her face. She wiped them away with her veil, then tossed it to the wind. Hands placed upon her belly as though protecting the babe, she said, ‘‘Your concern may be misplaced, milord. I'm surprised you haven't heard already—especially with Sir Ivor so busy spewing poison into every ear that will listen. This babe I carry may not be my husband's.’’ She took a step closer to him, her eyes meeting his. ‘‘There's just as much chance 'tis Dermot MacCarthy's child.’’

Chapter Five

Moira watched—waited—to see the look of shock cross Lord Connor's face, to see condemnation or distaste fill his dark brown eyes. When it did not, she simply stood there, uncertain what to do.

What more could she say, after the revelation she'd just made?

He nodded finally. "I had wondered what could have forced your husband to meet a man half his age in hand-to-hand combat. Now I understand. MacCarthy took you captive?" He glanced down as a flush tinted his face, then looked up and held her gaze, his eyes earnest, intent. "Raped you?"

More tears filled Moira's eyes, tears of relief—of disbelief. How was it that this man, who knew nothing of her, did not immediately believe she'd willingly given herself to Dermot, and that her husband had found out?

'Twas what Sir Ivor thought. He'd made no secret of it.

But Lord Connor was wrong in his account, as well, though she'd no intention of sharing the complete truth of the matter with him.

With anyone.

"MacCarthy waited till Lord Brien and a troop of men

left Gerald's Keep—lured him away, I've always believed, though I'd no way of proving it. The MacCarthys came in force soon after, their army flush with reinforcements from some of the other Irish families hereabouts.'' The sound of their war cries, the clash of battle and the moans of the dying echoed in her mind, sending a chill down her spine. ''It had been quiet here, peaceful, for a long time. We grew lax, relaxed our vigilance too much. They found it a simple matter to overcome our defenses, since most of our fighting men had gone with Lord Brien.''

''What did they do?'' he asked.

''Once they'd fought their way into the keep itself, they gathered all our people into the bailey.'' She closed her eyes, reliving again the terror, the helplessness that had nearly overwhelmed her, until she'd realized that only she remained to fight for the people of Gerald's Keep. That knowledge alone had permitted her to master her fear, to meet their invaders with her head high, her courage renewed.

''I come from a family of warriors, milord.'' She laughed, the sound as harsh as the memories prompting it. ''My father was infamous as a man who would fight over the most trifling matters. And my brothers are worse.'' Meeting Lord Connor's gaze, she added, ''But I've never met, before or since, anyone who took such pleasure from war as Dermot MacCarthy did. He gloried in it, savored every moment he held sway over his opponent.'' Her voice shook; she took a deep breath and waited, hoping 'twould calm her, but it made no difference.

Lord Connor took her hand and led her back to the rock where they'd sat before, releasing her as soon as he'd settled beside her. ''Such a man is not a warrior, milady. That is not honorable behavior.''

''There was nothing honorable about Dermot Mac-

Carthy,'' she said, sorrow closing her throat till she could scarce say the words. ''But I did not realize that fact until 'twas too late to change the course I had set upon.'' She stared out at the sea, at the gulls wheeling and swooping on the wind. Their freedom made a mockery of her life, pulling tight upon the tangled threads she'd woven about herself....

And everyone within her milieu.

How she wished she could send Lord Connor away, before he found himself wound firmly within this sticky web! But 'twas already too late for that, she knew, too late for all of them.

God alone knew how this would end. All she knew was that it could only end badly for her.

She prayed no one else might suffer for her folly.

Lord Connor touched her arm, his hand gentle, until she met his gaze again. ''Milady, I know it must pain you to relive this. I'm a stranger to you, and you likely wish me to the devil for pressing you, but I must know what happened here if I'm to protect you and your child, your people. I beg your forgiveness, but I *will* learn the truth of it, and soon.'' He sighed. ''I believe I'll hear a more honest account from you than from d'Athée. 'Tis clear he's no friend to you, or to anyone with Irish blood flowing in their veins.'' He nudged her with his shoulder, his mouth curling into a faint smile. ''The fool.''

Moira couldn't help but smile in return, though the thought of Sir Ivor and his lies wiped away the brief sense of sharing she'd felt. ''You've the right of it, milord, but 'tis not because I'm Irish that Sir Ivor hates me—at least that's not the only reason. He's always borne me a grudge, whether from jealousy or something else, I cannot say. He was very loyal to Lord Brien.''

''Whatever the cause, I doubt he's capable of speaking

on the topic of the MacCarthys—or you—for more than a word or two without his true feelings tainting everything he says.'' Connor shifted on the rock so that he bore the brunt of the wind pounding at them. ''I'll take my chances with you, milady, and trust you won't prove me wrong to have done so.''

As Connor watched her, he could see the internal struggle she waged revealed on her face, in her eyes. He doubted she could lie with any success at all. He hoped he was right, for he needed the truth from *someone* here, and she appeared the most likely candidate.

At last she focused her expressive blue eyes on his face, as though judging him, weighing *him.* ''I thank you, Lord Connor, for your trust—and your honesty. I will try to live up to it, I promise you.'' A shudder passed through her. ''You've the right of it, though 'tis a hard thing to admit to you what a fool I was. Stranger or no, 'twould be difficult either way.'' She huddled deeper into the loose folds of her gown, tempting him to wrap his arms about her for warmth, for comfort—for whatever she needed. Willpower alone kept him from doing so; she'd not welcome such familiarity from a stranger, nor did he wish to tempt himself further.

Sitting next to her, being enveloped in her nearness, her scent, the *feel* of her, was temptation enough as it was.

She laid her hand on his forearm, surprising him. ''I trust *you* to do all you can to help me protect my child, milord. I know your brother to be a kind and honorable man. 'Tis clear to me that you are no less so. The FitzCliffords have dealt fairly with the FitzGeralds till now, and I believe you'll continue to do so.''

''You honor me, milady.''

Sighing, she turned her gaze to the sea. ''I cannot tell you these things to your face, milord. 'Tis too embarrassing. I hope you don't mind.''

"Nay, do what you must." Since he already found it difficult to distance himself from her, perhaps this might help.

"When MacCarthy gathered everyone in the bailey, his brother Hugh dragged the maids and me from my solar, where the men had sent us when the assault on the castle began. Hugh is a rough man, coarse of tongue and foul minded. 'Twas only Brigit's intervention that kept him from stripping me to my shift before we reached the bailey. As it was, he'd ripped my tunic and unbound my hair, bruising my face and arms in the process. He forced me to stand before them all looking as though I'd just..."

As her voice faded away, she reached out and grasped Connor's hand in a tight grip. Her words made his blood run hot; when he finally met Hugh MacCarthy, he'd see that the bastard paid for what he'd done that day.

"It looked as if he'd taken me already," she continued. "His men proved as foul mouthed as he, shouting their filth and stirring my people into a frenzy, though they could do nothing to protect me." Her fingers tightened. "Indeed, the MacCarthys' men used it as an excuse to lay about with fists and cudgels once again. My servants were no threat to them, yet they seemed to take great pleasure in 'subduing' them."

The picture she painted did not surprise him, though he found it disgusting. He knew well the pleasure some men took in wielding whatever power they had over any within their reach who could not—or would not, he thought with a frown—fight back.

He turned his hand beneath hers and laced their fingers together. "I'd expect no less from dishonorable men."

She looked at him, her eyes bright with tears, but didn't free herself from his hold. "Dermot joined us on the landing then. He looked nothing like his brother or his men—

he was clean, his garb fine, of good quality. He approached us and bowed to me most courteously before knocking Hugh off his feet with one blow. I thought then that he would prove different from Hugh and the others, perhaps free my people, or at least cease their torment. He'd treated me with courtesy.... But 'twas all a sham.''

Connor's respect for the woman beside him grew with each word she spoke. 'Twas obvious she was the daughter and sister of warriors, for she had a keen eye and a clear manner of describing what had happened. She must have been frightened at the time—terrified, more like—yet she'd taken notice of her surroundings, made judgments based upon what she'd seen. ''What did Dermot do?''

''He stepped over Hugh, still sprawled on the landing, took me by the hands and led me away from his brother. 'I will spare your people,' he told me. I was so pleased, for they'd done naught but serve their rightful lord. They had no choice in the matter, and didn't deserve to be punished for it.''

''That wouldn't stop most men in MacCarthy's position from doing so,'' Connor said. ''It happens all the time. Given what you've said about his family, I find his offer surprising.''

''I did as well,'' she whispered. ''Still, I couldn't help but be glad they'd be spared any further punishment. I should have realized as soon as he said the words that *someone* would have to pay the price for his generosity.''

'''Twas you who paid,'' Connor muttered, disgust at such cowardice making his voice shake. ''He took you in return for sparing them.''

''He gave me a choice,'' she said quietly. ''A night's passion with him in return for their lives. He'd already taken Gerald's Keep. Considering I had nothing else to offer, and no way to best him, it seemed little enough sacrifice when so many might be saved.''

''You are a brave woman, Lady Moira FitzGerald.'' Connor made no effort to hide his admiration. ''Few noble ladies would trade their virtue to save the lives of servants.''

'''Tis not as though I were a virgin,'' she murmured, so low he could scarce hear her.

He reached out to smooth an errant strand of hair away from her face, letting his hand linger against her cheek, attempting to provide the comfort he could see she needed. ''Your experience—or lack of it—matters little. For him to force an unwilling woman to his bed is despicable.''

Though her eyes remained dry, he could not mistake the depth of her pain. He wanted to take her into his arms, to give her comfort, but it was not his place to do so.

Nor could she possibly wish that from him. By the rood, she'd think him no better than Dermot MacCarthy!

He slipped his hand from her cheek. ''You gave him what he asked for?'' She glanced away, nodding once. ''And he kept his part of the bargain?''

''Nay,'' she whispered. ''He simply waited till he'd taken what he wanted from me before he ordered his brother to resume his torment of my people.'' She pressed her hands to her face, covering her eyes for a moment as though she might shut out the memory. ''Five people died before my husband returned with his troops and fought his way inside.'' Her body shaking, she slid her hands into her lap, fingers clenched together so tightly her knuckles showed white. ''Dermot taunted Lord Brien with what he—what *we*—had done, threw the words in his face like a gage to challenge my husband, to enrage him to the point of foolishness.''

Connor leaped to his feet and spun to face her. "No man could ignore such an affront to his wife!"

She looked as though his words confused her. "'Twas the affront to his own honor he fought to avenge, not mine, milord."

Then he was a fool, Connor thought, though he didn't express that sentiment out loud. 'Twould serve no purpose to speak ill of the dead, especially to the man's widow.

"If I hadn't accepted Dermot's offer, my husband might still be alive, milord."

"Or you might be dead, and many of your people with you," Connor said flatly. "Most likely MacCarthy would have had you anyway. I doubt he'd have allowed your refusal of him to stand in the way of taking what he desired."

"Perhaps." Without the shield of his body beside her, the wind whipped at her hair and molded her loose gown about her rounded figure, making her appear a part of the lush land surrounding her—untamed, alive, ripe. He shook his head to clear away the fanciful image.

"'Tis my sin to bear that I caused my husband's death, however long it took to occur. I'll do penance for that, and for my infidelity, for as I long as I live. Yet despite everything that has happened, I cannot be sorry, for by my actions I saved all but five of our people." Opening her hands, she cupped them about her rounded belly. "And perhaps created this child." She looked up at him, her blue eyes dark, intense. "I cannot regret this child, no matter what the circumstances of his making. But I cannot allow his existence to lead to more deaths, more fighting, either. That is why we need your help."

"What do you mean?" he asked, though several possibilities, none of them appealing, came to mind.

"The MacCarthys seek revenge for Dermot's death, milord. They desire it nearly as much as they continue to want

Gerald's Keep for their own. But now they believe they've the perfect weapon, an indisputable way to gain this stronghold, milord. They believe the babe I carry is Dermot's. They'll stop at nothing to gain control of him, and through him, this castle."

Chapter Six

Moira accepted Lord Connor's assistance as they left the headland and headed back to the keep, but they made the short journey in silence.

She'd shocked him, no doubt. How could it be otherwise? He was a decent man, a moral one. That much had already become clear to her in the brief time she'd known him. He wouldn't want to stay here, to continually risk his life and the lives of his men, to defend an admitted adulteress.

She knew how it would be. Once they reached the hall, he'd excuse himself and distance himself from her as much as possible for the remainder of his stay here.

And he'd stay no longer than necessary.

Or else he'd decide to do as the MacCarthys wanted, and hand her—and her child—over to them.

Though how that would help, she'd no idea, for she doubted the FitzCliffords would agree to hand over Gerald's Keep as well.

And *that* was what the MacCarthys truly desired.

Besides, she couldn't believe that Connor FitzClifford could be so vicious as to turn her over to the men who had abused her.

How he would resolve their troubles with the MacCarthys, she had no idea. But she could not allow him to do anything that might jeopardize her child's life.

He steadied her on her feet once they reached the postern gate. Desperation gave her the courage to reach out and catch his arm, to stop him before he opened the barred door. "I realize I've no right to ask this of you, milord, but I'll do so anyway. Promise me you won't give my child to the MacCarthys. Do whatever you wish with me once the babe is born, but don't allow them to take my child!"

"What kind of monster do you think me?" His face had blanched at her words, making splotchy freckles stand out across his cheeks. His dark eyes held hurt, confusion; had what she'd said been so surprising? "I would never harm a child, nor separate a babe from its mother," he said, the conviction in his voice ringing true. He stared at her hand, pale against his dark sleeve, until she released him.

Heat flooded her cheeks. "I beg your pardon, milord," she muttered, unable to meet his gaze any longer.

"Don't look away now, Lady Moira," he said. His quiet tone, at odds with the air of command his words carried, compelled her to obey. She stared at him, bemused, as he held her gaze with his. "Perhaps you've not known any men you could trust before now, but I swear to you upon my honor, milady, you can trust me."

The wind buffeted them, whipping her hair about, winding the strands around them both. He ignored it and held out his right hand to her. She placed her hand in his, palm to palm, letting his warmth seep into her chilled fingers.

"Will you trust me?" he asked. Still holding her motionless with his eyes, he brought her hand to his lips, turned it to kiss her palm, then closed her fingers and pressed her hand to his chest. "Please."

His heart thundered beneath her touch as he awaited her

answer. With his eyes staring deep into her soul, his life-blood pulsing against her palm, 'twas a bond as binding as a vow. How could she refuse him?

"I will try, milord. 'Tis all I can promise—I will try."

He released her hand and broke the spell he'd cast. "Thank you," he murmured, looking away. Turning, he reached for the latch and pulled the door open.

Her mind in turmoil, her body exhausted, Moira followed him into the bailey.

Connor spent the remainder of the day examining the defenses of Gerald's Keep and observing the battle readiness of its men. By dusk, he'd learned enough about the place and its people to realize that resolving the situation here was sure to prove a greater task than either he or Rannulf had anticipated.

He'd also discovered the depth of Lady Moira's entanglement in the circumstances leading up to their current problems. Not only through her unborn child.

It appeared her brothers were involved, as were nearly half the Irish nobles in the area. Opinions about the O'Neills ran strong among Lady Moira's people. Most everyone agreed that her brothers treated her as naught but a pawn to manipulate whenever they wanted something from her, or needed her Norman husband to bail them out of some trouble or another.

They saw their lady as next to a saint for her care of her people—not to mention her sacrifice on their behalf. It seemed to him that d'Athée's opinion of her was not widely held. Instead, those Connor spoke with were very loyal to her, and would be to her child, as well.

Connor entered the hall, tired and filthy, intending to head straight for the chamber he'd been given on the third floor of the keep. A maid had informed him earlier that

Lady Moira would not be joining them in the hall for supper. He looked forward to a quiet meal, without any of the emotional turmoil she seemed to generate within him whenever she was near.

Will hailed him from a corner near the stairwell as Connor set his foot on the first riser.

"'Tis glad I am to see you, milord," he said, his voice devoid of its usual cheerfulness. He motioned toward the stairs with the drinking horn he held, sending adrift the scent of mulled wine. "I've news aplenty to share."

"Come join me, then," Connor said. "And if you've any of that left, bring it along."

Will disappeared into the shadowy hall and emerged with a battered silver pitcher and another drinking horn. "Milord." He followed Connor up the stairs.

Will had proved himself indispensable in keeping d'Athée busy and out of Connor's way today, although it was clear that his efforts had taken their toll on him. Apparently Sir Ivor had managed what Connor had believed impossible—to wear through Will's usual good humor and even temper, reducing his smile to a scowl and painting shadows of weariness across his face.

"You owe me more than you can ever repay for this day's work, milord," Will said as soon as they entered the room.

Connor closed the door and nodded for him to take a seat by the fireplace. Someone had been here recently, for a small peat fire burned in the hearth and a branch of candles on the table by the bed cast a welcoming glow about the simple chamber. Connor unbuckled his sword belt and set it aside, then stretched his arms toward the low ceiling. "Share some of that wine and tell me what you've learned."

Will poured wine into both horns, handed one to Connor

and set the pitcher on the hearth. He sank onto the cushioned settle with a sigh. "You'll be well served if you can find someplace else to send d'Athée, and without delay," he said. He raised the cup to his lips, lowering it untasted. "He's treachery waiting for a chance to strike. Of that I have no doubt."

Connor tasted the wine, savoring its fragrant warmth before pulling a rough-hewn chair closer to the fire and easing himself into it. "I feared as much. He made no secret of his hatred for Lady Moira, both last night and this morn. And his dislike of the Irish is well known—"

"He's lucky someone hasn't slit his throat for him," Will countered. "The man's a fool, no mistake. But he's the kind who'll stir up trouble every chance he gets." He drained the horn and leaned over to grab up the pitcher from the hearth. "By all accounts he fair worshipped Lord Brien, to the point where he was jealous of the man's wife." He made a sound of disgust. "By Saint Winifred's bones, where's the sense in that? Most men spend more time with their men than their wives anyway, save for your brother and Gilles—I'm sorry, the Lady Gillian," he added with a grin. "I still have to remind myself that the 'lad' I fought with as a child is 'my lady' now, married and a mother." He replenished his drink and held the pitcher out, offering it to Connor, who took it gratefully. "'Twould take a pike to separate her from Lord Rannulf most of the time."

"Unlike the FitzGeralds. Lord Brien spent little time with his wife, from what I've heard," Connor said. "She was naught but breeding stock to him."

"Yet he didn't live to see her bear his heir." Will set aside the horn and sat forward on the settle, leaning his elbows on his knees, his expression solemn. "Though there's some question whether 'tis FitzGerald's child she carries, milord."

"So I've heard from the lady herself." Though Connor knew 'twas common knowledge, still it felt odd, unsettling, to be discussing the topic with Will. It seemed a betrayal...or an invitation for Will, for anyone, to see Lady Moira as a woman who had sinned, and whose husband had died because of it.

Connor didn't trust himself to remain calm, uninvolved, should *anyone* treat her without respect.

He tried to drown the uncertainty *that* thought engendered with a deep draft of the wine, but it didn't help. No woman had ever caused the feelings of protectiveness that haunted him now.

Not even his mother, when his father had been on one of his rampages.

Aye, he'd imagined what it would be like to try to bring a halt to his father's madness, but he'd never carried the thought to fruition.

He would to protect Lady Moira.

"I don't want our men—nor the ones here—gossiping about Lady Moira or her child," Connor said firmly. "See to it that anyone who does is sent to me for punishment."

Will nodded, sending him a surprised look. "Of course, milord. You know I meant no disrespect by what I said—"

Connor waved a hand to cut off the apology. "I know, Will. You were doing exactly what I wanted you to do. Given d'Athée's attitude, however, I doubt there's been any effort to quell the rumors about their lady. I simply want it understood that any further gossip about her will not be tolerated."

He straightened and finished off his wine, realizing how heated his voice had become. How had this come about? She was a woman like any other, he told himself. 'Twas normal, fitting, to wish to protect a mother and her child. But what he felt now went deeper than mere decency.

"Milord, do you want more wine?" Will asked.

Connor started and tightened his grip on the drinking horn. "Nay, I thank you. I've much to consider, and wouldn't want to muddle my head any more than usual," he added with a mirthless laugh.

"Are you all right, milord?" Will's gaze sharpened. "Can't let anything happen to you, else I might as well not bother returning to l'Eau Clair. Gillian'd have my head for certain." His mouth curled into his usual grin. "Lop it off herself, most like."

The image of his sister by marriage, sword in hand, helped Connor force his concerns aside and join in Will's laughter. "Aye, that she would." Gillian had brought joy and laughter to his twin, and some semblance of family to the FitzCliffords when before they'd had none. Connor had come to care deeply for his brother's fiery-haired wife.

At least Gillian had Rannulf to watch over her; Lady Moira had no one.

Connor rose and paced the length of the chamber, stopping by the window and nudging aside the shutter to look out at the setting sun. Moira FitzGerald would face her troubles alone no longer.

Like it or not, she'd have Connor FitzClifford as her champion.

He turned to Will. "Tell me what else you learned today. Perhaps if we pool our information, 'twill become clear what we should do next."

Connor managed to avoid Lady Moira for the next few days—both a blessing and a curse. Fortunately he didn't see her when he rose before dawn for his morning ritual, for if he'd had the slightest inkling she was anywhere near, 'twould have distracted him worse than he was already. Try though he might, he could not keep her out of his thoughts.

But he spent that valuable time alone, settling his mind and exercising his body as best he could.

He'd need a clear head and strong arms for what might lie ahead.

By the time the sun cleared the horizon, Connor was ready to lead out a troop to explore the territory around Gerald's Keep. With either d'Athée or Will in charge of the garrison he left behind—for he didn't dare leave the castle unprotected—he set off each day to familiarize himself with the terrain and the inhabitants of the area, and to seek information about the MacCarthys.

He and his troops would return to the castle near dusk, weary and sore. Each night Connor retreated to his chamber as soon as possible after receiving a report from whichever man he'd left in charge, to rest up for more on the morrow.

'Twas a punishing routine. Though it didn't keep his thoughts away from Lady Moira, at least it kept his *body* out of temptation's way.

Lady Moira's estimate that nearly everyone who lived close to the castle either had been killed or had abandoned their home appeared correct. The chill surrounding Connor's heart grew colder with each burned-out farm or crofter's hut they found, with each crudely marked grave. Though the MacCarthys apparently didn't have the strength or influence to lay siege to a castle or attack a large troop without help, they weren't above doing everything else within their power to instill fear into people who had already suffered at their hands.

How many had died, Connor wondered, so that the MacCarthys could drive the Normans from Gerald's Keep?

They would not succeed, he vowed as they rode toward a small manor set just outside the demesne of Gerald's Keep. Sir Robert de Montfort, a minor vassal of Lord Pembroke's, had welcomed Connor when he'd gone there the first day, and had promised to ask among his people if anyone had word of Hugh MacCarthy's plans.

Now, after four more days of searching and unsuccessfully seeking any word of the MacCarthys, Connor could only pray Sir Robert had news to share.

Sir Robert's wife led Connor and Will into the small hall and settled them near the central hearth with mugs of ale, sending a boy to bring her husband from the stables.

"'Tis no bother for us to seek him there, mistress," Connor told her, but she would not hear of them leaving. Once he'd answered several of her carefully phrased questions about Lady Moira, he realized why he was being grilled. 'Twas clear that concern for Lady Moira's well-being ran high among her acquaintances, who'd seen and heard nothing of her since Lord Brien's death.

"Poor lady, to lose her husband so near her time," said Sir Robert's wife, wiping away a tear with the edge of her wimple. "And to have to raise her child alone! Lord Brien so wanted a son, you know." She shook her head and blotted her eyes. "Such a tragedy!"

'Twas a relief to learn that here, among the Normans, it appeared the specifics of Lady Moira's ordeal at the MacCarthys' hands remained unknown. Connor had wondered if she'd be shunned or disgraced—and perhaps she might be yet, if all the details came out—but at least for now, people were concerned for her and willing to help her.

Connor also gave silent thanks that he'd brought Will with him today, not Sir Ivor. Though d'Athée remained silent on the subject of Lady Moira these days, Connor wouldn't have trusted him to hold his tongue in this situation.

Sir Robert strode into the hall and joined them, casting a patient look at his wife, whose face wore stark evidence of sorrow. She wiped her hand over her quivering cheek and poured her husband a cup of ale.

He took it from her with a murmured word of thanks. ''My dear, I know you've duties awaiting you,'' he said, his voice kind. ''I'm sure Lord Connor and Sir William will understand if you leave us.''

''Of course.'' Connor stood and bowed politely. Will, who'd risen when Sir Robert entered the room, bowed as well.

''Please convey my best wishes to Lady Moira,'' she said, still sniffling as she made her way out of the hall. ''I shall hope to hear soon that she's been safely delivered of a fine, healthy child.''

''Please excuse my wife,'' Sir Robert said as they resumed their seats after she left. ''We were not blessed with children, and my lady feels that lack deeply.''

''I understand,'' Connor said, though in truth, he felt confused. He'd been surprised by Sir Robert's patience and tolerance of his wife's behavior; this apology surprised him even more. Connor knew there were married couples who had so caring a relationship; indeed, he need only see Rannulf and Gillian together to know such solicitude existed. But he hadn't expected strangers to show their feelings so openly in his presence.

''Have you anything to report, Sir Robert?'' he asked, impatient for news after days of finding nothing.

''Aye, I have,'' the older man replied. He leaned closer and lowered his voice, though Connor had noticed no one else in the room. ''You must look to the cliffs, milord.''

''The cliffs? The cliffs below the headland?'' He couldn't imagine anyone successfully attacking from that direction.

''Gerald's Keep sits atop the ruins of an ancient fortress, a fortress that was in MacCarthy hands many years ago.''

Sir Robert started when a manservant entered the hall carrying a basket of peat for the fire. He motioned for the fellow to leave, and waited to speak until he'd set the basket on the hob, bowed and departed.

"Sir Robert, 'twas not my intent to put you in danger," Connor said, rising to his feet and setting his cup on a table. "But from your actions, I fear I must have done so."

Sir Robert stood as well and glanced about the hall yet again. "Nay, milord. 'Tis just that some of our servants are Irish, and I've no way of knowing who might be related to the MacCarthys. These people carry tales... You cannot imagine, Lord Connor, how swiftly news can travel here."

By the rood, did no Norman have anything good to say about the Irish? Connor bit back the words he knew he should not say to their host—despite the provocation—and sought deep inside himself for courtesy enough to hold his temper.

For now.

"I assume you've nothing further to tell me?" he asked.

Sir Robert shook his head, then brought his ale to his lips and drank deeply. "Just look to the cliffs for the answers you seek, milord. I can tell you nothing more."

"Look to the cliffs?" Will said, glancing at Connor through the thickening dusk as they rode at the head of the troop. "What the hell does that mean? Are the MacCarthys goats, that they can climb up to the castle from the sea?"

Connor shook his head and nudged his mount closer to Will's. "From what Lady Moira says, the headland cliffs are too sheer to be scaled. Besides, even if one or two men could manage it, they couldn't overcome an entire garrison."

Sir Robert's words haunted him for the rest of the journey back to Gerald's Keep. There must be *some* truth to them, else the man wouldn't have bothered to relay the information—nor been so nervous about it.

Perhaps there might be someone among the Irish families currently living within the castle grounds who would know what Sir Robert's words meant.

The torches mounted on the gatehouse sent a welcome glow through the lowering night, a far cry from the darkness that had greeted their arrival a sennight ago.

As was the sight of the drawbridge, already dropping into place. They rode straight into the bailey and dismounted near the stables.

A man-at-arms approached Connor as soon as he climbed from the saddle. "Milord." He bowed. "Lady Moira invites you—and all your men—to join her in the hall tonight for supper," he said. "If it please you, milord."

"A moment," Connor answered. He handed the reins to a stable lad and, frowning, left the soldier and walked over to Will. The young knight stood near the stable door, talking earnestly with Cedric, one of the men they'd brought with them from l'Eau Clair.

"Something wrong, milord?" Will asked.

"Nay, unless you count that Lady Moira has invited us to join everyone in the hall this evening," Connor said, removing his helm and running his hand impatiently through his hair. Dear God, but he was tired! Not that he'd any time to sleep. "I'd planned to start exploring, see if we can discover the truth of what Sir Robert told us."

Will nodded. "Aye, milord, 'tis important. But do you believe we could see anything at night that we haven't noticed—so far—in daylight? And the men are tired, milord, and growing as dispirited as everyone else here, so Cedric tells me."

"I know. And you're right, 'tis too dark now to start looking." Connor frowned. "Especially when we don't know what we're looking for.'' Resigning himself to wait until the morrow, he clapped Will on the back. ''We've dragged the men far and wide the last few days. They deserve a bit of fun. We'll double the guard on the headland portion of the wall, and halve the time for each watch. Everyone not on duty may join us in the hall tonight.'' Seeing Cedric's wide smile, he warned, ''Be certain they stay sober enough to remain competent. I'll not have the garrison reduced to a pack of drunkards, lest we have need of them.''

''Aye, milord,'' Cedric agreed. ''Thank you!'' Bowing briefly, he hurried away to spread the news.

''Will you see to mounting the guard?'' Connor asked Will.

''Of course, milord.''

Connor nodded his thanks. ''I'll see you in the hall then.''

After Will left, Connor returned to the man-at-arms. ''Tell your mistress that my men and I would be pleased to join her, as soon as we've had a chance to wash away the dust of travel.''

After the man left, Connor sighed wearily and crossed the bailey to the stairs leading into the keep.

As if he didn't have enough to bewilder his tired brain, now he must find the strength within him to spend the evening in Lady Moira's presence...without revealing to her or anyone else just how tempting he found her.

Chapter Seven

Moira spent the days since she spoke with Lord Connor on the headland cloistered in her solar with her maids, spinning and sewing. She had time aplenty to berate herself for telling him anything of what had brought them to this coil, and to try—without success—to convince herself that he held the power to carry them through their troubles to a happy resolution.

There *was* no way out of this without more pain, more sorrow. When had life held aught else?

But never had she felt more powerless than she did at this moment.

She paused at the head of the stairs and listened to the hum of noise rising from the hall. 'Twas louder than usual—not surprising, given that their numbers had nearly doubled with the addition of the men Lord Connor brought—but the sounds seemed more cheerful, as well. The reinforcements had given back to her people the sense of hope they'd lacked since Lord Brien's death. Tonight they'd have the opportunity to celebrate that fact.

They'd kept hope alive throughout the first few months of Lord Brien's illness, for hadn't he vanquished a much younger foe? 'Twas surely a sign that God smiled upon them, or so Father Thomas told them.

Though Moira had done all she could to save her husband, and had prayed as long and solemnly as anyone, deep within her heart she couldn't stifle her fear that all their prayers and hope would not prevail. Guilt nagged at her—guilt that her sins were so much worse than anyone knew.

She had not dared confess the depth of them even to Father Thomas, for what if he should turn against her? She knew 'twas God's forgiveness she needed, not the priest's, but she feared to lose the gentle cleric's support when she—when they all—needed it most.

'Twas sheer cowardice on her part, she knew. Though it was yet another sin to stain her soul, her pride was all she had left to sustain her.

But every word of comfort offered to her twisted the blade of guilt deeper into her heart, until she wondered if there was penance enough in all the world to atone for everything she'd done.

A door opened on the floor above her, and the sound of voices—Lord Connor's and another man's—carried down the stairwell to her, bringing her useless, maundering thoughts to a blessed end. She tugged at the loose folds of her gown to straighten it, and realized as she was about to turn to greet them that her cheeks were wet with tears.

She'd never cried so much in her life as she had the last few months! She used the trailing end of her linen veil to blot her face before they reached her, though 'twas likely they'd still know she'd been crying. 'Twas the babe that made her weep, Brigit claimed, a convenient excuse for the fact that Moira had turned into a sniveling coward.

And a nervous fool. She drew in a deep breath. What did it matter that she'd not seen Lord Connor in days? He'd been in her thoughts often during that time—too often.

Both men had dressed more formally than usual, as had she, in keeping with the spirit of celebration. Lord Connor's dark green tunic fit him well, the soft wool outlining his muscular shoulders and arms and causing a strange warmth to fill her. Though it appeared he'd bathed, for his hair was still damp, he hadn't shaved. The shadowy whiskers covering his jaw, coupled with the scar on his cheek, lent him a dangerous air she found all too appealing. With her heart pounding wildly, she lowered her gaze.

Enough of that, she berated herself, and forced herself to face them. "Lord Connor, Sir William," she said, her curtsy awkward, but as proper as she could manage.

Lord Connor steadied her with his hand beneath her elbow, though her reaction to his touch nearly sent her reeling again. "Milady, you need not be so formal." He led her deeper into the hallway, released her and bowed. "'Tis not necessary on my account, nor would I have you tumble down the stairs."

Sir William bowed as well. "And you don't have to call me 'Sir William,' milady. I'll think you're talking to someone else," he added, chuckling. "'Will' is fine with me."

"But you must have worked hard to earn your spurs, Sir Will," she said, smiling in response. "There's much that's different between Irish and Norman, but proving yourself a worthy fighter remains the same. Once my brothers achieved that status, they'd not permit anyone to forget it."

"Nor should Will," Lord Connor said. "He's proved his worth as a warrior many times in service to Lady Gillian, my sister by marriage, and to my brother since Rannulf and Gillian wed. 'Tis a measure of his ability that Rannulf sent him here with me."

"Don't let him deceive you, milady," Sir Will said. "'Tis only that I've known Lady Gillian since she was a child—fought with her then and since.'' He laughed. ''Fought with her and for her, I should say.''

His words brought a strange vision to Moira's mind, of a warrior woman clad in armor and armed with a sword and shield. That could not be the case with Lady Gillian, but Moira would have to wait to question Sir Will further, for the gong sounded, calling them to dinner.

Lord Connor held out his hand to her. ''May I escort you, Lady Moira?''

Surprised by his gallantry, she was nonetheless pleased to accept his assistance. ''Thank you, milord.'' She placed one hand atop his and gathered up her skirts with the other, then glanced at him from beneath her lashes. ''You do realize, if I trip, my weight would carry us both to the bottom,'' she warned, unable to resist teasing him. ''Perhaps you ought to send Sir Will ahead of us, in case I start us rolling down the stairs.''

Lord Connor appeared as startled by her words as she was that she'd said them. His brown eyes intent, he scanned her face, lingering on her eyes for a moment, before gifting her with a slow smile. ''I trust you'll not drag me down apurpose.''

His words could be taken in more ways than one, and the meaning that filled her mind drove away the sense of playfulness that had so briefly washed over her. She lowered her gaze. ''Nay, milord, I will not,'' she said, her voice flat.

Unaware of her change of mood, Sir Will raced lightly down the stairs and waited for them at the bottom. ''Come along,'' he called. ''If you don't hurry, I'll go on without you.''

She took a step toward the stairs, only to be brought up short by Lord Connor's hold on her hand. He tightened his clasp on her fingers and moved closer. "What troubles you, milady?"

"'Tis nothing," she murmured. "They'll be waiting for us in the hall—we must go."

He leaned down, making her aware of his size, his strength, though not in a threatening manner. "I wish you would tell me. But perhaps 'tis too soon," he added, so quietly she barely heard him.

"There's naught more to tell," she replied.

He stared deep into her eyes for a moment, then shook his head. "I wonder."

Straightening, he eased his clasp on her hand and led her down the stairs, matching his steps to her slow ones. They entered the hall and were immediately surrounded by revelry.

More torches than usual lit the huge chamber, casting a flickering golden glow over the room. 'Twas easy to see that the people of Gerald's Keep had been glad of this opportunity to celebrate. Folks laughed and smiled, many of the women had livened their garb and hair with bright ribbons, and some of the men appeared cleaner than usual.

It seemed they'd welcomed Lord Connor's men into their midst already. Life at Gerald's Keep had been dark and solemn for months, and 'twas clear everyone needed a respite from those days.

Moira returned smiles and happy words of greeting, as Lord Connor led her across the long room to the table set upon the dais at the far end. Her heart swelled with gladness to see her people's joy.

Her pleasure dimmed somewhat when she stepped up onto the dais and discovered Sir Ivor waiting for them, arms folded tight across his chest, his handsome face twisted in a mocking sneer.

Once Lord Connor pulled out the bench for her, bowing

over her hand before stepping away and taking a seat to her right, she motioned Sir Ivor closer. "Good humor and revelry are the order of the day, Sir Ivor. I will not allow you to cast a pall over this meal with your ill temper."

His sneer turned to a frown, but he gave a curt nod and took his seat—thankfully, as far away as he could be from her.

Lord Connor's questioning look changed to a commanding glare as he glanced from her to Sir Ivor. "Ignore him, milady. I don't plan for him to be here much longer."

The level of noise tapered off as people took seats at the tables ranged below them in the hall. Moira rose and clapped her hands together, silencing the last snippets of chatter. "I am so pleased to see smiles and hear laughter," she said, smiling herself as she gazed about her. "It's been too long since we've had something to smile about. But that has changed." She turned to Lord Connor. "Our overlord, Lord Rannulf FitzClifford, has heeded our request for assistance and sent his brother with troops to help us. I know you'll continue to make them welcome and to lend them whatever aid they need. We've hard work ahead of us, but for tonight, let us celebrate our newfound good fortune." She reached for her goblet of wine and raised it to salute the man seated beside her. "Our thanks, Lord Connor." She sipped the drink as the crowd echoed her words, then placed the goblet on the table before her and sat down.

Father Thomas rose and blessed the food, and the servers carried the platters among the trestle tables below. A young man, tall, slim and unfamiliar to her, knelt and held a basin of scented water for her to wash her hands. "My squire, Padrig," Lord Connor told her. "He's come into my service only recently, but already he's proven himself a valiant assistant."

Color flooded Padrig's pale cheeks at his master's words,

and he turned his attention to offering her a linen towel to dry her hands. "Thank you, Padrig," she said. "I can see that you perform your duties well."

His flush darkened and he bowed his head. "I'll do my best to serve you, milady," he said before turning away.

"He's a brave lad," Lord Connor told her as he served her meat and cheese from the platter before them. "You'd not know it to look at him now, but 'twas not long ago that he lay near death with a lung fever. He recovered quickly, and could not wait to get out of bed and to his lessons in swordplay. He'll make a fine warrior."

As the talk turned to courteous pleasantries, the level of sound filling the hall rose once again. A motley group of musicians had assembled near the hearth, their music lending a festive air. Moira tried to keep her attention focused upon their lively songs and the activities of those seated in the hall below them, but the man at her side proved a most formidable distraction. All she could do was remind herself, again and again, that she'd nothing to offer any man now.

Nor would she put any man at risk through her actions.

A guard in mail and helm made his way through the hall and approached the high table, carrying silence in his wake. Even the music came to a jangling stop. He halted at the foot of the dais, tugged off his helm and bowed awkwardly to her. One of Lord Connor's men, for she didn't recognize him. "Pardon, milady. Milord, there's a messenger outside—"

Lord Connor cut him off with a gesture and motioned for him to join them on the dais. "There's nothing wrong," he called out in the near silence. "Please, carry on with the revels."

"A messenger from where, Henry?" he asked once the man stood beside him.

Henry leaned close and whispered his reply, too quietly for Moira to hear.

Lord Connor frowned, then nodded. "Bring him in." He cast a swift glance at the gaiety once more surrounding them. "Let him see that we're not cowering in fear behind the walls."

Henry bowed to them again, turned smartly and hurried toward the door.

"Who is it, milord?" she asked as soon as he'd left.

Connor picked up the goblet, raised it to his lips, then set the drink down untasted as he realized what he'd done. "I should have asked your permission before giving the order, milady. This is your home—it should be your decision who enters here," he said. "I apologize."

"'Tis nothing. I'm content to leave matters of our defense to you, milord." She picked up the wine ewer and topped off the goblet, sliding it closer to him. "This does concern our defense, does it not?"

"Aye, it does." Should he wait, have her learn who had sent the man to them, or warn her now? In her condition, 'twould be best if she were not overset by shock or surprise. "'Tis a messenger from the MacCarthys."

He thought she grew pale, though it was difficult to tell in the flickering torchlight. He'd been wise to tell her, to give her time to prepare herself.

The door from outside opened with a thud, heralding Henry's reappearance and silencing the revelry once again. The guard stood aside to allow a tall, bearded stranger into the hall, followed by two more of Connor's men. One pulled the door closed while the others escorted the stranger toward the dais.

The messenger, his dark brown garb worn, his reddish-brown hair and beard curling wildly around his face, strode through the crowd as though he hadn't a care in the world.

He stopped before them, standing at his ease with the three guards ranged behind him.

Lady Moira gasped and tried to rise, but Connor remained seated and held the bench firmly in place close to the table. He leaned toward her and whispered, "Stay where you are, milady. There's no reason for you to greet MacCarthy's man by leaping to your feet. I doubt he's worthy of that honor." She clutched the edge of the table with one hand, her knuckles white with strain. Her other hand lay atop the mound of her belly—which moved as he watched. By the saints! Did the babe feel her tension? "Besides, it cannot be good for a woman in your condition to be jumping about like a mountain goat," he added, hoping his poor jest might ease the tension that held her wound so tightly.

"You don't understand, milord," she said, her voice low, frantic. Her eyes were fixed on the man standing below them.

Ignoring the guards, he took a step closer, grinned and made a mocking bow. "Is this the way you greet me when 'tis been so long since last we met?"

Who was he? Connor shoved back the bench and stood, ready to vault over the table if the man didn't change his attitude soon.

"And who might this be?" the man asked, all signs of humor gone in an instant. "Don't tell me you've replaced Brien—and Dermot—in your bed already, sister dear."

Chapter Eight

"'Tis my brother, Aidan O'Neill." Her body shaking, Lady Moira braced her hands on the table and slowly levered herself to her feet. The glare she sent her brother should have felled him where he stood, but his grin widened in response. "Aidan, this is Lord Connor FitzClifford, my overlord's brother."

O'Neill moved forward, hand outstretched. Connor ignored the overture and remained where he stood, lowering his own hand to rest on his sword hilt. Henry and another guard came forward, their faces dark with anger, grabbed O'Neill by the arms and tugged him back.

Taking his time, to give himself a chance to cool his temper, Connor made his way around the table, then stopped in front of it. The urge to leap off the dais and grab O'Neill, to throttle him till his smug smile disappeared, was strong—too strong. Lady Moira might not appreciate it if he strangled her brother, despite the fool's disrespect toward her.

Instead he leaned back against the table, his hand still resting on his sword. "'Tis your good fortune that you're Lady Moira's kin, else I'd slay you here and now," he growled. "I just might do so anyway." He glanced back at Lady Moira, weighing her response—not that he'd take the words back.

She appeared stunned and weary, nearly swaying on her feet; he doubted she had even noticed what he'd said. He'd guess the shock of her brother's arrival, coupled with what the lout had said to her—loudly enough for everyone in the hall to hear—accounted for her reaction.

Connor turned his back on O'Neill and rounded the table again. "Milady, are you well?" he asked, taking her by the arm. The expression in her pain-filled eyes struck him like a knife to the heart. "Sit, lady. Rest." She resisted his efforts to ease her down onto the bench. "Would you rather retire to your solar or your chamber?" he asked quietly. "We need not continue this discussion here. 'Tis no one's business but your own."

She turned so they faced away from the others. "Thank you, milord. The solar will be fine," she whispered. "And I'll go there on my own two feet," she added when he would have lifted her in his arms.

He nodded. He understood how important it was for her to remain in control, especially in light of her brother's insults. Connor stepped away from her as she turned toward the crowd watching them in near silence. "Henry, please bring my brother to my solar," she ordered. "And post a guard in the corridor."

"Aye, milady." Henry bowed, then motioned for the guards to carry out her command. They tugged O'Neill around and urged him toward the wide path that had opened up in the midst of the gathering, leading straight to the stairs at the opposite end of the hall.

Lady Moira drew in a deep breath and clapped her hands—not that she needed to capture anyone's attention. All eyes had shifted back to the dais once O'Neill disappeared from sight into the stairwell. "We gathered here to celebrate. Please, let the revelry continue.'' After a discordant start, the musicians struck up a lively tune that was swiftly accompanied by the hum of renewed conversation.

The others seated at the high table had remained silent throughout the byplay, but now Will rose and drew Connor aside. ''What would you have me do, milord?''

Connor glanced about the chamber, his gaze coming to rest upon d'Athée's satisfied expression. While he doubted d'Athée had had any part in bringing O'Neill here, that he'd enjoyed the man's insults to Lady Moira was obvious. ''Send Padrig to make certain Henry kept a strong guard posted, and have him learn what he can about how O'Neill came here,'' he said in a low voice. ''Send word to the guards along the cliffside to redouble their vigilance. You stay in the hall and keep watch over the revelers,'' he added, with a meaningful glance at Sir Ivor. ''Lady Moira has worries enough without more being heaped upon her.''

''Do you need any help upstairs?''

He shook his head. ''With three guards there already? You've a poor opinion of my abilities.''

Will grinned. ''Nay, milord. 'Tis just that I hate to miss any of the excitement.''

''I doubt it will be exciting,'' Connor said wryly. ''Maddening, I've no doubt. But Lady Moira's presence should be sufficient to keep me from strangling her brother—unless, of course, she decides she wants me to.''

''The bastard deserves it,'' Will said, his smile gone, his voice cold. ''Simply for what he said to her, never mind anything else he might have done.'' He raked his hand through his hair. ''But since she's a gentle lady, she'll not let you harm him.''

''You might be surprised,'' Connor said, recalling Moira's determination to defend her child. If she thought her brother—or anyone—represented a threat to the babe, she'd do whatever necessary to protect it.

He'd do well to remember that himself, should he and Lady Moira disagree about what was best for her.

He clapped Will on the back and gave him a push toward the table. "Go on, keep them busy while I find out why O'Neill came here."

Will caught sight of a buxom maidservant headed their way with a platter of food. "I'll do my best, milord," he said. His grin restored, he motioned Padrig to his side.

Satisfied that Will would keep everything here well in hand, Connor left the hall.

Moira stood in the corridor outside her solar and waited for Lord Connor. Only the guard's presence beside her door kept her from slumping against the plaster wall and giving in to the despair enveloping her.

If she sought refuge within her bedchamber, she'd never find the courage to leave it while Aidan remained within Gerald's Keep. No matter how much she dreaded—and needed—to hear what her eldest brother, her least favorite, had to say.

Why had Aidan come here? Why now? Henry had said the messenger came from the MacCarthys. Did this mean her brothers had decided to join forces with her enemy once again?

Anything was possible with the three of them. If they believed they'd gain some advantage from such a scheme, they'd forge an alliance with the devil himself.

Well she knew the lengths they'd go to get what they wanted. When they'd decided 'twas necessary for them to form a connection with the Normans who'd risen to power in Munster, they'd seen her wed to Lord Brien.

Not that it had done them much good, she thought dryly.

Her husband felt they were too wild, too erratic to be of much use to him. He'd thrown that fact in her face more and more often as the years passed, barren years when she did not provide him with the heir he'd married her to gain.

A chill ran through her as she recalled Lord Brien's last months. She rubbed her hands over her arms, but the usually soothing motion could not chase the bone-deep cold away.

When he'd first realized she was with child... 'Twas fortunate for her he'd been too ill to rise from his bed, else he'd surely have struck her dead. How he'd ranted about old warhorses and young stallions, claiming 'twas her fault his seed had fallen on fallow ground while MacCarthy's had ripened.

His words had embedded themselves in her mind to taunt her, making her wonder again and again if there could be any truth to them.

Was everything that had occurred her fault?

As time passed, her husband's ire had abated. Though he had never apologized for his accusations, eventually they ceased. The last month or two before his death—as her belly grew bigger, making every glimpse of her a reminder of all that had happened—he'd changed his stance completely. In both word and deed he'd claimed her child as his own.

What should have been a blessing, however, felt more to her like a curse, for it became a constant reminder of her guilt.

The noise rising from the hall masked the sound of Lord Connor's footsteps on the stairs. She looked up and he was there, standing at the top of the steps, watching her.

Though she wanted to look away from his probing glance, she met his gaze, raised her chin in challenge.

Pray God her thoughts had not shown themselves upon her face, else he'd know all her secrets.

"I thought you would have gone inside by now," he said, closing the distance between them, his eyes still focused on her with uncomfortable intensity.

"I'm too big a coward," she said. "I've no wish to meet him alone."

Lord Connor came forward and took her arm, the warmth of his touch soothing, lending her strength. "You need not speak to him. If you'd rather, I can question him about why he's come. Though I admit I'd find your presence a help." He gazed down at her, his expression apologetic. "It's not my intention to insult your family, but your brother doesn't strike me as trustworthy. Since you know him, you may be able to judge if he's telling the truth."

"I suppose such a miracle is possible, but I wouldn't depend upon it."

"That he'd be truthful, or that you'd be able tell if he lied?" he asked. "He's your brother—wouldn't you know?"

"If you have the unfortunate pleasure of coming to know my brother better, you'll realize that fact matters not a whit." Her laugh sounded bitter, as close an emotion to what she felt toward Aidan as any. "Indeed, if he comes to know *you* better, 'twill only supply him with more weapons to use against you."

"Then I hope you'll come in with me now," he said, drawing her along with him to the door. "For I know your opinion will prove useful."

Taking a deep breath to calm her quaking stomach, she gave him a weak smile. "Such flattery, milord. Though in this instance, your need dovetails well with my desire." He raised an eyebrow in question. "I want to know what he's doing here, why he's come now."

He nodded and raised the latch, but hesitated before opening the door. "Do you want me to go in first?"

She didn't understand why he asked, but as she weighed his serious expression, she realized what he meant. "Nay—he'll not harm me, with you and two guards here. His tongue was ever his favorite weapon, milord. I assure you, I'm used to it."

"As you wish." Lord Connor pushed open the door and stood back so she could enter the solar.

Two branches of candles had been lighted, and the fire in the hearth sent off the homey scent of burning peat. The chamber should have felt welcoming and cheerful, but the scene laid out before her made her want to scream with frustration, not smile with pleasure.

Aidan sat sprawled at the head of the table, his chair tipped back on two legs, one booted foot resting atop the fine polished tabletop. He held a goblet in his hand and wore a taunting grin on his face.

'Twas just as she'd imagined; he'd make himself comfortable anywhere, whether he was welcome or not.

Henry stood by the window across the room, his hand clutched about the hilt of his sword and his face twisted into a scowl as he stared fixedly at Aidan, while the other guard, his visage emotionless, maintained a position just inside the door.

Aidan raised the goblet in salute, then tipped it back and drained it. "Moira, my darling little sister. Not so little now, though, I see." He scanned her from head to toe, his grin changing to a leer. "You *have* been busy since I saw you last." He swung his foot off the table and thumped the chair legs down on the floor. "The brat you carry must be slowing you down. I thought you'd never get here." Banging the empty cup onto the table, he belched and reached for the ewer of wine set before him. "I'd think you'd be eager to see me, after all our time apart."

For a brief moment she considered ignoring his crudity, but she knew how much worse he could get—especially once he was drunk. Best if she stopped him now, if possible, before he had the opportunity to show himself to be a bigger fool than he'd already done.

She crossed the room and snatched the pitcher of wine from his hand. "As always, Aidan, you abuse my good nature and expect me to thank you for it."

"What are you saying?" Scowling, he tugged at his beard, a sure sign that he knew exactly what she meant.

She stepped away from him and held the wine beyond his reach, not that it stopped his attempts to take it from her. She slapped his hand aside and moved back, wishing his chair were still tilted, so she might have the pleasure of knocking it from beneath him. "Do you think you can come here, insult me and my guests—"

"Enough, Moira." He glanced past her to Lord Connor. She looked back over her shoulder and saw that, other than folding his arms across his chest, he hadn't moved since he'd entered the room and taken up a position near the closed door. "I hope she doesn't nag at you like this, milord. I warn you, she can be a vengeful shrew when the mood strikes her."

"You always did have that effect on me," Moira said quietly. She pulled out the chair opposite Aidan and motioned for Lord Connor to take it. "Here, milord. Sit, if you please. 'Tis not proper for you to stand while he sits there, allowing his mouth free rein."

Unwilling to stand by and watch Lady Moira and her loathsome brother spar any longer, Connor came forward and grasped the seat she offered, holding it out for her. "You first, milady."

She sank onto the chair, her faint smile thanks aplenty. Connor took a stool from near the hearth and, setting it between Lady Moira and her brother, turned to the guards. "Henry, Louis—we'll not need you in here. Louis, you and Ralph can return to the gatehouse while Henry stands guard outside this chamber."

Henry nodded. "As you wish, milord," he said, though he looked as though he'd rather remain in the room.

Connor would rather he did not, since there was no telling exactly what Aidan O'Neill was apt to say or do. Until they discovered O'Neill's reason for coming to Gerald's Keep, Connor preferred to keep their conversation private, for Lady Moira's sake.

He waited till the two guards left and shut the door behind them before he sat down. "Now that we're alone, O'Neill, you'd better cease your insults toward your sister—which I will not tolerate further—and tell me why you're here."

O'Neill slumped back in his seat. "So you're FitzGerald's overlord?"

"My brother is."

O'Neill scowled. "We'd heard that Lord Rannulf—he's your brother?" he asked abruptly, his pale blue eyes shifting restlessly between Moira and Connor.

"He is." Connor limited his impatience to a sharp nod.

"We'd heard he'd come.... The fellow swore 'twas him," he added, suspicion coloring his tone, his expression. "The message I bear is for him, not his lackey."

Did the fool believe he was Rannulf pretending to be Connor? What purpose would *that* serve?

Most important, *who* had told O'Neill—and the MacCarthys, presumably—that Rannulf had come to Ireland?

What did it matter?

Connor pushed aside the questions plaguing him and focused his attention on O'Neill and the information he could supply.

"You'll have to settle for me," he said flatly. He sat back and glanced from O'Neill to Lady Moira. "Your sister knows my brother. She can verify that I'm not Rannulf, not that I understand why anyone would think that—"

"You *are* twins, milord," she said. "There's more than a slight resemblance." Though she sounded polite, alert, he could hear the weariness tainting her voice.

A swift glance at her face, tense and pale, confirmed it.

"Aye. 'Twould account for it, I suppose, though we don't appear exactly alike." He gestured toward the scar on his face.

"You're alike enough, especially from a distance. I assume the spy is not someone from within these walls?" she asked her brother.

"Nay, 'tis not." O'Neill shoved away from the table and raked a hand through his tangled hair. "Though I don't see what difference it makes," he snarled.

"It matters to me!" she cried. She looked at Connor. "To both of us, I'd imagine."

"Aye." Connor rose and went to the hearth, staring into the flames dancing there as though they might contain the answers to ease his restless mind.

How could he question O'Neill properly, when all he wanted was to grab the fool out of his chair and smash him into the wall for his manner toward his sister? Not to mention the fact that he wasn't certain the questions he'd ask would be the correct ones.

He wanted to do this well, to prove Rannulf had been right to trust him. He picked up the poker and stirred the fire.

And though it should not matter, Connor didn't wish to

appear an ignorant fool before Moira. She was depending on him. He didn't want to disappoint her.

Never had he felt his lack of experience more keenly than at this moment!

He reminded himself of the conversations he'd had with his brother before Rannulf sent him here. Rannulf knew better than anyone of the uncertainty that plagued him.

Behave as though you have the answer to every question, Rannulf had told him. *As though the answers don't matter. Only then have you any chance of hearing the truth.*

Connor glanced from Moira to her brother once more, weighed what he saw. He could sense O'Neill's impatience, etched in every line of his body.

Good. He could use that impatience to his advantage in questioning him.

But he could not drag this out much longer, he realized as he observed Moira. One hand rubbed her belly as though it pained her, and the other clutched the lower edge of the table, a sign of tension visible to him, but not, fortunately, to her brother.

His movements slow and measured, he gave the fire a last stir, laid the poker on the hearth and returned to the table. "The hour is late, O'Neill, and your sister grows weary." He caught Moira's angry glare from the corner of his eye, but he ignored it and straddled the stool. "I'm the only FitzClifford you're like to get, so if you've a message to deliver, start talking. Otherwise, I'll escort you from Gerald's Keep myself, for I'll not allow you to remain here a moment longer than I must." He reinforced the threat with a steady glare. "Not after the way you've insulted your sister."

O'Neill's impatience transformed to anger and he leaped to his feet. "You've no right!" he shouted, one hand going to his waist and clutching at air where his sword hilt should have been.

Connor remained seated, outwardly relaxed, though poised to spring into action should it prove necessary. ''Who are you to tell me otherwise?'' he asked, amusement flavoring his voice, lips curled in a faint smile. ''Deliver your message and be done with it.''

O'Neill moved away from the table and leaned back against the wall near the shuttered window—out of reach, Connor noted, the amusement he felt now genuine. ''Hugh MacCarthy lays claim to Moira and the child she bears, through her liaison with his brother, Dermot.'' He straightened, his stare a challenge. ''I'm to bring her back with me on the morrow.''

Mind reeling, forcing himself to ignore Moira's outraged cry, Connor concentrated upon keeping his expression neutral. ''Did MacCarthy truly believe—do *you* believe—I'd simply hand her over to him as if she were a cow that had strayed from its byre?'' He didn't dare look at Moira to see how she took those words. ''And how can *you* think of giving her over into the hands of the family who abused her?''

Amazingly, what appeared to be righteousness lit O'Neill's eyes. ''We wed her to FitzGerald, and now that he's gone, 'tis our right—my brothers' and mine—to give her where we will. Might as well send her where she'll do us the most good.''

His attention caught by O'Neill's words, Connor didn't notice that Moira had risen from her seat until she passed him. He stood and reached out to catch her about the waist before she could get to her brother.

''Release me at once,'' she cried breathlessly, fighting Connor's hold. ''I'll not allow him—'' She kicked out, her soft shoe connecting with Connor's shin. Though she cried out in pain, she didn't cease her struggles.

O'Neill backed away from them, likely his wisest act since he'd arrived at Gerald's Keep.

Connor slipped his arms about Moira's middle and held her clasped to him, her back to his front. Her body fairly vibrated with rage. Though he'd love to release her and let her give her brother what he deserved, he feared she'd harm herself. "Easy," he whispered in her ear. "Hush. He'll not take you anywhere unless you wish to go. I swore to you, remember?" He felt the fight slip from her until she slumped against him, his arms holding her upright. "All right?"

She rested her arms atop his and clasped her hands tightly around his wrists. "Aye, milord," she murmured. Once her fingers eased their grip and she stood on her own, he released her, though he stayed close behind her. "How could you join forces with them, Aidan? After all they've done, how could you agree to give me to them?"

"'Tis for the best, Moira," O'Neill said.

"Best for *you,*" she said, her voice cold. She turned to Connor, her eyes dry, but filled with pain. "I should have expected this. My brothers have ever seen me as coin to barter for their betterment."

Connor glanced past her to her brother. "She's yours to bargain with no longer, O'Neill," he said. "Tell MacCarthy that Lady Moira's fate rests with the FitzCliffords now, and they refuse to hand her over to anyone against her will."

Chapter Nine

Moira knew she'd never forget the expression on Aidan's face when Lord Connor refused to hand her over, for after the way her brother—nay, all her brothers—had treated her over the years, 'twas a pleasure worth savoring to witness one of them thwarted in his desire to use her again.

Nor could she forget the warmth that flooded her at the feeling of support Lord Connor's arms about her waist, coupled with his words, had supplied. Though that was a memory she'd do well to erase from her mind and heart at once.

She'd wanted to follow as Lord Connor and Henry escorted Aidan from the keep, but Lord Connor had refused to allow her to come along. Her temper simmering, she'd obeyed.

But she didn't plan on remaining silent when Lord Connor returned, as he'd said he would.

Connor led the way to a small storeroom on the ground floor of the gatehouse and held the stout, iron-bound door open while Henry led Aidan O'Neill inside, then brought in a blanket and a bucket. Dismissing Henry to return to his duties, Connor removed a lantern from its hook on the wall next to the door and entered the room, closing the door behind him.

Something rustled and squeaked in the far corner of the chamber.

"I see I'm to be given all the comforts Gerald's Keep has to offer," O'Neill said dryly. He shook out the blanket with a snap, wrapped it about his shoulders and settled onto the floor, resting his back against a sack of grain.

Connor hung the light from a peg on the wall and leaned back against the door, arms folded across his chest. "What did you expect—that your sister would hear what you had to say, then greet you with open arms?"

"She ever was a contrary lass," O'Neill said with disgust. "Never willing to do what we wanted."

"If this latest plan of yours is an example of your wishes where she's concerned, I can understand why. Did you truly believe she'd agree to give herself and her child up to the men who abused her?" He watched the Irishman's face carefully, but saw only honest confusion displayed there.

"They'll wind up in Hugh MacCarthy's hands sooner or later anyway," O'Neill said with some heat. "No offense to you, milord, but you cannot expect to thwart Hugh. A more pigheaded man has never lived!" He shook his head. "Hugh won't rest till he's taken what he wants—or dies in the process."

Connor straightened and stood at his ease—outwardly, at least. "Hugh MacCarthy will find there is a huge difference between terrorizing a dying old man and his defenseless peasants, and facing me and my men."

"So you say, milord. But what'll you gain, eh? This keep isn't yours, 'tis your brother's. And Moira..." He laughed. "Do you honestly believe having her in your bed will be worth the bother of dealing with MacCarthy? The man sees this as a holy quest—"

The sneer on O'Neill's face changed to shock as Connor lunged toward him and, snagging the front of his tunic, lifted him off the floor. "You'll cease talking of your sister as though she was a whore," he snapped, raising the man higher and shaking him. "Else you'll be lucky if you can crawl out of here." Connor threw him against the piled bags of grain and watched him slide to the stone floor, all his strength focused upon not closing the distance to finish off the mouthy bastard.

O'Neill lay unmoving, staring up at Connor. Then, reaching around to rub the side of his head, he slowly sat up. "Christ, you've a temper on you!" He smoothed his hair back and gave his beard a tug. "Wouldn't have thought it of a Norman," he added with a grin.

By the saints, was the man mad? Connor wondered. Toss him aside like an empty ale horn, and he became more friendly? Jesu! Perhaps he ought to bring Will in here, see if *he'd* any notion how to deal with someone like O'Neill.

"Your mistake," Connor said. His gaze cold, he picked up the blanket and tossed it down next to O'Neill. "Seems I'm Irish enough to want to kill you where you sit, but I've sufficient Norman blood to stay my hand."

He reached for the lantern, then paused before opening the door. "Have you anything you'd care to tell me before I leave you and the rats to enjoy the remainder of the night together?"

"Nay, milord—not a thing," O'Neill said in a lazy drawl.

"Perhaps something will come to you by morning," Connor said as he left the room without a backward glance, closing Aidan O'Neill in utter darkness.

His mind awhirl, he headed back to the keep. He doubted he'd learn any more from O'Neill come morning than he had tonight. And he hesitated to question the fool about the

MacCarthys' plans too closely, lest he inadvertently give O'Neill some snippet of information about their situation to carry back with him.

Connor paused outside the door leading into the hall, closing his eyes and savoring the silence of the bailey before braving the noisy revels.

He didn't intend to tarry there long. He'd told Lady Moira that he'd return once he'd seen her brother settled for the night.

What he'd say to her once he saw her again, he had no notion.

He opened the door and let the sound pour over him. It should have heartened him, but only served to underscore how tired he felt. He lingered to speak with Will and assure himself that his orders had been carried out, then mounted the stairs to Lady Moira's solar again.

Moira's temper had cooled by the time she heard a knock at the door, but she'd worked herself into a mass of nerves as the time crept by. What if Connor believed Aidan's plans had merit? What if he decided she and her child were too much bother, and handed her over to her brothers? No one would see anything odd about such a decision, for many a widow returned to her family after her husband's death.

But she'd rather go anywhere—save to the MacCarthys—than return to her brothers' none-too-loving arms.

In her heart, she could not believe that Connor FitzClifford would do such as thing. But in her mind... In her thoughts, anything seemed possible.

When the knock sounded, she set aside the spindle she'd been working in the fruitless hope of calming herself, rose and pressed her hands against her gown to still their trembling, then crossed the room and pulled open the door.

He was alone, she noted with relief. At least she'd not have to hear his decision for her future before witnesses.

"Milord, come in." She held the door wide, then closed it behind him. "I trust my brother gave you no trouble?"

His face revealed nothing of his thoughts, but she could tell something weighed heavily on his mind. "Nothing I couldn't handle," he said absently.

What did he mean by that? The words gave her no ease, since she doubted there was much this man *couldn't* handle.

Something he would not wait till morning to discuss.

"I know the hour is late," he said as they stood in the middle of the room. "And you must be exhausted. But I wished to speak with you now."

Because if he delayed, he might lose his courage? she wondered as she met his dark eyes and he glanced away. He looked as though he wished to be anywhere but here, yet here he remained.

Despite her curiosity, she wasn't sure she wished to know what could cause this mighty warrior to appear so uncertain. Yet waiting till the morrow would serve no purpose save cause her a sleepless night.

"Come, sit down, milord." She gestured toward the chairs by the table. "I can send Brigit for food. You had little opportunity to eat at supper, and you must still be hungry."

"Food would be welcome. Will you join me?"

"Aye, milord." She went through the doorway to her chamber, where Brigit sat by the fire, sewing. She sent the maid to fetch a tray of food and a pitcher of warm spiced wine. Perhaps a cup or two of the wine might ease Lord Connor's discomfort.

When she returned to the solar, she found him near the hearth, sword belt in hand. "I hope you don't mind." He leaned the weapon against the wall and knelt to build up the fire.

"Not at all. Please, milord, relax and be comfortable. Brigit will return with food and wine soon," she said.

While he tended the fire she replaced several guttering candles in the stand by the table and removed the goblet and pitcher Aidan had used.

If only she could make Aidan's words disappear so easily!

Lord Connor remained near the hearth, staring into the flames, while she wandered to the small loom set up beneath the window. 'Twas too dark here to try to weave, but she once again took up the spindle lying next to it and spun a bit of thread. Surprisingly, she found the silence between them pleasant, comfortable.

Brigit returned, followed by Lord Connor's squire, Padrig, carefully balancing a loaded tray. "Set it on the table, there's a good lad," Brigit ordered. While Padrig laid out the food and drink, Brigit turned to Moira. "He wished to serve his master," the maid said, her wrinkled face alight with humor. "Who am I to tell him he cannot?" She gave a dry laugh. "Besides, you'd like as not have had to send me back for more if I'd attempted that trek, since I doubt I'd have made it up the steps without spilling something."

"I didn't intend for you to carry the tray up here yourself, Brigit," Moira scolded. She set aside the spindle and joined them by the table. "As you well know. As it is, I'd not have sent you down the stairs again tonight, had there been anyone else up here to go."

The maid chuckled again and patted Moira's hand. "I know, milady, I know. You're a good lass to a crotchety old besom, that you are. I just hoped to make you laugh, 'tis all."

Moira gave the maidservant the smile she'd wanted.

"You do, Brigit. Only there doesn't seem to be much to laugh about, not with my brother here."

"You ignore whatever that bastard says, beggin' your pardon, milady. He's never done anything unless he thought he'd gain from it, and well you know it." She glanced past Moira and her face creased into a look of welcome. "You'll keep her safe from her brothers, won't you, milord? A strong young fellow like you should be able to fend off the likes of the O'Neills."

Moira turned; Lord Connor stood behind her, dusting off his hands. "I'll do my best," he said. "I can guarantee that the only way your lady's brothers will enter Gerald's Keep again is if they can fight their way past me and my men. And O'Neill won't bother anyone for the rest of the night, I warrant."

Moira wondered at the amusement she saw in his eyes. "I thought you intended to put him out tonight."

"Morning will be soon enough," he said. "I haven't quite decided what I want to do about him."

"So long as he's not wandering about the place," Brigit said with a decisive nod. "We'll be safe from him, then. Thank you, milord." She cast a glance at them, then looked over at Padrig, standing at attention beside the table. "Come along, lad, and leave your master and the lady to their business."

"Milord, do you need me for aught else?" Padrig asked.

"Nay. Go find Will, see if he has need of you," Lord Connor said. He smiled. "If he doesn't, I'm sure you can find something to occupy you until I need you in the morning."

"Aye, milord, thank you," Padrig said in a rush. His bow so hurried he nearly tripped over himself, he raced for the door. He halted just inside the room, however, and turned. "By your leave, milady," he said, surprising Moira with the fact that he'd slowed his headlong pace for her.

"I thank you for helping Brigit, Padrig," she said, hoping she could return his serious expression and not offend him by smiling at his sudden gravity. "God grant you a peaceful rest."

He swept another bow, more formal this time, then negated the effect when he dashed from the chamber. Brigit, chuckling beneath her breath, bobbed a curtsy and followed him out with far less haste.

The door creaked closed, leaving Moira alone with Lord Connor. "You don't think he's off to his bed already, do you?" Lord Connor asked with a smile. "The revels were still going strong when I passed through the hall."

"You're probably correct, milord." Suddenly uncertain what to say or do, Moira gestured toward the table. "Shall we see what Padrig brought for us?"

The smell of roast mutton and spices reached her on a gust of wind coming through the drafty shutters, setting her stomach growling. The babe chose that moment to kick and squirm. "All right, I'll feed you," she whispered, laying a hand on her belly.

Lord Connor's laugh brought a flush to her cheeks. "Demanding, is he?" He reached for her free hand and led her to her chair, easing her into it. "We cannot let the poor child go hungry, especially since there's so much to choose from. Padrig has brought us a feast, by the look of it." He picked up the wine and poured a measure into a cup, handing it to her. "Do you think he meant for me to have any of this, or is it all for you?" he asked, casting her a teasing glance.

Despite the color still heating her face, Moira allowed her gaze to roam over him as he piled mutton onto a trencher and placed it in front of her. Her eyes lingered over the breadth of his chest before stopping once she encountered his. "You're much larger than I, milord. Perhaps 'tis the other way around. He's *your* squire, after all."

'Twas not embarrassment that warmed her face now, but awareness of him. His height alone made her feel small, dainty—she who could scarce lay claim to such a description, especially now. His muscular build made her feel safe, despite her many fears, as though no one could harm her or her child.

As for his manner toward her... When had a man *ever* treated her with such respect as Lord Connor did? 'Twould be so easy to believe she meant something to him, had value to him for herself, not for what she could bring him.

'Twas a seduction more tempting than any sins of the flesh.

And it was a dangerous way to think, to feel, dangerous for both of them. She could not trust herself in the presence of a young, virile man. Her previous actions told her that well enough.

And embroiling *this* man within the tangled web of her life could not be safe for him, either, not with the MacCarthys, the O'Neills and Lord only knew what other Irish families eager to gain possession of Gerald's Keep through her and her child.

One man, no matter how strong, could not overcome such odds.

They ate in silence. As Moira drained her cup of wine, she glanced up and found Lord Connor watching her.

When she would have looked away, he reached for her hand. He drew in a deep breath and finally, the Virgin be praised, lowered his gaze. "Moira, what is wrong? Every time we begin to truly talk, when I believe we'll begin to know each other, 'tis as though a shutter closes within you, keeping you from me. I've not been here long, and I know that you've suffered a grievous loss, but you must realize that I would never cause you harm. Not you or your child."

"I know." How could she make him understand her reticence, her fears, without explaining everything?

Before she could try, he spoke again. "Circumstances have placed you within my care, milady. As the guardian of this place and all who dwell within it, I *need* to know everything that could cause a threat, a danger. Beyond that lies the man who wishes to know you better, if you will allow it. But his needs cannot hold dominion over yours."

How did he know all the right things to say, to make her want to trust him?

She closed her eyes, turned away. She should not have succumbed to the temptation to be herself—to *flirt* with him... She shook her head and barely resisted the urge to bury her face in her hands.

"Moira—"

Her eyes flew open and she spun toward him. "I've not given you leave to call me that." After a swift glance at his face—handsome, honest, understanding—she focused instead on the intricate design embroidered about the neckline of his finely woven green tunic.

"I've called you Moira several times, and you've not seemed to mind till now."

She could feel his gaze upon her, but she refused to glance up, to meet his eyes. He saw too much, saw her too clearly. "I didn't notice," she said, making her tone cold, indifferent.

He slid his chair nearer to hers, leaned close and caught her chin in his hand, gently forcing her to look at him. "You didn't care," he said, his voice soft. "Any more than you care now." His fingers grazed her cheekbone, sending a shiver of awareness skittering down her spine and startling her into meeting his eyes. "Do you, Moira?"

"I..." She didn't wish to lie to him.

"I've vowed upon my honor to lay down my life for you, Moira. Allowing me to call you by name—and you calling me by mine—is a small price to pay, don't you think?"

This close, she could see the faint flecks of gold in his dark brown eyes, feel the warmth rising from his skin. His hair fell in soft chestnut waves to his shoulders, tempting her fingers to reach out to smooth it away from his brow.

She fought the urge, though her fingertips nigh tingled with anticipation. So intent was she upon the myriad sensations flooding her, she didn't notice he'd moved closer still until his muttered curse broke the spell. "Forgive me—I cannot resist," he whispered against her mouth, then pressed his lips to hers.

Chapter Ten

Moira sat motionless as Connor brushed his mouth over hers in a featherlight caress. He slipped from his chair and knelt in front of her, sliding his hand into her hair beneath her veil as he continued to sip lightly at her lips.

Warmth spread from his touch, a healing balm carried in her blood to all the aching, needy places in her soul. Giving in to the compulsion to touch him as well, she raised her hand and buried it in his hair. Softer than she'd imagined, it sifted through her fingers, sending shards of sensation to stoke the heat she felt to a gentle burning.

She'd been five years wed, had lain with a man not her husband, yet she'd never known a man's kiss until now.

Never in her wildest imaginings could she have believed it would be like this.

Tears filled her eyes as Connor continued to press his mouth to hers. The feeling building within her rose so swiftly, she feared 'twould rend her heart in two. "Connor," she murmured, then gasped when he traced his rough fingertip over the sensitive flesh beneath her ear.

She slipped her fingers along the neckline of his tunic, making him gasp. Her lips curved into a smile against his, even as a tear slid free.

He drew back far enough to scan her face, frowning as he raised a finger to follow the trail of moisture down her cheek to her mouth. "Dearling, what's this?" He echoed the path with his lips. "Have I hurt you? What have I done to make you cry?"

"Nothing," she whispered. She outlined his jaw with her fingers, savoring the rasp of his whiskers against her skin. "They are tears of happiness, Connor, not sorrow." Cupping her hand over his cheek, she tried to smile. "Your kisses were a joy I've never known. I thank you for them." Reluctance making her linger over the task, she eased her hand away and settled into the chair. "But you must not kiss me again."

He sat back on his heels, catching hold of her hand and cradling it within his larger one. "You said you enjoyed what we shared, so you must not have found it distasteful. I don't understand… I would not force myself on you, nor do I believe that I'm every woman's dream." His face flushed. "I know I'm scarred, too big and clumsy, but I swear to you—"

"'Tis no fault in you, Connor," she told him, his words making tears fill her eyes once again. "I did not mean for you to think 'twas something wrong with you." She tightened her grasp on his hand. "You are not too big or clumsy—you've a strength and grace to catch any woman's eye. I watched you as you practiced with your sword, Connor, so do not try to tell me otherwise. The scar—" she traced its length with her fingertip, holding his gaze with hers all the while "—it simply adds a mysterious appeal to a handsome man." Lowering her hand to her lap, she added, "Lord Rannulf is handsome. You, my lord, are intriguing."

He still bore a trace of red on his cheeks, but he seemed more at ease. "Your flattery makes me wonder all the more why you say you'll not allow me to kiss you again. 'Tis because you're newly widowed. I should not have..." He raked his disheveled hair back from his face and stood; she felt a sense of loss immediately. "I've no wish to make you uncomfortable." There was a remoteness in his face, a chill in his eyes that she'd never intended to cause.

But perhaps 'twas for the best. What kind of woman was she, to trifle with a man she knew she could not have?

"I told you before that I had something to discuss with you." He surprised her by moving his chair close to hers—so close their knees nearly touched. He sat down and poured wine for her before filling his own cup and taking a sip. "I wish there was some way I could take away the sting of your brother's words, but other than refusing to allow him to come here again, I'm not sure what else I can do about him. I doubt you wish me to kill him."

"Nay, do not!" Moira cried. "His words were an embarrassment, but 'tis his way to be so blunt. I may not love my brother as I ought—"

"*He* doesn't treat *you* as he should," Connor said flatly. "You owe him nothing, so far as I can see."

She barely stopped herself from nodding in agreement. Such feelings were wrong.... How could she be a good and loving mother to her child, when she harbored so little love for her own family? "Nonetheless, I don't wish his death—especially not on your soul."

Connor met her gaze, searching her eyes, her face, till she wondered if he could see her every thought, all the stains upon her own soul. But the earnestness in *his* eyes never faded, so she had to be mistaken. "I'm keeping him locked up in the storeroom tonight in the hope he might reveal the MacCarthys' plans to me come the morn. After a night spent shut up in the dark, with naught but vermin to keep him company—"

"He should feel at home with them," Moira couldn't resist saying. "Though the rats will abandon him in no time at all, I have no doubt."

"You've a low opinion of him, but regrettably, 'tis well deserved, from what I've seen," Connor said. "I don't know if I can trust him to carry a message back to Hugh MacCarthy, but I plan to give him something. I don't know yet what I'll say. I hoped that you would help me decide what to tell them." He raked his hand through his hair once more and settled his gaze on her face. "I trust you're not offended that I locked him up?"

"'Tis more than I expected—and less than he deserves. His insults were no surprise to me, Connor." She frowned. "He said what many others believe, I'm sure. And 'tis similar to Sir Ivor's opinion."

"You're wrong about what people think of you. As for d'Athée, you won't have to listen to his ranting for much longer," he said. "As soon as I can spare him, he's leaving for Wales. Whatever happens to him once he's in my brother's keeping is Rannulf's problem, not mine. Rannulf won't stand for d'Athée's nonsense, and he has more options—and authority—to deal with that idiot than I have." Connor swirled the wine in his cup, staring at the ruby liquid. "One of the advantages of being the elder."

"Do you mind that Rannulf is the elder?" she asked, then wished the question unsaid. "I beg your pardon, 'tis none of my business."

Connor swirled the wine harder, then stopped and glanced up at her. "I used to mind, but that was long ago. We've put the past behind us," he said firmly.

Did he try to convince her of that fact, she wondered, or himself?

"My brother is dear to me, and I begrudge him nothing." He set down the mug and leaned toward her. "And

I don't mind that you asked. If you agree to part of the plan I have in mind, you'll have the right to ask me anything you wish."

"What do you mean?"

He looked away, as though marshaling his thoughts, then took her hands in his. "Fear not, I won't kiss you," he said, no doubt meaning to reassure her.

She didn't fear anything he might do; 'twas what she might do in return, or what could happen to him should he remain near her, that frightened her. Not knowing how to respond, she nodded.

"The MacCarthys are determined to take your child from you." He shook his head. "Enlisting your own brother to their cause is a mark of their desperation."

"That may be true, but 'tis also true that my brothers are easily swayed, when 'tis to their advantage." She slid her hands free and stood. "Couldn't you tell what sort of man Aidan is? I'm sure he'd have joined forces with Hugh MacCarthy even under different circumstances. The fact that I'm his kin simply means he's more apt to benefit from it." The babe, no doubt sensing her agitation, chose that moment to beat a hard tattoo beneath her ribs, robbing her of breath. She grabbed hold of the chair and lowered herself into it.

Connor half rose from his chair when he saw Moira's obvious pain, then sat down when she waved him away. "It cannot be good for the child when you become upset," he scolded. Was it his imagination, or did this happen every time he was near her? Was it his presence or what they were discussing?

Perhaps he should just leave her be, though he knew he could not do that. "Are you in pain? Should I get Brigit?"

Moira grabbed his hand and placed it atop her belly. The babe kicked—hard. "It doesn't hurt, but 'tis not comfortable, either,'' she said, gasping when the child thumped harder still beneath his hand.

''By the saints!'' he whispered, knowing he sounded like an awestruck fool, and not caring a whit. Watching her stomach, he shifted his palm until he held a sharply protruding limb cradled within it. ''He's right there, under my hand.''

Moira laid her hand atop his, her lips curved into a smile. Her beauty at that moment—a perfect moment—stole the breath from his chest and brought a sheen of moisture to his eyes. He couldn't have looked away if his life depended on it.

They formed a connection in that instant—mother, child and protector—that he knew he could not ignore. 'Twas as though the scheme he'd hatched, the plan he'd feared to reveal to Moira, had received divine approval.

''Such a strong lad,'' he murmured as the babe settled down to more gentle, erratic movement.

''Or lass,'' Moira teased. ''There's no way of knowing till the birth.''

''Whichever it is, it seems a healthy child. Very active.'' Realizing the movements beneath his palm had ceased, he reluctantly eased his hand away.

The sense of loss was overwhelming. Had he ever felt such a bond with another? Most likely not since he'd been in the womb himself, sharing it with his twin. Once he and Rannulf had been born into the cold, harsh world, it seemed that everything had conspired to drive them apart. Until a short time ago, the link joining them had been stretched until only the considerable force of will they shared had kept the bond alive.

''It appears that tonight's performance is over,'' Moira said, her voice still alight with laughter. Sighing, she sat up straight and sipped her wine. "It's time to rest while I can."

"Does this happen every night?"

"Aye—and other times of day, as well. The babe is very lively." She reached behind her to press on her lower back, the motion thrusting her bosom into greater prominence. Connor shifted his attention to her face, lest he be tempted to stare where he should not. "But in the evening it's apt to continue after I've sought my bed."

He couldn't imagine what it must be like. Until his recent sojourn at l'Eau Clair with Rannulf and Gillian, he'd not been in close proximity with a pregnant woman. Even so, all he knew about it was that Gillian had been greatly relieved when their daughter, Katherine, was born.

Though as he recalled, her delivery of the child had taken a long time and been fraught with danger.

The thought of Moira in a similar situation—of the danger involved in bearing a child—caused worry to close about his heart like a fist. She was strong, he reminded himself. After all she'd endured already, surely she and the babe would survive.

Moira, sipping her drink, gasped again and began to cough as she choked on the wine. Connor leaped to his feet and bent over her, thumping her back carefully until the paroxysm eased. "Better?"

Breathless, she nodded and began to smooth her hands over her belly.

"The babe is still awake?"

"Aye."

"When I touched you before, the child seemed to quiet. May I do it again?" he asked, already reaching out as she nodded her agreement.

She took him by the wrist and laid his hand high on the mound of her stomach. The bump beneath his palm felt different than before, larger and less bony. "What do you think I'm feeling this time?" Maintaining the contact, he lowered himself down to kneel beside her chair.

"I cannot guess," Moira said, her voice as quiet and solemn as if they were at Mass. "Sometimes I think I can recognize a hand or foot, but other times, like now, I'm not sure." She shifted his hand to follow the baby's movement. "Every so often it seems the babe has more arms and legs than it should."

"Could there be more than one child?" *That* situation could compound their dilemma mightily, for he could well imagine the MacCarthys' response. They'd demand that one child—the boy if there was one, or the elder son if both were male—go to them, the other to Moira.

Or, considering what Connor had learned of them, 'twas as likely they'd demand both of Moira's children should there be two of them.

"Brigit assures me there's but one—and that it bears the proper number of limbs." She cupped both her hands over his and smiled. "I believe the babe likes your touch better than mine, milord." When he raised an eyebrow in question, she added, "Connor. When you laid your hand over the child, it settled almost at once."

"Perhaps the warmth from my hand is greater because I'm bigger." Whatever the reason, the thought brought a surprising pleasure. He glanced up at Moira's face, gilded by candlelight and at ease once more, and savored the wave of contentment carrying him in its wake.

The scheme he'd concocted to protect Moira and the child rose to mind again, a plan that seemed less shocking now than it had earlier. There might never be a better time to suggest it than this moment.

Before he lost his courage, Connor shifted on his knees to face Moira more fully. "Milady, the hour grows late, and I've yet to tell you about my plan for thwarting the MacCarthys' schemes."

An eagerness lit her eyes, and the hint of a smile on her lips widened till he could not mistake it. "Please, tell me what you've decided."

He dragged his free hand through his hair and ordered himself to stop stalling. "Lady Moira, will you marry me?"

As his words sank into her brain, Moira's heartbeat stumbled, then began to thrum so fast 'twas a wonder she could think at all. Her fingers tightened around Connor's hand and she stared at him in the flickering light. His dark eyes held honesty, as sincere as the expression on his face—and uncertainty as well.

Marry him?

Shock turned to panic as the full import of his words flooded her mind.

"W-w-we cannot wed," she stammered. "You don't understand. I cannot marry ever again."

She wished he would move away, take his hand off her stomach. Cease this assault upon her senses so she could *think.* But he had surrounded her with his heat, his scent, his touch, till she could think of nothing else but him, and the images his offer had planted in her brain.

If they married, she could be assured of his company—most welcome to her already—whenever she wished it. And somehow 'twas clear to her that he'd be a steady husband, lending her his support, his protection—

Nay! For that reason alone, she could not accept. "I'm sorry, milord," she said, trying to infuse her voice with strength as she shook her head and fought back tears. "You honor me greatly by your offer, but I cannot marry you—or anyone."

The babe chose that moment to renew its kicking. Connor shifted his hand and the child settled. "You see? I can help you with this—and with much else, if you'll let me."

Tears filling her eyes, she pushed her chair back and dragged his hand off her stomach. "Enough, milord! Please, do not..." She averted her face and scrambled from the chair, nearly sliding to the floor before she caught her balance and lurched to her feet.

"Moira, have a care." Connor reached out to help her as he stood as well, but she slipped away from him and moved to the opposite side of the table. He righted the chair she'd abandoned and shoved it aside, shaking his hair back from his face. "There's no need to run from me. I'll not harm you," he said, his voice low and calming.

For some reason, that fact roused her ire. "Why should I believe you would?" she demanded. "And why should that make a difference? I told you nay, and nay I meant!" She picked up a chunk of cheese off the table and raised it to pitch at him, then reconsidered. The childish action would solve nothing. She choked back a burst of hysterical laughter; she'd really look a fool if her aim was off and she missed.

She let the cheese drop to the table, and tugged her disheveled gown into place before glancing across at him. The position of the candles left one side of his face in shadow and bathed the unscarred side in soft golden light. 'Twas odd, but she found that seeing Connor without the scar was like gazing at a stranger. At least that made it easier to apologize. "I beg your pardon, milord. I didn't mean to startle you." She drew in a calming breath. "You didn't frighten me."

He held out his hand to her, but when she ignored the gesture he let it fall to his side. "'Tis late," he said, casting a look at the dying fire. "I'll leave you to your rest now, but we'll continue this conversation on the morrow, I assure you."

"I don't—"

"Tomorrow, Moira," he said firmly. "Perhaps we'll both view things differently then."

Since there didn't seem to be anything she could say to dissuade him, she didn't bother to try. He'd soon learn that she could be stubborn—to the point of madness, so she'd been told.

Mayhap *that* would convince him he'd no wish to bind himself to her for the rest of their lives.

He rounded the table and took her by the hand. "Come, to bed with you." He tugged her forward and led her to the door to her bedchamber. "I'll snuff the candles and bank the fire before I leave."

Why must he continue to be courteous to her? she wondered, ready to scream in frustration.

Instead, she nodded her thanks. "Good night, milord."

He bowed over her hand, turning it and pressing a kiss into her palm. "Until tomorrow," he murmured.

As soon as he released her hand, Moira opened her door and fled into the sanctuary of her chamber.

Chapter Eleven

Once Moira had retreated into her room, Connor built up the fire, extinguished all the candles save the ones near the hearth, and opened the door to the corridor a crack to listen. The earlier sounds of merrymaking rising from the hall had died away, leaving a blessed silence in their wake. He gave a satisfied nod and silent thanks that he hadn't had to call a halt to the revels. While he knew everyone had needed the respite, *he* required able-bodied fighters on the morrow.

If not sooner.

He eased the door shut and drew a chair close to the fireplace. He wasn't ready to retreat to his chamber yet, and this room was already warm and comfortable. A cup of wine in hand, he sat and stared into the dancing flames, brooding over all he'd learned today.

He could scarcely wait till morning to begin their survey of the headland and the cliffs. They'd best make a thorough inspection of the cellars as well, in case there was some sort of tunnel or passageway leading from the cliffs into the castle itself.

Though how that could be with no one in Gerald's Keep the wiser, he couldn't fathom.

Still, he'd not ignore any possibility.

He sipped at the wine, the rich brew sending its pleasant warmth flowing through him, easing his tension and spurring his imagination. Could Aidan O'Neill possess any information that might help them? Connor couldn't imagine anyone with any sense entrusting the obnoxious fool with important knowledge—but from what little he'd heard about Hugh MacCarthy, he'd guess the man was ruled more by emotion than sense.

Connor decided he'd question O'Neill again in the morning, then draft a message for him to carry back to MacCarthy.

As for the other part of his plans, he wished Moira would agree to wed him, for several reasons—not the least of which being that he hoped making her his bride would dissuade MacCarthy from any further claims upon her and her child.

Connor sat up and set aside his wine. Was MacCarthy unwed? No one had mentioned the fact one way or the other. It would certainly make Moira—an unmarried Moira—a *very* attractive lure for the Irishman. Capture her, marry her, and no one could deny his right to the child.

Nor to his trying to secure a birthright for the babe.

Of course, MacCarthy had left out one important detail in that plan, Connor thought with a grim smile. The FitzCliffords would not give up what was theirs.

Gerald's Keep belonged to them, by right of blood and conquest. 'Twas their duty to protect their land and people.

Including Moira, their vassal's widow.

For him to marry Moira seemed the most logical solution to her dilemma. Once she was his wife, the MacCarthys could scarce expect him to turn her over to them, and *he'd* be in the perfect position to lay claim to the child she carried.

He'd spoken to her too soon—he could see that now—

but the situation didn't look to improve with the passage of time. Instead 'twas apt to grow worse, the nearer they came to the child's birth.

And once the child was born... They'd never know a moment's peace, nor safety for the babe.

Moira's refusal of his offer hadn't surprised him. They knew little about each other, and she had every right to wed where *she* chose this time. It was clear her marriage to Lord Brien had not been a happy one.

However, wedding Connor might not seem any better to her—or for her.

What did he know of being a husband, a father? His experience of family life was no recommendation for it, though he knew 'twas possible to create a different situation. Rannulf and Gillian had managed to do so. From all he'd seen, they'd succeeded. Unlike his parents, Rannulf and his wife had found happiness together, forged a union made stronger still by the birth of their child.

But Rannulf had lived away from FitzClifford, from their father's complete domination of his wife and younger son, since childhood. He'd seen how other people lived, had not been forced to endure Bertram FitzClifford's iron fist hovering over every aspect of his life, poised to smash to bits the slightest hint of the softer emotions.

A lifetime spent skulking in the shadows to escape his father had not prepared Connor for much of anything save cowardice. Since Bertram's death, Connor had schooled himself in the art of war.

But in the matter of love, of devotion, he knew he was ignorant.

The foreign emotions that had swept through him when he'd felt Moira's child move beneath his hand made him wonder if that could change. Made him wonder at the miracle of it all. He'd felt protective, tender, and though he hoped she hadn't noticed, his eyes had been damp with tears until he'd mastered the unexpected reaction.

Whether his feelings would be adequate for a parent, he could not judge.

Taking Moira as his bride would be no hardship. If he must wed someday, why not to a woman of such strength and beauty—beauty within and without—as Moira?

She drew him to her, without any effort on her part. He could not deny his attraction toward her, nor the fact that his respect and admiration for her grew with every passing day.

Her desire to protect her child was so fierce, so profound… What would it be like to have that intensity directed at him, to be the recipient of her love and caring?

If she loved with that passion… The memory of Moira's lips pressed to his swept through him, hit him just as hard as it had when they'd kissed, carrying with it a wave of heat rivaling that rising from the hearth. Her taste, the sweet feel of her rounded body alongside his own…

But that was lust, an emotion familiar to him, not that he'd had much opportunity to indulge it. Though what he felt with Moira seemed deeper somehow than the mere yearning of the flesh he'd felt before.

He'd certainly never believed a pregnant woman could be as appealing as he found Moira. There was a richness, a ripeness to her—like a fine wine to be savored, an indulgence to the senses. It had taken all his willpower to keep their kiss light, not to crush her to him, snatching from her all he could take before she pushed him away.

Though she'd denied him anyway. Perhaps she'd known what had been going through his mind while they kissed. It would certainly explain why she'd told him not to kiss her again.

And then, fool that he was, he'd suggested they should wed.

He drained his wine, grimacing when he reached the bitter dregs at the bottom of the cup. The late hour, coupled with all this soul searching, had made him maudlin.

He'd do better to reconsider everything on the morrow, as he'd suggested to Moira.

Perhaps then 'twould become clear to him what course they should follow.

Moira stood in the corridor before first light, prepared to follow Connor once he descended from his chamber. She planned to join him when he visited her brother. Aidan's words still rankled, still pricked her sense of guilt. Perhaps if she saw him again, she could appeal to him, beg him to help her keep Hugh MacCarthy *away* from her and her child.

Though 'twould likely be a waste of breath even to try, she realized, since she'd nothing to offer Aidan in return.

Her mind seemed clouded, overwhelmed, overburdened. She gave a mirthless laugh; she could scarce recall when she'd felt any different. Only since Connor's arrival had she known even a moment of happiness, a sense of her troubles being lifted from her shoulders. Some of her weariness this morn, however, could be laid at Connor's door. She'd barely slept, though there was nothing new about that since the child had grown so large and become so restless. But in the past, she'd had only her usual guilt and sorrow to fill her thoughts as she waited for the night to end.

Last night, however, thoughts of a completely different kind had sustained her through the darkness. Thoughts of Connor FitzClifford—of the warmth of his kiss, of his gallantry and support of her…

Of his offer to make her his wife.

Before impatience could overwhelm her completely and send her running like the coward she knew herself to be, she heard his footsteps coming down the stairs from the floor above.

Pushing aside her nervousness about seeing him again—for she wasn't certain she could behave toward him as she had before his startling offer—she hastened toward the stairs to meet him. As she did so, she debated whether she should pretend their meeting was a coincidence or simply tell him the truth.

"Good morning, Moira," he called before she could decide. He bowed politely. "If you think to see your brother again before I release him, I strongly suggest you do not."

"But—"

"I need to question him about some information I received yesterday, and I'm not certain he'll be willing to say anything if you're there."

She drew herself up to her full height and met his challenging look, opening her mouth to refute his statement. But then the truth of it melted her indignation and she sighed. "You're probably right," she muttered. "He's never been one to say aught of value in a woman's presence, unless he's boasting. And in that case, you cannot believe anything he says."

Connor took her by the arm and drew her back down the dimly lit corridor toward her solar. "I should have asked you this last night, but I—" he dragged his hair back from his forehead and a touch of red colored his face "—I became distracted."

'Twas good to hear that she wasn't the only one affected by their kiss.

Not that it should matter.

He glanced around the empty hallway, then stopped beside the door to the chamber at the end. "Have you ever heard anything about a way into the castle from the cliffs?'' he asked, his voice low, urgent.

''The cliffs?'' she asked, not bothering to hide her surprise. ''Nay. If I knew anything of that nature, I'd have shared it with you before now. You've seen them—how could it be possible to get in from there?'' She couldn't imagine such a thing; in truth, she'd never even considered the possibility. ''Why do you ask?''

''I was told to 'look to the cliffs,''' he said. ''But I haven't a clue what that means.''

''I doubt that Aidan can tell you anything useful. He's not a man people share secrets with, since he cannot keep one to save his soul,'' she said derisively. ''Though it would not hurt to ask.''

Connor nodded, looking preoccupied. ''*Do* you wish to see him again before I let him go?''

''Nay,'' she muttered, infuriated at the mere thought. '''Twould accomplish naught but to feed my anger again. I've yet to recover from my shock at seeing him here, though I can't say I was surprised to learn he's joined forces with Hugh MacCarthy once more.'' She frowned, though she felt like screeching in dismay. ''Nor that he'd offered me in trade yet again.''

Connor reached for her hand and clasped it tightly. ''You know I won't permit him to use you thus again, Moira. No matter what our relationship might be,'' he assured her.

His touch felt too good, too warm and comforting. She couldn't allow herself to grow used to it; she must learn to stand on her own. It would be difficult enough already to let him go. ''Thank you,'' she said, slipping her hand free. ''I doubt you want Aidan within these walls for any longer than necessary, so I'll let you go about your duties.'' She edged past him and opened the door to the solar. ''Until later, milord.'' Not giving him a chance to respond, she shut the door.

Unfortunately, she feared she couldn't shut him out of her mind—or her heart—so easily.

Connor had decided to get straight to his duties this morn, without taking the time for his usual exercises. Though he could have benefited from a clear head when he drafted his letter to Hugh MacCarthy, he thought with a rueful laugh. He'd spent nearly an hour scratching away on a piece of parchment, writing and rewriting, before he'd been satisfied that he'd achieved his objective—a missive warning the MacCarthys away from Moira, her child and Gerald's Keep, while hopefully not enraging the fools to the point where they descended upon the castle like a plague.

However, that might be the best solution—draw them out and have at them. The idea made him itch to be armed and fighting. Waiting and wondering—being *patient*—was not his way. Only the thought that he must protect Moira stayed his hand from sending MacCarthy what would amount to an invitation to combat.

'Twas no wonder his muddled thoughts didn't promise to untangle anytime soon.

Certainly not whenever he was in Moira's presence.

He wished he knew more about women—*this* woman, at least. Every time he believed he'd begun to know her a little, she showed him another facet of herself—and confused him completely.

He raked his hands through his hair in frustration. Was there naught in his life at this moment that made a whit of sense?

He ran Will to ground in the barracks as the sky lightened. 'Twas a cool, misty day—perfect to make exploring the cliffs more dangerous than usual. ''A quiet night?'' he asked as they approached the gatehouse.

''Aye, milord. The most excitement we saw all evening was when Cedric challenged Jean to an arm wrestling match for the favor of a buxom wench,'' Will said with a grin. ''Though I can't be certain whether 'twas her charms or the fact that she works in the kitchen that attracted them to her.''

''Considering that each of them eats as though he'll be denied the tiniest crumb tomorrow, 'tis likely the promise of extra food that drew them,'' Connor added wryly. ''Who won?''

''They got so involved in trying to best each other, the maid left them for someone who'd pay her more notice.''

''Likely just as well. If they grow much bigger, we'll have to get the armorer to add more links to their hauberks.'' Connor paused outside the door to the gatehouse. ''But 'twas quiet on the walls?''

''Aye, else I'd have sent word to you at once, milord. Nothing of note happened last night...'' His expression serious, Will stopped as though lost in thought. ''Nothing except that Sir Ivor surprised me by speaking up after you took Lady Moira's brother away.''

''Indeed?'' Connor's lips quirked in a mirthless smile. ''And what great revelations did he decide to share with you?''

Will's face didn't change. ''Seems he's been thinking about whatever 'twas you said to him before, and his assumption about the lady and the MacCarthys. He didn't care to hear her brother call her a whore, I can tell you that.''

''Nor did I.'' It was a vast understatement. Connor hadn't believed he'd ever find a reason to agree with Sir Ivor on much of anything—and certainly not something involving Moira. ''Any idea why he's changed his stance? I cannot believe 'twas anything I said that accounts for it.''

Will shook his head. ''All I know is what he told me, milord. Could be he suspects you plan to send him away and hopes to change your mind. But considering he vowed his hatred of the Irish less than a week ago, that doesn't make sense, either. I wouldn't trust him any more today than I did then, God's truth.''

''You've the right of it, Will.'' Something more to mull over when he'd naught else to occupy his mind, Connor thought with a frown. Who could guess what plots Sir Ivor had running through his brain? ''I cannot send him to Ranulf quite yet, however. D'Athée's a decent fighter, and we'll have need of him before we're through here, I have no doubt.'' He led the way into the gatehouse and removed the key to the storeroom from the pouch on his belt. ''Ready for another futile conversation?'' he asked, eyebrows raised.

''Perhaps we'll be lucky,'' Will murmured.

Connor stopped with the key poised near the lock. ''Are you certain you didn't overindulge last night? Perhaps 'tis a surfeit of wine that makes you so hopeful.''

''Nay, milord,'' Will said, his laugh deep and full. '''Tis my cheerful nature.''

Laughing as well, Connor unlocked the door and swung it open.

An ear-splitting snore came from the man curled up on the pile of grain sacks, sound asleep. Rolling his eyes, Will took the lantern off the wall and carried it into the storeroom, opening the shutter wide and bending to shine the light into O'Neill's face.

''By Christ's eyeballs!'' the man snarled. He tried to leap up, but slid on the uneven pile and fell to the floor with a thump. ''What's a fellow got to do to get some sleep here?''

Connor stared at O'Neill in disbelief. ''If you want to sleep, find someplace else to do it.'' He stood by the door, arms folded, and waited while O'Neill picked himself up and set about brushing himself off and straightening his garments.

Not that he looked any different once he'd finished.

By the rood, how was it possible that this fool was blood kin to Moira? Was *she* the exception in her family, or was Aidan?

''''Tis a busy place, with men stomping up and down the stairs all the night long.'' O'Neill shook his head, his sharp gaze focused on Connor. ''You must have a powerful garrison, indeed.''

Connor breathed a silent sigh of relief, for he'd begun to wonder if he'd erred in locking O'Neill away here. But perhaps he'd unwittingly done something right. ''Aye, and so you may tell MacCarthy when you see him.''

''Oh, I've much to tell Hugh,'' O'Neill said, his gaze considering. ''Of course, perhaps you and me, we might come to a better bargain than I have with him—if you'll meet my terms.''

''And what might they be?'' Connor asked, though he could well imagine.

O'Neill drew in a deep breath and grinned. ''Well, 'tis like this. If you could see your way to returning Moira to the loving arms of her family, I just might be able to find out what Hugh's plans for you are.'' He relaxed his stance, his grin widening. ''After all, I don't figure you for a man who'd want a shrew like my sister around for long. She can't be of any use to you, now could she? Especially in the shape she's in at the moment.''

Connor had just finished closing his hands around

O'Neill's throat when Will grabbed him by the back of the tunic. Connor tightened his hold for a moment—just long enough to give O'Neill a taste of his strength—before he allowed Will to drag him away.

Will took up a position between the two of them—not that he'd be able to stop Connor if he decided to grab O'Neill again—and tugged down the cuffs of his shirt. "I know he's a boil on the backside of decency, milord, but I doubt Lady Moira would appreciate you throttling her brother." He glanced from Connor to O'Neill and shrugged. "Then again, mayhap I'm wrong."

The sight of O'Neill rubbing at the marks on his neck filled Connor with satisfaction, not that he intended to show it. Instead, taking his time, he reached into the pouch at his waist and drew out a folded sheet of parchment sealed with wax. "The only bargain I'm offering you is your neck—if you get the hell out of here and stay out of your sister's life." He held out the parchment, waiting with a patience he didn't feel until Aidan snatched it from his hand. "Moira is not yours to use, O'Neill, not again. If you *ever* forget that fact, I swear I'll hunt you down and finish what I started."

Chapter Twelve

Connor sent for Henry to escort Aidan O'Neill from Gerald's Keep—and to make certain he left the area. Frustration filled him as he watched Moira's brother leave, though he had to admit he was glad to see the last of him. But if the man had been more reasonable, might he have learned something useful from him?

Since "reasonable" didn't describe O'Neill in the least, Connor would have to discover what he wanted to know on his own.

The payment O'Neill demanded in return for information was simply too high.

"I understand why you didn't want to keep him here, milord—but why didn't you question him about the cliffs?" Will asked as they approached the door leading from the bailey into the undercroft of the keep.

"He wouldn't have told us anything," Connor said flatly. "You know it as well as I. All he cared about was working things to his own advantage." He yawned and, handing Will the lantern he carried, carefully worked the large iron key he'd brought into the lock on the heavy wood-and-iron door leading to the cellars. Considering the lock's battered appearance, the key turned with surprising ease. "He wouldn't have given me any information without first haggling over the price—and we both know he'd not have made any bargain unless it brought Moira into his hands."

"You've the right of that, milord." Will's frown echoed his own. "I still cannot imagine her brother—her own *blood*—treating her so badly."

"You might be surprised at how poorly some people act toward their relations," he muttered as he focused his attention on wriggling the key out of the misshapen lock. He ignored Will's questioning look and gave the door a shove; hinges squealing, it swung open, enveloping them in a cloud of cool, musty air.

"If the Irish think to come in through here, we'll hear them," Connor said, his voice dry. "Or smell the stench." They entered the undercroft of the keep and he pushed the door shut with another nerve-jangling screech. He grimaced. "From the top floor."

"What are we looking for, milord?"

"I haven't any idea." Connor took the lantern and headed for the rough stone foundation of the opposite wall. "A hidden door, or the entrance to a cave, perhaps? Sir Robert's information was so vague as to be almost useless." He sighed. "'Twas just enough to whet my curiosity."

"Still, 'tis a place to start," Will pointed out.

Considering Sir Robert's obvious fear, they were fortunate to have learned anything at all. "Aye. I should be grateful he was willing to tell me that much." Raising the lantern high, Connor pointed at the wall before them. "This faces the headland. Seems as good a place as any other to begin."

After spending the entire morning investigating but one room of the dank, vaulted area, they were filthy, hungry and desperate for a breath of fresh air. Connor preferred to carry out this chore himself, in the company of men he knew and trusted completely, rather than send in men-at-arms from the barracks. He had no desire for word of precisely what he was doing to leak out. 'Twas limiting, but necessary.

However, he decided he'd have to depend on d'Athée to help, for he wanted to explore the cliffs himself. After questioning Sir Ivor closely and deciding that the man's fierce loyalty to his dead master—if nothing else—would keep him honest, Connor swore him to silence and sent him to search the cellars with Will after the midday meal.

He managed to put off Moira's servants, who sought him out as soon as he entered the keep, and to somehow evade the woman herself. Once he'd eaten and given d'Athée and Will their orders, Connor stole out of the keep to the headland. He wanted to search for answers to give Moira, to show her he was doing all he could to protect her and her child, to keep them safe.

Until then, he planned to stay away from her—and the distraction she presented.

Memories of Moira in his arms, of her rare smile, of her lips pressed to his, were distraction enough.

Later that day, hot, filthy and soaked with sweat, Connor gathered up his discarded tunic and weapons from the edge of the cliff and set off along the headland toward the castle. The sun, which had burned through the mist at midday, began to paint the sky with vivid streaks of color, and the wind, thankfully little more than a faint breeze while he'd climbed about on the rocks, had risen to howl around him like a swarm of ghosts.

When he reached the rock where he and Moira had rested the day she'd brought him here, he decided to sit and enjoy the relative quiet as the light faded. Perhaps the silence would help him determine what to do next, for his search this afternoon had been as unsuccessful as the morning's. He'd count the day wasted, save for the fact that he'd had the chance to familiarize himself more closely with the strengths and weaknesses of Gerald's Keep.

Though he'd found nothing to indicate that anyone planned to assault the castle from the cliffs, he *had* learned that the headland did not provide so impregnable a barrier as he'd been led to believe. He'd climbed down to the sea and back up again without a rope or anyone to help him. It had been a challenge, 'twas true—and his strength was likely greater than many a man-at-arm's—but it *was* possible.

Of course, if there were some way into the keep *through* the cliff, that task would be much easier to accomplish.

The wind whipped his hair about and plastered his shirt against his chest, cooling his body. He closed his eyes and tilted his head back to let the breeze blow the cobwebs from his mind, then jumped when he heard the crunch of loose stones behind him.

Sword in hand, he jumped up and spun around, startling a shriek from Moira. "Moira! What are you doing out here?" he snapped, lowering the weapon and letting the tension ease from his muscles.

She left the path and crossed the swath of grass separating them. "I thought to catch you before you returned to the keep." She swept past him and sat down on the rock. "It seemed that you might not escape me out here." She gazed out at the sea. "Besides, 'tis a beautiful evening, and quiet. There's little enough of that within the castle walls." She glanced over at him, her expression challenging. "I'm pleased to have caught you before you disappeared again."

"I was avoiding you earlier," he admitted. And likely would have done so again this evening, not that he'd tell her that now. He took a step closer to her, propped one booted foot on the rock and rested his forearm on his thigh. "I hoped you'd have a chance to rest today, but I see you did not." Noting the shadows beneath her eyes, he reached out to brush his fingers across her cheek, then noticed how scratched and moss stained his fingers were in contrast to her smooth, pale skin. He drew back, but she caught his hand in hers and turned it palm up.

"What have you been doing?" she cried. She traced a finger over a long, thin scrape on his thumb.

The shiver passing through him owed little to the cool wind and everything to her touch. "'Tis nothing." He closed his free hand into a fist as he sought to keep from reaching for her.

She bent and pressed her lips to the cut, the simple gesture sending a bolt of heat from his hand to his loins. The wind lifted her hair and whipped it around his arm, ensnaring him as completely as if she had bound him to her.

Sliding his hand from her grasp, he knelt before her and gathered her to him in one smooth movement, his mouth capturing hers with a hunger he could not deny.

She returned his kiss with equal fervor, burying her hands in his hair and pressing close to him. Her kisses held a surprising innocence, but she followed his lead as he swept his tongue across her mouth, then nibbled at her lower lip.

"You taste so sweet," he murmured against her mouth. He reached up and tugged off her veil, sinking his hands in the bounty of her hair and freeing it completely. The wind caught the long, dark strands, billowing them about, enveloping him in her scent of flowers and spice—of woman. He smoothed his fingers through the fragrant mass, the feel of its softness brushing against his skin sending shards of heat to stoke the fire of madness burning through him.

She stroked his scalp, his neck, before caressing his shoulders. ‘‘You’ve such strength,’’ she whispered, closing her hands about his upper arms as she drew away from him and met his eyes. ‘‘Yet you are so gentle with me.’’ She looked down for a moment, then met his eyes again, her own a smoldering blue. Tracing her fingers over the flesh exposed by his rolled-up sleeves, she added, ‘‘’Tis an exciting combination.’’

’Twas a miracle he didn’t leap out of his skin to escape the wave of desire washing over him. His entire body burned for her. He had become so sensitized to her touch that the mere brush of her hair over the back of his hand seemed enough to send him hurtling over the edge like an untried boy. Her fingers upon his bare skin proved irresistible.

Connor ran his hands through the length of her hair, then sat back on his heels and stroked her arms. ‘‘Your beauty makes me feel the strongest of men,’’ he said. He cupped his hands lightly about her neck, then slowly smoothed them down, outlining the fullness of her bosom, the mound of her belly, halting with his hands clasped about her hips. ‘‘And the weakest of fools.’’ He leaned forward and pressed his lips chastely to her mouth. ‘‘We should not be doing this,’’ he said with regret. Brushing his mouth over the velvet softness of her cheek, he shifted to hold her, burying his face in her hair.

Moira returned the embrace, giving a soft sigh and nestling deeper into his arms. Despite the desire still raging through him, Connor had never felt more at ease. Yearning and a curious sense of satisfaction joined within him as he held Moira, a contentment he'd never known existed until now.

When the wind lessened and the vivid streaks of color began to fade from the sky, Connor released her, reluctant to let the moment end, but knowing they shouldn't remain there. She turned away, but not before he saw the tears slowly welling from her eyes. He reached out and touched her damp cheek. "Dearling, what is it?"

Moira gave Connor a shaky smile and leaned into his touch. "We should go back, but I don't want to leave. Not yet." Her eyes filled with tears, she scanned the churning sea, then turned to stare at the towers of Gerald's Keep silhouetted against the darkening sky. If only he knew how badly she wanted to burrow back into his embrace, to borrow from him the strength to face the troubles plaguing them! 'Twas a blessing he didn't know the depth of her desire, for 'twould likely send him rushing away from Gerald's Keep as swiftly as he could.

Simply because he'd offered her the security of his name didn't mean he wanted *her,* clinging to him like a leech.

As for the other desire she felt, the yearning for Connor himself... He couldn't possibly want her in that way, so near her time with another man's child.

Hadn't she learned better than to give in to desire? Though she hadn't cared for Dermot in the least—particularly after she realized her error in accepting his bargain—she couldn't help but mourn the fact that her actions had helped lead to his death.

How, then, could she even consider accepting Connor's offer? Although she didn't know him well, already she'd come to care for him, far more deeply than she'd have believed possible.

Tears welled in her eyes yet again as she considered her dilemma. Was she willing to risk Connor's safety, possibly sacrifice him, to protect her child?

She pressed her cheek against his shoulder, as much for

comfort as to hide her tears. Sitting here in his embrace, feeling his heart beating strong and steady, how could she choose?

Connor laid his hand on her shoulder, his touch alone giving her comfort. "We can stay till the sun sets, if you wish," he said quietly. He sat next to her on the stone and slipped his arm around her, then used his free hand to turn her face toward him. "Moira," he murmured, brushing away the tears on her cheeks. "Dearling, tell me what's wrong."

She shook her head; she'd not be able to force the words past her lips, not here and now.

His own lips firmed into a frown as he scanned her face; it felt as though his eyes could see into her heart, her mind, into the shadows hidden deep within her. But she refused to look away.

Let him stare, she thought fiercely, let him wonder. Perhaps he would see the truth of her, spare her the shame of revealing to him the stains upon her soul.

She could feel the rush of heat as a flush mounted her cheeks, and still he watched her. If she had any courage to spare she'd have asked him what he sought, what he *saw,* but it took all her resolve simply to hold his measuring gaze.

Finally she could resist its power no more. "I don't know if I'm strong enough!" she cried. "If I can *be* strong enough."

His expression softened, and he nodded. "Then let me be strong for both of us." He picked up her hand from where it lay on her lap, entwined his fingers with hers and raised it to his lips to press a soft kiss upon her knuckles. "You *are* a brave woman, Moira FitzGerald. I do not doubt the depth of your strength for a moment. You've withstood much sorrow, and your concerns are far from over." He lowered their joined hands to her lap, but didn't release her hand—or her gaze. "For now, while you're here with me, you needn't worry, or think of anything but yourself." He cradled her against his side. "This is what I would give to you, Moira—someone to share the bad and the good, a strong arm to protect you."

Moira felt a sense of loss so overwhelming, 'twas all she could do to breathe. Never had she wanted anything so much as she wanted to accept Connor's offer—to accept him.

She forced herself to move, and struggled out of his hold. "No more, I beg you," she whispered, standing before him. She covered her face with her hands and fought for calm. Lowering her hands, she wiped the moisture from her cheeks and faced him. "Do you think I want to cause your death as well?"

Connor rose and held out a hand to her. "Have you so little faith in me, Moira? When I make a vow, I keep it come what may."

Tears flowed from her eyes unchecked. "What will come is Hugh and his allies. They will not stop until they've taken what they want—my babe. It doesn't matter to me *who* fathered my child. I am its mother, and I refuse to allow them the opportunity to turn my son or daughter into one of them." She pressed her hands over her belly, taking comfort from the babe's gentle movements. "But neither do I want them to destroy *you.*"

"They'll not harm me," he said firmly. "Or if they do it matters naught, as long as you are safe." He raked his hand through his hair and looked out at the roiling sea.

His words cut deeply into Moira's heart, laying bare to her how much she'd come to value him—to care for him. But she couldn't allow that to stand in the way of protecting her child, she reminded herself. Her child must remain her primary concern.

Then shouldn't she give in to Connor, accept his proposal, no matter the harm it might bring to him?

As long as she kept her babe safe.

She could not do it, not yet—could not find the determination to endanger Connor when there might be another way to protect the babe and him both, and to keep the castle out of Hugh MacCarthy's hands.

Never mind how her heart urged her to selfishly seize the comfort and support that Connor offered—the chance to be his wife in truth, in every way that mattered to her. When Connor returned his attention to her, he wore an expression so fierce she might have been afraid, had it been any other man but him. "How do you suggest we protect the child? How do we protect you?" he asked, his tone as intense as his appearance. "From what you've told me about Hugh MacCarthy—by the saints, from what I've seen of your own brother—you're not safe here, Moira. If I believed I could spirit you away from here and send you to Rannulf, I would. But I doubt we'd travel a league before we'd be attacked."

"I doubt they'd harm me, lest they hurt the child." Small comfort, should she fall into MacCarthy's hands.

Clenching his fists at his sides, Connor took a step closer to her. "There's no telling what might happen to you in a battle, Moira. 'Tis not orderly and neat—you know that. No matter how closely we guard you, there's no guarantee we can shield you from them. And the journey to England is long and hard. What would happen if the child came while we were on the road?" He shook his head. "I will not allow you to put yourself into harm's way."

"But I'm to permit *you* to risk harm yourself?" she demanded. "To save me?" She closed the distance between them and met his stare. "I tell you now, I will not have it. I don't care if we continue to hide behind these walls until every MacCarthy in Ireland is dead, if it keeps *everyone* safe."

"But that's the problem, Moira," he told her, his voice quiet, almost sad. "Hiding behind the castle walls won't keep you safe. Not if MacCarthy finds a way in."

She closed her fingers in the voluminous skirt of her gown to keep from grabbing Connor by the shirt and shaking him. "What do you mean?" she asked, her voice quavering despite her attempt to sound calm. "Have we a traitor in our midst?"

God help them if that were so.... Though it could not be, else Hugh would have struck by now, wouldn't he? Before Connor had arrived with reinforcements?

"No traitor that I know of," he said. "So far as I can tell, the threat remains outside the walls. But it won't be long before they find their way in, if what I've heard is true." Connor reached down and tugged her wrist till she released her grip on her gown, then took her by the hand. "Come, you look as though you're ready to fall over," he said. He led her back to the rock and, taking her by the shoulders, urged her to sit down. Even in the rapidly fading light she could see his concern. He joined her and let go of her hand. "I planned to tell you—tonight, most likely, if I could find a moment to speak with you without an audience."

She weighed the sound of his voice, his expression and the fact that he didn't meet her gaze, and came to her own conclusion. "Don't think to mislead me now. I may not know you well, but 'tis clear to me you'd no intention of sharing whatever you've learned until you had to." He opened his mouth to speak, but she covered it with her hand and shook her head. "Don't," she warned him. She pressed her fingers tighter over his lips when she felt him try again to speak. "Don't deny you've been avoiding me. If you'd rather not spend time in my presence, 'tis your right. But 'tis *my* right to know if we're in danger." Resisting the urge to cup Connor's whisker-covered cheek in her palm, she moved her hand away.

Connor promptly caught it in his grasp and brought it to his lips, pressing a soft kiss to the inside of her wrist. "'Tis true, I've been avoiding you." He entwined his fingers with hers and added, "This is one reason why."

Heat suffused her face at the warmth in his voice, his eyes. It swept through her to settle in parts of her body she hadn't realized could feel such yearning.

"You cannot..." Heart thumping wildly, she shook her head and tried to pull free of his clasp, but he continued to hold her, with his hand and his gaze. "You cannot want me in that way!" She gestured toward her stomach. "Look at me! I am huge with another man's child. I was never beautiful, but now—"

"You *are* beautiful, Moira—the babe simply makes you more so. I find you lovely, enticing..." He brought her hand to his lips once again, then loosed his light hold and stood. "Which is a good reason why we should not remain out here by ourselves," he added, glancing out into the gathering dusk. "'Tis too dark to be here now, at any rate." He picked up his sword and tunic, then held out his hand to help her up off the rock.

"We can continue this conversation inside the keep, with Will and Sir Ivor present." He sighed and moved his grip from the warm intimacy of her hand to an impersonal clasp of her arm to help her over the uneven ground. Pausing for a moment, he tightened his fingers. "I swear you'll have no reason to fear being alone with me, Moira. But perhaps 'tis better if I limit myself to visiting you only when others are present."

She could scarce see him in the murky twilight, but she couldn't mistake the sincerity vibrating in his voice. "I have never feared you, Connor. I know of no reason why I should."

Connor heard Moira say the words, felt them settle over him like a blanket of peace, security—trust.

She trusted him, when *he* did not know if she should.

Was he capable of living up to her trust? he wondered as he led her through the darkness.

Or would his father's legacy prove too strong to overcome?

Chapter Thirteen

As they silently made their way back to the castle, Connor helping her over the rough ground, Moira wondered yet again if she should simply give in, accept his proposal of marriage. It would strengthen her position greatly, for 'twould be difficult indeed for Hugh MacCarthy to wrest control of her from Connor if she were his wife.

And if, God forbid, Connor were killed… Nay, she'd not think of that! She stumbled against him and had to fight the urge to clutch him to her as he caught her by the arms and steadied her. Despite the pain such a horrid, morbid thought caused her, she should approach the situation sensibly, she reminded herself. If some harm should come to Connor, as his wife she'd have the full power of Rannulf FitzClifford behind her, more so than she did now—for Rannulf would be more likely to protect his sister by marriage than a mere vassal's widow.

Though hadn't Rannulf already provided her with the best defense he could by sending his brother to her?

That being the case, the best security she could provide for her child would be to marry Connor without further delay.

The harm that decision might bring to Connor sent a chill

through her. By the Virgin, she thought, casting a sidelong glance at him as they crossed the torchlit bailey, contemplating her dilemma was enough to drive her mad!

They entered the hall, where Sir Will and Sir Ivor sprawled upon benches drawn up before the hearth, drinking horns in hand.

"Milord—well met," Sir Will called. "We were just about to go looking for you."

"Were you?" Connor asked, giving Moira a glimpse of his skeptical grin before he hastened across the hall to join them. "You'll pardon me if I doubt that." He paused on the dais to wait for her, then, once she reached him, tugged another bench closer to the massive fireplace and motioned for her to sit down.

She settled on the bench with a weary sigh, sliding over a bit to make room for Connor.

"Mead, milady?" Sir Will asked, holding aloft a pitcher.

"Nay, I thank you," Moira said. Of late, mead made her sleepy. While she could use a decent night's rest, at the moment she needed her wits about her more than she needed to sleep.

"Milord?" Sir Will had already begun to pour the drink.

"Aye," Connor said. "All my quest this afternoon accomplished was to kindle an immense thirst." He raised one arm and stretched it high above his head, then reached for the horn Sir Will held out to him. "And sore muscles."

She glanced at the two knights, their garb dusty, their heads and shoulders liberally festooned with cobwebs. "Where have you been?" she asked.

To her surprise, 'twas Sir Ivor who straightened, set down his drink and replied. "Lord Connor sent us into the undercroft, milady, to seek a hidden passageway." He looked a different man, his face relaxed, his eyes alight with excitement.

"Indeed?" Moira scarce knew how to respond to this new side of Sir Ivor. What could account for the change in his demeanor? Whatever the cause, she didn't dare trust him any more now than she had when he'd snarled and insulted her. She turned to Connor and asked, "For what purpose?"

Connor drank deeply of the mead and gave a satisfied sigh. Glancing about the large chamber, he sent the few servants at their end of the hall scurrying with a single look. "As I told you before, Moira," he said, his voice pitched low, "I've heard that the threat to Gerald's Keep will come from the cliffs. I don't know if that means from within the cliffs, or in the walls of the castle itself. Will and I searched in the cellars this morn, and I sent Will and Sir Ivor to continue looking beneath the keep while I investigated outside."

"Do you think we ought to move someplace else to talk about this, milord?" Sir Will asked. "The servants'll be coming in to set up the trestles soon, won't they, milady?"

Moira nodded. "They should be about their work already." She rose. "'Tis nigh time for supper to be served, milord. I should send the servants in here at once. Where would you care to go for this discussion?"

Connor eyed the great hall, then stood as well. "I'm certain you're heartily sick of your chambers, so we'll not consider your solar." He looked over the table and benches on the dais. "If we move these back, farther from the main floor, we should be able to speak freely so long as we're quiet about it."

Moira approached Connor and, taking him by the arm, led him away from the others. "Are you certain, milord?" she murmured. "'Twill be noisy here—"

"All the better to drown out our words," Connor interrupted. He stared at her for a moment. "Shall I send Will to carry your message to the servants? You look weary."

She gave a quiet laugh. "Such attention, milord! You'll turn my head for certain. Who knows what I might agree to if you keep it up?" Sighing, she lowered herself onto the bench. "But I thank you for the offer. I'll be more grateful than I can say to sit and rest."

Connor sent Sir Will and Sir Ivor off to carry out their orders, then returned to join her on the bench. "Would you rather I helped you to your chamber and sent Brigit to you?"

"Nay. Too many of our conversations have been cut short because of me." He rose, snatched several cushions from the settle beside the fireplace and piled them into her lap. "I'll be fine here, especially since I can see that you plan to coddle me," she said, smiling.

"'Tis the least I can do." Frowning, he scooped her, pillows and all, into his arms and deposited her on the settle he'd just cleared. "You're supposed to use them to make a more comfortable seat," he said. He took two from her and wedged them behind her back, then moved a low stool closer and knelt to prop her feet upon it. "What else shall I fetch for you, milady?" he asked as he stood, making a sweeping bow, his wide smile infectious.

Her face red, Moira picked up the remaining cushion and held it poised to toss at him. "Enough, Connor!" Laughter bubbled through her, along with a tide of warmth. She lowered her voice and tried—unsuccessfully—for a stern tone. "Do you wish for everyone to see how helpless I've become?"

Connor leaned toward her, still smiling, his dark eyes bright with amusement. "Not helpless, milady—cosseted, as you deserve." He took the pillow from her and slipped it beneath her feet. ''How can anyone think less of you for that?''

'''Tis doubtless a blessing that Sir Ivor isn't here,'' she said, sobering. ''Else I'm sure he'd have something uncomplimentary to say.''

Connor sat down beside her. ''It seems his opinion is changing,'' he told her. ''According to Will—'' He broke off as the two knights reentered the hall and approached the dais.

She couldn't hear what they were saying as they crossed the floor, but she nearly slid off the settle, so great was her shock, when Sir Ivor let out a roar of laughter and clapped Sir Will on the arm.

She glanced at Connor, who appeared as surprised as she. He merely raised an eyebrow in response to her questioning look before his face settled into a noncommittal expression.

A trail of servants followed hot on their heels. In no time, the hall had been prepared for the evening meal and the chamber began to fill with noisy diners. Sir Will and Sir Ivor drew the furnishings on the dais as far from the main floor of the hall as they could, and as they ate, Connor laid out the details of what he'd learned.

Sir Will and Sir Ivor had discovered nothing during their search of the undercroft, and Moira could see that all three of the men were frustrated by the lack of progress. She, too, wished that some helpful bit of information would turn up soon, for at this point, it seemed that immuring themselves within the castle indefinitely was their only alternative to giving in to Hugh MacCarthy's demands.

Everyone left the hall after the meal was over, the men heading for the barracks outside the keep tower and Moira wearily seeking her bed. But once she climbed beneath the covers and settled herself, sleep abandoned her.

She stared at the fire in the hearth through the opened

curtains at the foot of the bed, letting her mind wander where it would and hoping the low, dancing flames might lull her into slumber. The warmth and comfort relaxed her body. Her mind, however, refused to stop worrying about the question of a secret entrance into Gerald's Keep.

Where could it be? The men had inspected barely half of the undercroft. 'Twas a dirty, time-consuming task, especially since they knew nothing about the arrangement of the supplies stored there. They'd have been better served to have taken her with them—she knew the storerooms more thoroughly than anyone else at Gerald's Keep, save Brigit, perhaps.

Now that she considered it, she recalled several places where the tower foundation incorporated stones far older than those used to build the castle—from the ancient fortress that once stood there, most likely. What better place to hide a passageway?

And if 'twas from the old fortress, perhaps 'twould explain how the MacCarthys had learned of it.

Excitement coursed through her veins, making her restless, eager to finally have something useful *she* could do. She threw aside the bedcovers and dressed in an old, shabby gown, drawing a cloak about her shoulders against the cellar's constant chill. There were no lanterns here, but she could find one near the door from the hall to the bailey. Making certain she had her ring of keys, a flint and steel in the pouch suspended from her belt, and her eating knife in its sheath, she left her chamber.

Staying to the shadows, Moira crept past those sleeping on the floor of the great hall, took up a lantern from the hook by the door and went outside.

The bailey was deserted, lit only by a few flickering torches set at intervals on the stone walls. She paused beneath a torch not far from the door to the undercroft to light the lantern, swiftly shuttered it, then stole the rest of the way, her soft shoes noiseless on the cobbles.

She knew the trick to making the lock work smoothly and silently. Picking up the lantern, she entered the noisome depths of the cellar and pulled the door closed behind her.

Connor spent a short while in the barracks with the men, as much to judge for himself whether any of them might be a traitor as to observe how well the soldiers of Gerald's Keep had combined with his troops. Satisfied that the rigorous training program he'd instituted hadn't sent Moira's men to their pallets, he'd also been pleased to see their spirits remained surprisingly high, and that they seemed eager to fight.

Now all he needed was a real foe for them to face, instead of vague threats from a spineless coward.

A foe who remained *outside* the castle walls.

A flicker of light across the bailey caught his attention, but it disappeared before he could see anything more. Tightening his hand on his sword hilt, he glided closer in time to hear the faintest creak of metal against metal.

But he saw no one.

Senses alert, his suspicions aroused, he seized a torch from the wall and crept toward the door to the undercroft. A tug at the handle showed 'twas locked, as it should be, but the sound had come from here. He felt in the pouch on his belt for the key that Will had returned to him tonight. Snuffing the torch and laying it aside, he unlocked the door.

He managed to get it open without creating a racket this time, but whoever had gone inside was bound to hear the faint squeal of the hinges. Connor shut the door, blocking the faint glow from the bailey and pitching the area into total darkness.

* * *

Clutching the partially shuttered lantern in one hand and holding her skirts up off the damp floor with the other, Moira passed quickly through the large storage rooms near the entrance to the undercroft. When she reached the winding passageway leading to smaller chambers deep beneath the keep, she set down the light and wrapped her cloak more securely about her. The chill of the place seemed to seep straight through the heavy wool of her clothes.

Her movements awkward, she looped the hem of her gown and cloak up over her arm and slipped her eating dagger free of its sheath. She doubted she'd find anything but rats here, but she knew better than to go unarmed. Indeed, she should have drawn the knife as soon as she came through the door. She sighed. Clandestine endeavors such as this were clearly beyond her.

At least no harm had come of her lapse this time. The babe gave her a kick beneath the ribs—its usual nighttime activity—as, lantern held high, she wended her way along the stone corridor until she reached a heavy, iron-bound door.

The light glittered off the heavy lock, wet and rusting, that hung open on the latch.

The lock should have been closed. She'd swear it had been, the last time she'd ventured this deep into the cellars.

When had that been? She could scarce recall the last time she'd made a thorough examination of the entire undercroft. The previous spring, perhaps?

Her blood ran cold. Whenever it was, she knew for a certainty that she hadn't been here since before the MacCarthys had come to Gerald's Keep.

Had they used their brief time within the castle to explore the place? They could have.... They could have done *anything* while they had everyone gathered together in the hall and bailey and Moira occupied in her old bedchamber, with none of them the wiser. She drew in a deep breath and fought to quell the panic sweeping through her.

What might she find beyond this door?

She'd never know if she stood here like a coward. Her hands shook, making the light waver wildly, but she managed to slip the lock from its mooring. Gathering her resolve, Moira opened the door.

The loud creak of the hinges echoed after her as she passed through the portal. The way grew narrow at once, and the stones more rough. Here she could sense the walls crowding in on her, feel the bulk of the keep tower and the walls pressing down on her. 'Twas a fearsome experience, making her breath seize tight within her chest and the babe shift restlessly.

She let the lantern drop to the floor, setting her shadow to dancing on the wall as the flame wavered, but thankfully didn't go out. Moira leaned back against the stones and closed her eyes. Smoothing her hands over the squirming child, she searched within herself for a drop of courage to carry her the rest of the way.

However far that was.

Once her heartbeat slowed and her breathing eased, the slow, measured tread of footsteps suddenly caught her attention. Her pulse thundered in her ears once again, but didn't drown out the sound. She couldn't tell whether it came from behind her or ahead of her; either way, 'twould be trouble. Who else would be down here at this time of night save someone who shouldn't be?

Herself included.

Moira opened her eyes and adjusted her fingers about the knife hilt, pushing away from the wall and broadening her stance. The footsteps sounded louder now—and they were definitely coming from behind her.

"You've trapped yourself this time," she muttered under her breath. "How will you get out of this?"

The tip of a sword edged past the half-open door. Not knowing what else to do, Moira raised her puny eating knife and lunged toward the doorway, screaming at the top of her lungs.

Soon after Connor entered the undercroft, he caught a glimpse of light and set out in pursuit of it. Skulking along in the intruder's wake, he kept to the shadows, never coming close enough to see who it was he followed. The floor became uneven, slowing his progress further as he tried to move quietly.

He caught up when they reached a series of smaller chambers that afforded some cover, wincing when the screech of metal against metal split the air and echoed throughout the place. The light stopped moving, and the footsteps ceased.

The cellars couldn't go on any farther than this! Perhaps he'd cornered the intruder? Eagerness singing in his blood, he drew his sword and crept forward.

A narrow opening lay before him, light glowing brightly beyond it. Sword first, he crept toward the half-open portal.

He realized 'twas Moira standing before him just as she screamed and dove at him with a knife. Dropping his sword in the cramped passageway, he grabbed for her wrist as the blade slashed toward his face. "Trying to give me another scar?"

He released her arm and caught her as she slumped against him, her knife falling to the floor. "By the Virgin," she gasped. "I might have cut you!"

Holding her steady with one arm, he stooped to retrieve their weapons. "You might try," he said, surprised to feel himself grinning. He flipped her knife around and, catching it by the blade, presented it to her hilt first. "But I think I've strength enough—barely—to protect myself."

"'Tis nothing to laugh about," she scolded, making Connor want to smile all the more. Hands shaking, she snatched the knife from him and shoved it into its sheath on her belt. She seemed genuinely concerned for his well-being.

From her frown and the way she slapped him on the chest, he guessed his pleasure must have been obvious to her. "You're determined to do me harm." He captured her hand in midslap, brought it to his lips and kissed her knuckles. "You're freezing!" Catching both her hands in one of his, he tugged her cloak closer about her.

Then he gathered her into his arms and held her. Once her shaking stopped he loosened his hold, though he didn't release her. Instead he pressed his face to her unbound hair, savoring the sweet fragrance that even their musty surroundings could not overcome. "What are you doing down here, Moira?" he asked, the words a whisper rather than the stern demand he'd intended. "What if someone other than me had followed you in here?" The mere thought made his heart trip and falter.

She drew back and met his gaze, her blue eyes shining with eagerness. "I remembered something, Connor—remembered a place down here that could be what you were looking for."

"You couldn't wait till morning to check?" he asked dryly. "Or send for me to come with you?"

"'Twas late—I thought you might already be abed." Some of the excitement faded from her face. "And I couldn't sleep," she added, lowering her gaze, a trace of pink staining her cheeks.

Did he have anything to do with her sleeplessness?

There's arrogance, he taunted himself. By the saints, Moira had troubles aplenty to keep her from her rest.

"But nothing happened," she said. "I've come to no harm."

Connor lowered his arms and stepped back, then froze as a steady thumping—pounding?—came from somewhere down the passageway. Moira clutched at his arm. "What was that?" she whispered, her eyes huge in her pale face.

He held up his hand to silence her. The noise continued, faint but distinct. Should he send Moira back for help and go on himself, or take her with him? Either way, they would have to proceed silently and in total darkness, lest they alert the interloper. He eased his sword free and leaned close to murmur in her ear. "Go back, Moira. Tell Will we heard something, and that I've gone on to investigate."

She drew herself up beside him, resting her hand on his shoulder and tugging him down to her level. "I will not," she said in an angry whisper. "By the time I leave, find Sir Will and come back, who knows what might happen to you?" She drew her blade. "There's barely room ahead of us for men to fit, Connor, let alone to fight. We'll be lucky if you can stand up in the corridor. It becomes much narrower just ahead."

By the rood, he'd no desire to drag her along behind him, but neither could he ignore this opportunity to discover what was causing the noise. The answers he sought might lie straight ahead of them!

Other sounds joined the muted pounding. "All right," he muttered. "You needn't go back. I'll go on, see what's ahead of us. But I want you to stay here." Glancing ahead of them, he noted how far the lantern's light spread. "I'll be back soon." He cast one last, measuring look down the corridor, then bent and doused the light.

Moira stared hard at the place where she'd last seen Connor, naught but a black void in a sea of darkness. She knew he'd moved away because she could no longer sense his nearness—the warmth of his body, the nigh-indecipherable scent of him. But he made no sound as he crept down the passageway.

Could she manage to move so quietly? she wondered.

Edging past the lantern, she tightened her grip on her dagger and set off to find out.

Chapter Fourteen

Moira gingerly felt her way along the dank passage, biting back a shriek of terror when she slid her hand across something cold and slimy. Her heart thundered so hard she couldn't tell if the sounds Connor had gone ahead to investigate continued. They could have grown louder, for all she knew.

The darkness wrapped about her like a cold, damp blanket. She began to shiver again, so hard 'twas all she could do to keep moving.

But she could not let Connor face whatever—whoever—awaited him at the end of the corridor alone, no matter what he'd told her to do. At the least, she could go back for help if he *did* run into trouble.

The way became so narrow her shoulders brushed against the walls, and the floor grew rough, littered with bits of stone and debris. She wished she had light, for the end of the corridor must be near, and she had no desire to come crashing into Connor and startle him.

She halted and held her breath, straining her ears for any sound. But she heard nothing save the steady drip of water and the rapid thud of her pulse.

Without warning, a large body backed into her. Biting

back a cry, she lost her footing and fell hard on her backside, with her attacker sprawled atop her legs.

"By the saints!" Connor growled, following the words with a string of curses the likes of which she'd not heard since she'd left her brothers' home. "Can't you do as you're told, Moira?" He rolled off her. "I ought to blister your backside...."

"There's no need," she muttered through her tears. "'Twill be black and blue already." The floor beneath her throbbing buttocks must be made up of jagged stones.

"Are you all right? I didn't harm the babe?" He reached out and touched her legs, following them up her body till he could clasp his hands about her middle. "Can you stand?"

She'd force her legs to work, if necessary, to get up and away from the debris still poking into her. "Aye." He hefted her off the floor and set her on her feet, keeping his hands at her waist until she steadied. "We're both fine," she assured him.

"Listen," he whispered. They stood motionless.

The only sound they heard was their own quiet breathing.

Connor muttered something beneath his breath. "We must have frightened them off." He sounded as disappointed as Moira felt. "Come on, then." He caught her by the elbow and nudged her ahead of him.

"Did you find anything?" she whispered as she limped along.

"No." Though he kept his voice low, she couldn't mistake his ire. "And I'm not likely to now, after all the noise *we* made." The corridor opened up a bit, and he urged her to move faster. "Anyone who was here will have gone, if they've any sense. I was coming back for the lantern—" he tugged on her arm and brought her to a halt "—though

I doubt there'll be anything to see now. Still, it can't hurt to look."

The lantern rattled as he leaned past her and picked it up, followed by the sound of flint striking steel. He kindled the wick and adjusted the shutter, the warm light bathing them in its welcome glow.

He wore tension and exhaustion in equal measure upon his face, and frustration in his eyes. Moira lowered her gaze. If she'd stayed where he'd left her…

Connor shifted the lantern to his other hand. "Stay with me."

"You're taking me with you?" she asked, then felt a fool for giving voice to her surprise. Besides, she shouldn't *be* surprised; he didn't trust her to obey him, most likely.

She followed close behind him, drawing her knife from its sheath before they'd gone far. 'Twas a tight fit for Connor in this passageway. If they encountered anyone, he'd not be able to draw his sword, though she noticed he'd armed himself with a lethal-looking dagger he'd drawn from his boot.

Though they were moving as quietly as they could, Connor couldn't hear anything save the rustle of their clothing as they crept along the ever narrowing passageway. He held up his dagger, motioning for Moira to stop. "Listen," he mouthed. They stood for a moment, but heard nothing. Frowning, he held the lantern out and scanned the corridor. "Look there—there's naught but a solid wall," he whispered, not bothering to hide his disgust. Three strides took him to it. He ran his hand over the roughly mortared stones, pressing on the joints to no avail. "There's no way through here."

"Not yet," Moira said. He abandoned his search and turned to look at her. "I'd suspect someone was trying to tunnel their way in, but there's naught but solid rock on the other side.''

Connor reviewed their path to this point, trying to determine where they stood in relation to the headland. ''There shouldn't be anything but rock on the other side—though if that is true, why didn't they simply incorporate it into the foundation?'' He smoothed his hand over the mortared stones once more before turning to Moira, his weary brain alight with hope. ''If it was solid, there'd be no need for mortar here.'' He took her by the arm and urged her ahead of him, enthusiasm brightening his outlook for the first time in days. ''Time to go back.''

''What are you going to do now?''

He paused and leaned forward to whisper near her ear. ''I'll tell you once we're out of here. There's no way of knowing if the rats are already in the walls, or where they might be.'' Moira nodded and remained silent as they made their way to the door.

He swung the heavy, iron-bound panel wide and looked closely at the sturdy metal hinges. ''Have you a key for this?'' he asked.

''I do, but it wasn't locked before.'' She shuddered. ''I think Hugh—someone—must have unlocked it when they were here,'' she told him. ''It was always kept locked before. I'm certain I haven't been this far back since before they came.''

''Are you the only one with a key?'' He unhooked the padlock from the iron loop on the latch and held it up to the light, shaking his head. ''Look—it's been forced, with a dagger most like.'' He pointed to the gouges in the rusty metal. ''Perhaps someone came down here while you were otherwise engaged.'' He met her gaze, hoping she wouldn't see the rage engendered by the mere thought of what she'd endured that night—rage directed at the MacCarthys, not her. "I don't know how they got into the undercroft itself without a key, though."

"There's more than one key to that door." She unhooked her ring of keys from her belt and sorted through them until she found the one she sought. "Will it still work?" She handed it to him.

"We shall see." With abrupt movements, he closed the padlock and unlocked it with the key. Motioning for Moira to go through the portal, he followed her, then threaded the lock onto the door, snapped it closed and dropped the key into the pouch on his belt. "Come," he ordered.

He took her by the arm and helped her over the uneven floor, setting a hurried pace in his eagerness to leave this dreary place, to explore the ideas teasing at his brain.

She pulled back and dug in her heels. "Enough, milord."

"What?" He spun about and shifted his attention to Moira.

Weariness radiated from her, shadowed her face and her voice. "You're moving too fast." She stared pointedly at his hand until he released her arm. "I cannot keep up with you, Connor," she said in a more even tempered tone.

Especially considering how sore she must be from falling down and having him land atop her. Jesu, was he turning into a thoughtless brute? "I'm sorry." He ran his hand absently through his hair. "I've much on my mind. I didn't realize..."

"I know. But dragging me behind you won't help." She held out her hand and clasped his. "Come on. If you stay *beside* me, 'twill be all right."

Again Connor heard the weariness in Moira's voice, could see it in the way she held herself. She should never have come down here tonight.

Perhaps if *he* were thinking more clearly, he'd have realized she might try to search for a hidden passageway herself. He felt his anger build again. How could she endanger herself, her child, by coming here alone?

He clamped his jaw tight and stared hard at the water dripping down the stone wall. He wanted to rage at her, take her to task for her folly, but in truth, the fault could just as likely be his own.

His mind was so muddled, he didn't trust himself to make a sensible decision about anything. He needed to sleep, to give himself a chance to mull over all he'd learned thus far, before he could determine what to do next.

Haranguing Moira now would serve no useful purpose—and might very well turn her away from considering any plan he put forth.

Best to hold his tongue till morning at least, wait to see how it all looked once he could think clearly again.

He allowed Moira to lead him through the remainder of the undercroft. After he locked the door to the cellars, he doused the lantern and escorted her to the stairs. He noticed she was limping when she tried to climb them. Muttering a curse, he handed her the lantern and picked her up, carrying her the rest of the way.

She uttered not a word of protest, proving to him how tired she must be.

'Twas past time for her to seek her bed.

They passed through the hall in silence as he wound his way among the sleeping servants and up the spiral stairs. He set her down at her door. "Will you be all right?" he asked. "Should I send for Brigit?"

"Nay, let her rest. I'd rather she not find out that I left my chamber and went down there," Moira said with a quiet, mirthless laugh. "'Tis best not to provoke her temper—especially since she'd be right to take me to task."

Since he agreed with her, Connor didn't know how to

reply to that. Deciding he'd be wise to remain silent, he simply nodded and opened her door for her.

"Good night." Shoulders drooping, she limped into her room.

He closed her door and leaned against the wall, resting his cheek on the cool plaster as he sought the strength to go back to the barracks. As much as he wished to climb the remaining stairs and seek his bed, he'd much left to set in motion. He needed to arrange for men to guard the undercroft till the morning.

He pushed away from the wall and made his way down the spiraling stairs, marveling yet again at the ease with which Rannulf commanded several keeps. His brother made the work appear simple, effortless, a skill Connor wondered if he lacked.

Or perhaps he merely lacked the training Rannulf had gained in his years away from FitzClifford.

By the rood, he'd gain nothing by treading over this well-worn path once more, Connor realized. 'Twas his weariness and frustration making him doubt himself, nothing more. He left the keep and stood in the bailey for a moment to let the cool night air clear his head. He'd do what he could tonight, then seek his bed.

After a night's rest, everything would seem better, he was sure.

A raucous din startled Connor awake as the sun cast its first light into the sky. Evidently Padrig hadn't expected to find his master still abed, for the lad sang a bawdy tale, his uneven voice mangling the tune, as he entered Connor's chamber and slammed the door against the wall.

"By Christ's bones," Connor snarled as he leaped from beneath the covers and grabbed his sword from where he'd rested it against the wall.

"Jesu!" Padrig cried, jumping back from the coffer at the foot of the bed and tossing the mound of clothing he held into the air.

A shriek sounded from the corridor. His sword still held at the ready, Connor glanced past his squire and saw a young maid, her hands clapped over her mouth and her eyes huge, standing in the open doorway staring at him.

He cast aside his sword, sending it clattering onto the floor. Cursing, he snatched a blanket from the bed and draped it around his waist to cover his nakedness.

A door down the hallway slammed. "What is going on out here?" he heard Moira ask. Light footsteps on the wood floor heralded her appearance. "Maeve, what is wrong with you?"

The maid pointed into the room. Moira joined her in the doorway, her serious expression changing to a smile. "Milord, I'll thank you not to terrorize the maidservants." Taking Maeve by the arm, Moira led her away and returned alone a moment later. "Now you'll have the silly lass mooning after you," she scolded, though he could hear laughter in her tone and see it in her eyes.

He gathered the blanket more securely about his waist. "You can thank Padrig for that," he said dryly. "If not for his screeching, I'd yet be abed, disturbing no one." He gave the squire, standing in silence at the foot of the bed, a grin to soften the words.

The lad's face remained pale and serious, however. "'Tis a jest, Padrig," Connor reassured him. Glancing at the light shining through the shutters, he added, "I should have been up and about my work long since." He met Moira's gaze. "It seems that recent events have exhausted me."

Let her take that however she would. He'd not slept well, though whether the memory of Moira's kisses, his worry over her wandering through the cellars in the dead of night, or something else completely had caused his restlessness, he didn't know.

He *did* know, however, that if Moira continued to stare at him, he'd soon need to adjust the fit of his makeshift garb lest his overeager body embarrass all three of them.

"Padrig, bring me water to wash," he ordered. Perhaps shifting his attention to something besides the near-physical touch of Moira's gaze over his body would help. The blanket dragging along behind him, he turned to the window and threw the shutters open wide, flooding the room with light.

Padrig knelt to gather up the clothing scattered about him on the floor.

"*Now,* Padrig."

The lad stood, glanced from Connor to Moira, lowered his gaze and bobbed a bow. "At once, milord," he said, his voice cracking. He darted for the door, snatching the water pitcher from the table as he passed.

Now that they were alone, the sensations caused by Moira's stare intensified despite the bright light filling the room. Connor sank down on the bed and bent to pick up his sword off the floor.

The door creaked shut and footsteps drew nearer to the bed.

"Unless you intend to join me here, Moira, I suggest you keep your distance," he told her, focusing his attention upon sliding the weapon into its sheath. "My body has dominion over my mind when I first wake. It wouldn't be wise to tempt fate—" he glanced up and found her standing so close, he could reach out and sweep her onto the mattress if he chose "—by giving me too much encouragement."

Her right hand settled onto his shoulder, her fingers cool

against his overheated flesh as she trailed them over the curve of his shoulder, along the muscles of his upper arm.

He sucked in his breath. ''Jesu, you'll drive me mad,'' he muttered, shutting his eyes to block out her intent expression.

It made no difference, for her face remained emblazoned upon his mind's eye.

She closed her hand about his arm and turned his back toward the window. ''Who did this to you?'' she asked, her outrage clear though he could barely hear the whispered words.

His eyes snapped open, and his stomach churned when he glanced over his shoulder and realized what had caught her attention.

''''Tis nothing.'' He tried to shrug free of her hold, but she kept her hand clasped firmly about his arm.

Unwilling to release Connor, Moira moved so that she had a better view of his shoulder and back. This close, in the clear morning light, she could see what hadn't been visible before.

Many scars, long and thin, showed white against the tanned, freckled skin. She smoothed her hand over his upper back and discovered some were more easily felt than seen. He'd had them a long time, she'd guess. They had the pale, faded look of wounds long healed.

She slid her hand back around to clasp the bulging muscles of his arm; with her free hand, she reached up and turned his face toward her. ''Connor?''

''Let it alone, Moira.'' The pain and turmoil in his dark eyes belied his flat tone. ''I told you 'twas naught.''

''Scars such as this don't happen by accident,'' she said, her voice quiet, but firm. She'd not rest till she discovered who could have done such a thing to him…to a child. Who could have beaten a young nobleman so badly?

She stroked her hand over his shoulder again, meaning naught by her touch but to soothe, but he caught her wrist in an unyielding grip and lifted her hand away. "Enough!"

Holding the blanket in place with one hand, he slipped past her and stood just beyond her reach, turned so his back remained hidden from her.

The pain in his eyes, however, was clear and visible, as was the anger smoldering within him.

That he'd not give her the answer she sought was clear. And perhaps 'twas not her business to dredge up painful memories from his past.

But how her heart ached for the young boy he'd been, for the hurt so deep the anguish of it still shone plainly from his eyes.

Anguish mixed with shame.

"Connor, I'm sorry." Sorry that he'd been beaten. Sorry that she'd upset him.

But not sorry she'd seen the scars, for they told her that there was more to this man than the strong, able facade he presented to the world.

In that moment, she saw him not as a warrior, a figure of authority, the image of a noble, but as a man.

She caught her breath as she realized the intensity of the attraction she felt for that man.

The door creaked open, startling them. Connor fairly leaped past her to the window; Moira, knees weak and heart racing, leaned back against the bedpost. Padrig came into the room, the water pitcher in one hand and a steaming bucket in the other.

"Shall I shave you, milord?" the squire asked, his cheerful voice sounding out of place. The lad seemed unaware of the tension still binding Moira and Connor together, for he whistled a merry tune as he poured water into the basin. He turned to pick up the clothing he'd dropped earlier, his gaze coming to rest on Moira, and quieted abruptly. ''I beg your pardon, milord. Lady Moira. 'Twas not my intention to interrupt your—'' he looked from one to the other and his cheeks flushed ''—your conversation,'' he concluded, his voice trailing away. He waved his hand toward the door. ''Shall I come back later?''

The lad's obvious embarrassment made Moira all too aware of how this must appear. Her face felt as hot as Padrig's looked. She straightened and stepped away from the bedpost, thankful he hadn't entered the room earlier, when she'd had her hands all over Connor. ''Nay, I must go,'' she said, already halfway to the door.

''Moira.'' Connor's voice stopped her with her hand on the latch. Gathering her courage, she glanced back to where he stood by the window. She couldn't see his face with the bright light surrounding him—a blessing, though to judge by his tone, he'd recovered his composure. ''We will talk, and soon.''

Hearing the promise in his words, she could only nod and slip out of the room.

Chapter Fifteen

After Moira left, Connor washed quickly and scrambled into his clothes. He hadn't intended to sleep so late, nor to skip his morning routine. Today he felt the need to clear his mind and relax his body more keenly than usual. Especially since Moira had stirred up unsettling memories of his past with her innocent question about the scars on his back. But he would have to wait to ease his tension, for today he must look to the present and the future—untainted by the past.

Despite his continuing fatigue, anticipation thrummed through his veins as he left the keep. Perhaps today he'd discover the answers he sought—the answers that would enable him to protect Moira and her babe, to give her peace of mind.

When he'd returned to the barracks last night—or this morn, more likely—he'd roused Will from his bed and sent him into the undercroft to guard the door leading to the narrow passageway. Though he wasn't pleased to be dragged from his bed, Will's mood had improved once he realized that Sir Ivor would be forced to endure the misery of spending the night in the cellars, as well.

As for d'Athée, Connor didn't know what accounted for

his apparent about-face, but the other man had grown quieter, more pensive the past few days, at least in his presence. Perhaps 'twas Will's influence on him, though Connor doubted it could be that simple. Still, he'd be an arrogant fool to deny that a man could change—change greatly—when he himself had worked so hard these last few years to effect such a change in his own life.

Though given his reaction when Moira had asked who'd scarred his back, he couldn't help but wonder if the changes in himself were on the outside only. The feelings coursing through him when she'd smoothed her hand over the faded marks had borne a strong resemblance to those he'd felt years before, whenever anyone noticed him. He'd felt then—and again this morning—as though all his faults and sins were laid bare, exposed for anyone to see if they but looked his way.

'Twas a terrible sensation, painful and frightening, one he'd believed—he'd hoped—never to experience again. That it was Moira who'd seen him thus made the angry child hiding within him want to howl in rage.

Or run away so she'd no chance of ever unmasking him again.

But one thing he *had* learned was that running never made his troubles disappear. It only made them worse. He would run no more.

He could only hope that the next time he saw Moira, he'd have the strength to push that cowering child deeper within himself, where she couldn't find him.

After leaving Connor's chamber, Moira kept herself busy, hoping her duties, and the demands of supervising the servants as they went about their work, would occupy her mind to the exclusion of all else.

It mattered little, however, for thoughts of Connor crept

into her head despite her efforts to avoid them. That she also saw him from a distance several times did not help. At least their duties kept them apart, a circumstance she prayed would last for a good while longer. The more time she spent in Connor's company, the more confused she became.

The more distracted from the course she knew she must follow.

He drew her to him with every new facet of his character that she discovered. It had taken her months—nay, years, more like—to know Lord Brien as well.

If she ever had.

But in the case of her husband, she'd found it no hardship to keep her distance from him whenever possible. She'd thought him a crotchety old man the first time they'd met, and marriage to him had done little to change her initial impression.

She'd found it easier to face the more intimate aspects of their union when he himself remained a mystery to her. At night when she sought her bed, she made certain all the candles in her chamber were out, the shutters closed to block out the moonlight, the fire died down to a few glowing coals. She'd been naught but a vessel for her husband's seed, and she'd done everything she could to maintain that illusion for both of them.

However, until Dermot MacCarthy came into her life, she hadn't understood what that fact meant to Lord Brien.

They'd met Dermot on several occasions, always among the groups of nobles at some feast or gathering. He'd been charming to *all* the women, from what she'd seen. Certainly she'd never noticed that he singled her out in any way, nor had he ever done anything—within her sight—to show that he'd any particular interest in Lord Brien FitzGerald's wife.

In her husband's eyes he had, she learned later, though

to this day she had no idea what that had been. But Lord Brien had become protective of her, attentive to her both inside their bedchamber and outside it.

And each sign of attention her husband lavished upon her made her dislike for him grow stronger.

Her mere tolerance of her situation turned to loathing as he redoubled his efforts to provide himself with an heir.

A legitimate heir.

Despite Moira's secret hopes to the contrary, her husband took no other women to his bed. It shamed her to recall how she'd prayed, when a new young maid had joined their household, that the girl would capture Lord Brien's attention and distract him from his wife. That her prayers had been unsuccessful was a blessing her stained soul no doubt did not deserve.

She'd always known Lord Brien desired a son, but she'd begun to suspect he had more reason than the wish to pass on his name. Did he fear that the FitzCliffords might remove him from his position at Gerald's Keep because of his age? He was their vassal, as well as their kin. Surely they had an obligation to him in return for his homage to them.

"—sit down, milady?" Brigit's voice, coming from behind her, broke though Moira's reverie as she climbed the stairs to her solar.

Hand pressed against the smooth plaster wall, Moira stopped and glanced down at the maid. "What is it, Brigit?"

The old woman, huffing for breath, halted at the bottom of the steps. "You must have been lost in your thoughts, milady," she said, her voice quavering. "I've been trying to catch your attention since you came into the hall from outside."

Guilt sent Moira slowly back down the stairs. "I'm

sorry, Brigit.'' She took the maid by the arm and led her to a bench at the edge of the hall. ''Here, sit and rest.''

Brigit sank onto the long, narrow seat and drew Moira down beside her. ''As long as you will as well.''

It *did* feel good to get off her feet and rest her aching back against the cool stone wall. '''Tis a fine idea you had,'' Moira said, sighing in pleasure.

''That it is. And a wise one, too, if you don't plan to work yourself into labor today. You're doing too much, milady,'' she scolded. ''It's not good for you or the child—and to my mind, 'tis still a mite too early yet for the child to be born, as I've told you before.''

Moira leaned toward Brigit and gave the old woman's hand a squeeze. ''I know.'' She gazed absently into the hall, where the servants worked at setting up the trestle tables for the midday meal. ''I hadn't realized 'twas so late. I'd thought to rest in my chamber for a bit before dinner.'' The night's exertions had caught up with her, especially since her sleep, once she'd sought her bed for the second time last night, had been far from restful. Worries about a secret passageway into the keep... *Nay, be honest,* she silently admonished herself. 'Twas thoughts of Connor FitzClifford that had replaced her usual round of worries to haunt her dreams.

She knew she should stand up, be about *some* business, but decided to wait a little longer before forcing her weary body into motion. Instead she shifted to a more comfortable position on the bench. ''You see, I *have* been listening to you,'' she added, smiling at Brigit's feigned look of surprise.

''I know you do, milady.'' The maid patted Moira's arm, her faded gaze sharp as she looked Moira over from head to toe and back again. ''You're not sleeping well. I can see it in your face.'' She picked up Moira's hands and held them, turning them this way and that. "And see how your fingers have swollen? Your feet are the same, I'd wager."

Moira nodded. "A little. But 'tis normal for them to do so—isn't it?" She knew she'd heard of it happening, quite often, now that she considered it.

"Some swelling is usual. But staying on your feet won't help matters any." Brigit let go of her hands, and Moira fought the urge to tug her skirts down around her ankles lest the maid take it into her head to examine them as well. "We've help aplenty around the place. At least now that Lord Connor's brought us some real fighting men, we do. Everyone can go back to their own duties." She shuddered. "We've been lucky so far, milady, that Hugh MacCarthy's left us alone. I hate to imagine how we'd have fared before, if we'd had to defend the place."

Moira looked up and saw Sir Will weaving his way among the busy servants, heading toward her.

A wide grin brightening his face, he stopped before her and swept her an elaborate bow. "Sir Will, you've no need to be so formal," she chided. Though she knew him for a jokester—and enjoyed his japes and jests—it left her feeling distinctly uncomfortable to be the recipient of his humorous brand of charm. Though 'twas harmless, she knew.

"As you wish," he said, assuming a serious expression in the blink of an eye. "Milady, I've orders from Lord Connor to bring you to him at once."

She'd not be able to avoid Connor any longer, so it seemed. And try though she might, she couldn't suppress the surge of heat, of excitement, that thought sent spilling into her veins. *Fool!* she chided herself. 'Twas folly to allow her emotions to overrule her good sense. Hoping her thoughts didn't show on her face, she gathered up her skirts to rise from the bench.

Sir Will held out a hand to help her. "Take your time,

milady, you needn't rush.'' Once she stood he placed her hand on his arm and led her with great care through the hall.

'Twas all she could do not to laugh by the time they reached the door. ''We'll be at this the rest of the day at this speed,'' she told him. ''I'll not collapse at your feet if we move faster, Sir Will—though I appreciate your concern.''

The knight met her gaze, and evidently noticed the amusement she couldn't quite disguise. ''As you wish.'' He lifted her hand off his arm and sketched another bow—a brief one this time. ''*You* may set the pace and lead the way, milady.'' Lips twitching as he held back a grin, Sir Will raised her arm and cocked it at the elbow, then placed his hand atop it. ''Thank you so much for your escort,'' he said, his voice pitched high in imitation of a woman's. ''Please, promise you'll be gentle with me,'' he added, fluttering his eyelashes.

Fairly bursting with the need to laugh, Moira waited to speak until they'd begun to descend the stairs and she'd mastered her voice. ''You, Sir Will, are a rogue through and through.''

'''Tis a pleasure to make you laugh, milady. Ivor laughs at little, though he's improving. I'll wear him down eventually.''

''It must be difficult for you, to be in his company all the time.'' She could scarce imagine a worse torture.

'''Tis not so bad. He forces me to think, to think hard, for how else can I argue with his ridiculous statements?'' he asked wryly. ''Jests are easy for me. Thinking is more difficult. And I've had little practice at it. At l'Eau Clair, no one expects anything of me but smiles and laughter.''

She'd never considered that would be a trial, but it appeared she was wrong. "Your skill is impressive, Sir Will. But I've no doubt your mind works with equal talent."

"Thank you, milady," he murmured.

"Where am I taking you, by the way?" she asked as they reached the bailey.

"To the undercroft."

A different excitement coursed through her now. "Connor has discovered something?"

"I'll let him tell you," Sir Will said.

Moira hurried to the door into the cellars, Sir Will close on her heels—ready to catch her should she stumble, no doubt, she thought with a smile. 'Twas strange to have such concern directed toward her, but heartening as well.

'Twas another aspect of the different mood prevailing here since Connor's arrival. The sense of hope, of comfort, of concern… She glanced around the bailey. If she didn't know better, she could almost believe she'd been magically transported to another place altogether.

A guard stood beside the door, well-armed and stern. He nodded respectfully to her, unlocked the door and opened it for them to enter. The telltale clink of the key turning after he eased the portal closed sounded even through the heavy panel.

Sir Will took a lantern from the pair hanging, lit and ready, on either side of the door. Others lighted along the way chased away the heavy shadows that had lent the cellars such an eerie feeling the previous night.

She followed Sir Will into the narrow passageway, then bumped into him when he came to an abrupt halt. "Pardon me, milady," he said. He moved back a few paces and gestured for her to go ahead. "If you don't mind going on alone, you'll find Lord Connor at the end of this corridor. I nearly forgot that I've other tasks yet to carry out."

The three of them wouldn't have all fit in the scant space ahead, so 'twas just as well she went on her own.

Besides, now she'd have no audience should she make a fool of herself when she faced Connor again. "I'll be fine," she assured the young knight. "Lord Connor will see that I leave here as safely as I came in."

Sir Will nodded, handed her the lantern and hurried away.

Moira paused near the door, pondering what course to follow when she reached Connor. Should she be cool, polite, remote? She gave a quiet snort of laughter. As if she could! She'd yet to carry herself as a proper lady ought, in Connor's presence, at any rate. But the image of him this morning, the vulnerability he couldn't quite hide, had haunted her ever since.

That, and the image of his near nakedness, the sun streaming over his lean, muscular form. That memory alone sent heat flowing through her body.

She had no shame, that much was clear. She smoothed her hand over her burgeoning belly, clanking the lantern against the stone wall in the process. She'd do well to remember how she'd found herself in this condition...and what her interest in Connor FitzClifford might mean to his continued safety.

"Moira, is that you?" Connor asked. The sound of loose debris crunching beneath his boots came closer.

She turned slowly toward the door, using the time to collect herself, to rid her expression of any trace of her unsettling thoughts. "Aye, milord. I'll be right there."

He came into view then, hunched over to avoid the ceiling, a lamp in his hand. When he reached her he straightened and smiled, his face alight with excitement. "Come." He took the lantern from her and set it in the doorway.

"I've something to show you." He took her hand and led her back the way he'd come.

They halted before the same mortared wall Connor had examined the night before. He set the lantern on the floor and knelt. "If I'd looked more closely last night, I'd have found this," he said. He slipped the dagger from his boot and used it to scrape at the mortar. She could see from the layer of plaster dust covering the dirt floor that he'd been doing this before she arrived. He stopped and turned to her. "Come and see."

She moved the light aside and leaned closer. Connor picked up a thin metal bar from the floor and used it to pry the stone from the wall—stone no thicker than the width of his dagger blade. "Are they all like that?" she asked. "Is it naught but a disguise?"

"Not all, but many." He got up off his knees and forced another stone from the wall. "Look at what lies beneath them."

She touched the flat, plaster-covered surface, then drew her own knife and scratched at the mortar until her blade scraped against metal and wood. "'Tis a door," she gasped. A very old door, to judge by the splintery condition of the boards and the age-pitted iron holding it together.

"Here, let me take off the other stones," Connor said.

She stepped back and gave him room to attack the rest of the facade covering the wooden panel.

He removed all but the last row of stones along the bottom of the door; surprisingly, the panel held. But a disquieting thought occurred to her as he raised the bar to complete the job. "Connor," she called, staying his hand. "What if there is someone waiting on the other side?"

He shook his head, his dark eyes intense in the lantern's glow. "I've had guards mounted on the walls facing the headland, as well as along the cliffs, since soon after I left here last night. I'm sure that whoever we heard then is long gone, and I doubt anyone could get in now without being seen.''

''But shouldn't we have someone in here—besides yourself—who can fight? In case you're wrong?''

He sighed. ''Anyone there now is a fool. We haven't been quiet. For all they know, I've an army in here—though I could hold this position myself with very little effort if necessary, while you go for help.''

She looked away and sought to overcome her uneasiness. He knew better than she the ways of war, of defense. As he knew his own abilities. She'd trusted him with all else in her life; she could trust him in this.

She met his gaze, imbuing her own with her confidence in him. ''Shall I see if I can find a way to open this?'' she asked, pointing her knife toward the area where a latch might be.

His eyes drew her in, held a warmth and approval she must surely be imagining. But when he smiled, his expression told a similar tale. Had he needed her approval? How could a man so strong, so skilled, have so little belief in himself?

Those questions would have to wait for another time. For now, she'd do all she could to show her faith in him. ''Connor?''

''Aye.'' He shoved aside the pile of rocks he'd removed. ''Just leave me room enough to take off these last few stones.''

Moira scraped at the mortar where she'd gauged the latch would be, but found nothing beneath it save the wooden panels of the door. She tried another spot, and once Connor had pried off the last of the facade, he used his larger blade to chip at the plaster that filled the gap between the door and its frame.

Connor's anticipation grew as they uncovered more of the ancient portal. He glanced down at Moira, scraping away with her small knife, and felt a sense of pleasure that under these circumstances should have been completely out of place. But right or wrong, the fact that Moira had accepted his assessment of the situation, had cast off her uncertainty, made him want to smile. The two of them working together felt right. That faced coupled with his growing certainty that they'd found the way the MacCarthys planned to use to conquer them... Perhaps they'd found the way to rout MacCarthy instead.

How could he help but smile?

He slid the dagger blade into the narrow space he'd cleared and felt it catch against a piece of metal near the top of the door. "I think I've found it," he told her. Removing the blade from the gap, he began to scrape at the thick layer of mortar that coated the upper half of the door.

Moira snatched the lantern from the floor and held it up near him. "Do you want me to help?"

He glanced over at her and saw how tired she looked. By the saints, he should never have sent Will for her; she should be in her chamber, resting. But he knew she wouldn't leave now. "Only by keeping the light here." She nodded, and he continued to carefully scrape away the plaster.

Finally he uncovered a lock—crude, but solid. "Now what?" he asked as he used the knife point to clear the keyhole. "I doubt you've a key for this."

Moira handed him the lantern and unhooked the ring of keys from her belt. "There's nothing here to fit that," she said. Passing him the keys, she leaned close and peered at the lock, then held out her knife, hilt first, to him. "This should work, don't you think?" she asked, moving back from the door.

He gave her back the lantern and ring of keys. ''Aye.'' His own knife clutched in his left hand, hers in his right, he slid her slim blade into the keyhole and, with hard-won patience, wriggled it about within the lock until something snapped. ''I hope that wasn't your knife,'' he muttered.

''It doesn't matter if it is,'' Moira replied.

''Ah, but it might—I don't want the blade stuck in there.'' Giving the hilt a gentle turn, he gingerly slid the knife free.

He heard Moira sigh, and turned to find that she'd set the lantern on the floor and stood resting against the far wall of the compact space, her eyes closed. Two short strides brought him to her. ''Are you all right?''

She opened her eyes, her lips curving into a smile. ''Aye. I'm just relieved—and trying not to hope too much. Perhaps there's naught on the other side of the door but solid rock.''

He checked the blade of her knife, surprisingly undamaged, and slid it into the sheath on her belt before bending to shove his dagger into his boot. Leaning closer to her, he smoothed the back of his fingers over the velvety softness of her cheek. ''If this turns out to be nothing, we'll find some other way to best them,'' he assured her. ''I promise you, Moira.'' He scanned her face once again in the flickering light. Though her skin looked pale, her blue eyes held relief—and anticipation. Not willing to face the temptation of her lips, he brushed a kiss across her brow. ''Come on, let's see what we've uncovered.''

He stepped away, took up the narrow bar he'd used to pry off the stones and wedged it into the crack between the door and the frame. ''You'd better stay back until I get this open.''

She nodded and moved off to the side. She'd drawn her knife, though how she thought to use it, he couldn't guess.

He gave the bar a hard shove and felt the door break free. Plaster and splinters of wood filled the area, along with a cloud of dust that blinded him. He felt a large body brush past him from beyond the door. Still unable to see, he drew his dagger and spun around just as Moira screamed.

Chapter Sixteen

"Connor!" Moira shouted.

A man cried out in pain, then let loose a frantic rush of Gaelic, too fast for Connor to understand.

Whatever he'd said didn't matter, anyway—not when Moira might be in danger. Connor swiped his sleeve across his eyes and tugged his dagger from his boot as he lunged toward them.

"Domnal O'Neill," Moira exclaimed. "By the saints, what are *you* doing here?"

Connor halted, blinking rapidly until he could see through the thinning haze of dust. Another O'Neill? All he could tell through the murk was that the man looked nigh as large as Aidan.

Connor's vision cleared. O'Neill stepped away from Moira and held out his left hand to her, palm up. "Look at this," he whined. "You cut me, Moira."

"Moira, are you all right?"

"Aye," she said, sounding vexed. "Ignore him, milord."

She appeared unharmed, so Connor glanced over and peered through the doorway. Naught but a cloud of dust. O'Neill was alone. Besides, would the man be sniveling to his sister if he'd come with a war party? Connor gave a grunt of disgust at the idea. Doubtful. Nonetheless, he'd best be cautious. He shoved closed what was left of the door and braced the iron bar against it.

Turning to them, he saw that Moira had slouched down and now sat on the filthy floor, her hands cupped protectively over her rounded belly. "You said he didn't harm you," he growled. He grabbed O'Neill by the tunic, whirled him away from his sister and held him pinned to the wall. Wisely, the young man clamped his mouth shut and didn't move.

She slowly stood, giving a muffled groan. "Moira?" Connor held her brother to the wall, but focused his attention upon her.

"I'm fine, Connor, truly—no thanks to Domnal," she added with disgust. She brushed at the coating of gray dust covering her from head to toe, to no avail. Pulling off her veil, she used the clean side to wipe off her face, then sneezed. "'Tis a miracle he didn't startle me into giving birth right here."

Connor tightened his grip and pressed O'Neill more firmly against the stone wall. "Did you come alone?"

"Aye, milord." O'Neill glanced over at his sister. "I'm sorry I frightened you, Moira. I didn't mean to. I didn't realize 'twas so close in here."

Connor eased his hold and allowed O'Neill to slump down onto his feet. "Do you swear you've no one with you?"

The youth—for Connor could see that O'Neill couldn't be more than sixteen—met his gaze without hesitation. "On our mother's grave, milord," he murmured.

"Moira?" Connor asked. "Should I trust him?"

She took a step closer to her brother. "Aye." To Connor's surprise, she reached down, unhooked the sword from her brother's belt and held it out for Connor to take. Even more startling to him, O'Neill made no protest, his dirt-smeared face merely twisting into a resigned expression. "But regardless of his honesty or lack of it, I suggest we leave here."

Connor nodded. He'd just as soon get Moira out of the dust and dirt; it couldn't be good for her or the child. He needed to send someone down to guard the doorway, as well. "You've the right of it," he told her, tucking her brother's sword beneath his arm and reaching over to claim his knife, too. He motioned for Moira to take the lantern and go ahead, before nudging O'Neill into motion. "I'll send Will and Sir Ivor down."

O'Neill paused and turned to him. "You should close it up, milord," he said urgently. "If Hugh and Aidan come back..."

"You can tell me more once we're out of here," Connor said quietly. "For now, I want your sister someplace safe."

"'Tis all I want as well, milord." He met Connor's gaze, his eyes intense. "Though I don't know if such a place exists."

Once they'd left the undercroft, Moira absently trudged along in Connor's wake as he sent laborers to block up the passageway, with Sir Will and Sir Ivor to guard the site.

She glanced at her brother yet again, her mind awhirl with reasons why Domnal might have been waiting on the other side of that door. Although impatient to discover his intent, she also felt a definite uncertainty. Whatever brought Domnal to Gerald's Keep, it couldn't be good.

And she didn't know how much more bad news she could bear.

Although Connor had released his grip on Domnal before they left the cellar, her brother stayed close without any urging that she could see—a definite change from the defiant youth he'd been the last time they'd met. However, the more she observed Domnal, the more she became convinced he was frightened. Terrified, in fact. Though terrified of what, she hadn't any idea.

The three of them were so filthy—covered in dirt and gray dust—that 'twas almost funny. To her surprise, however, no one laughed, or said a word, as they passed through the bailey and hall, though she heard a wave of muffled laughter following in their wake. Perhaps 'twas Connor's presence, or his stern expression, that accounted for it.

He appeared oblivious to it all, his attention clearly focused elsewhere. No doubt upon what to do next, or what he might learn from Domnal.

She hoped he didn't expect much from her brother, however. Aidan and Finan had never bothered to include the youngest O'Neill in any of their plans, beyond using him and his astounding prowess at arms when it suited their purpose to do so.

Much as they'd used her for their own gain, she realized. Mayhap 'twas time for her to view Domnal in a different light.

Connor sent the lad into the solar ahead of them, then paused, turning to lean back against the doorframe. "I never thought to ask, Moira—are you sure you want us entering your rooms in this condition?" He glanced down at his filthy clothing and her own, his mouth quirked in a wry smile. "Not that you look much better," he added, the glint of humor in his dark eyes tempering his words.

The answering spark of amusement that coursed through her slashed through the dismal murk clouding her mind and kindled a spark of hope within her. Connor was here—he would help her, share whatever news Domnal brought, good or bad. She felt her tension ease. ‘‘This is one of the more private places for us to talk to him, to question him.’’ She reached past Connor and pushed the door wide, flashing him a teasing smile. ‘‘Of course, you realize you’ll have to sit on the floor.’’

‘‘Only if you do,’’ he murmured, ushering her into the room.

Domnal stood at the hearth, gazing down at the dying fire. To Moira’s newly awakened notice, he looked filthy, cold—and more frightened than when they’d left the undercroft. Good. Perhaps if they gave his apprehension a bit longer to grow, he might be more truthful and forthright with them.

‘‘Would you stir up the fire?’’ she asked Connor. ‘‘I’ll be back in a moment.’’ He, too, cast a measuring look Domnal’s way before giving her a slight nod.

She crossed the solar and entered her room, calling for Brigit as she closed the door.

The maid, dozing in a chair by the fire, started. ‘‘Beg pardon, milady,’’ she said, then glanced up and gasped. *‘‘Lady Moira!’’* She lurched to her feet and hurried to her side. ‘‘Sit down—nay, you’d better lie down—at once,’’ she scolded. Before Moira could stop her, Brigit took her by the arm and led her toward the bed. ‘‘Look at you! You’re filthy, milady. What happened to you?’’ she asked, her worried gaze sweeping over Moira from head to toe. ‘‘Are you all right?’’

Moira gently freed herself and halted before the maid could nudge her down onto the mattress. ‘‘I’m fine, Brigit,’’ she reassured her. She took Brigit’s work-worn hand in hers and urged her to sit on the edge of the bed. ‘‘There’s no need to ruin the bedcovers with all this dirt. I’ll simply wash my face and hands and go back to the solar. Lord Connor is there with Domnal—’’

''Domnal?'' Brigit jumped to her feet. ''Your brother?''

Moira picked up the pitcher from the table and poured water into the basin. ''Aye, my brother.'' She wet a cloth and wiped her face with it, then rinsed her hands.

''What is he doing here?'' Brigit took the grubby rag from her and handed her a towel.

''I don't know.'' She dried her face and shook out the towel, frowning at the smudged linen. She was still dirty, but couldn't take time to do more about it. ''We found him in the passageway off the undercroft of the keep.''

''Do you think your brother has sent him to spy?'' The old woman's face went pale, and her voice rose with every word.

''Hush,'' Moira warned. ''Do you want him to hear you?''

''If he didn't come in through the front gate,'' she whispered, ''they're bound to have sent him to do you harm. What if they sent him to take the babe?''

''Nay, I cannot believe that of him.'' She laid a hand on Brigit's arm to calm her, casting a glance toward the closed door. ''I don't know why he's come—or how he got here, truth to tell. And the longer I linger in here, the less chance I have to find out.'' She smoothed her loosened hair back from her face. ''Send Padrig for food, drink and some water for the men to wash. I've let Domnal stew long enough.''

As soon as the door closed behind Moira, Connor went to the hearth and knelt to build up the fire, taking advantage of the lad's proximity to observe him.

Now that he saw Domnal O'Neill in the clear light of day, he couldn't mistake his resemblance to Moira. Unlike Aidan, Domnal had bright blue eyes and straight dark hair, and despite the lad's scraggly attempt at a beard, the similarity of their features showed through.

Though Connor had never seen that look of fear on Moira's face, despite the gravity of her circumstances.

He knew why she'd retreated to her chamber—one reason, at any rate, and one he agreed with. She wanted to build Domnal's fear. Considering how her brothers had treated her, Connor wouldn't have blamed her if she drew out Domnal's torment in retribution for past hurts, but he doubted that was her intent. More likely she hoped to frighten her brother into telling them everything he knew.

Raised voices sounded from Moira's chamber, though he couldn't distinguish the words. Still, 'twas enough to make Domnal jump, and his face—where he'd wiped away some of the dust—grew pale. "How fares my sister, milord? Is she well?" His voice held concern. Was it sincere, or naught but a ploy?

Either way, Connor's answer would be the same. The lad should be made aware of what effect her family's schemes had on her. "The babe tires her, but 'tis the press of worry over what the MacCarthys—and her brothers—might do," he added with a pointed look, "that weighs heaviest upon her."

Domnal turned away. Had his words sunk in? Connor wondered. He hoped they had. Kneeling on the raised hearth, he waited until the new layer of peat he'd laid upon the embers caught fire. He tried to mute the curiosity nagging at him, but 'twas futile; he wanted—nay, *needed*—to know what brought Domnal O'Neill to Gerald's Keep in such secrecy.

Evidently he wasn't the only impatient one; Domnal paced the length of the room, stopping near the window and reaching to open the shutters.

"Get away from there," Connor said, keeping his voice stern. He brushed off his hands and stood.

Domnal spun and faced him, an expression of guilt written plainly on his face. ''Milord?''

What had he been about to do? Did he think to send a signal, or to spy out the lay of the land from this lofty perch? Keeping the lad within sight, Connor dragged a stool away from the table and thumped it down. ''Sit.''

Domnal obeyed the terse command, slouching onto the seat and staring at the scar on Connor's face. ''Were you wounded in battle, milord?'' he asked, eagerness in his tone and curiosity replacing guilt on his face.

''Nay,'' Connor replied. He turned away and moved closer to Moira's door. He folded his arms across his chest and leaned back against the wall. What was keeping her? He listened carefully, but heard no sounds at all coming from the other room.

He glanced at Domnal again and suppressed a groan. He'd thought the chill of his answer would have quelled the lad's interest in the mark, but it didn't appear to have done so.

''''Tis a nasty scar, milord,'' Domnal said, his enthusiasm undimmed. ''What caused it?''

'Twas clear he'd have no peace till he gave an answer. Perhaps the truth would silence Domnal's prying before it went any further. Besides, Connor had no patience left to hide who he'd been—the man he'd become had more courage than to hide behind half-truths any longer.

He pushed away from the wall and came to stand by the window, nudging aside the shutters to let the sunlight pour over him—over his face when he turned toward Domnal. ''My father cut me with a dagger. He believed me a coward, and sneered at my feeble attempt to protect my mother from him. He'd the right of it, for I didn't even know how to defend myself from his blade.''

The door to Moira's bedchamber slammed shut. His

heart thundering in his chest, Connor shifted his gaze from the stunned lad to the woman hurrying to his side. "By the Virgin," Moira gasped. Her hand shook as she reached up and traced the slash across his cheek, her touch a balm that soothed his pride even as it spurred his pulse. Settling her hand on his shoulder, she leaned close. "Your back, as well?" she murmured, too low for Domnal to hear.

"Aye." Connor met her gaze and gave a silent sigh of relief. While he saw the sympathy he'd expected in her eyes, he also saw more. Pride, support…

Was it possible he could reveal the details of his past to her freely, without worrying that she'd view him as weak? He wanted her to know that he would always do his best to protect her.

She cupped his cheek with her palm and smiled. "Your valor astounds me, Connor. You are a very brave man."

Her words astounded *him*—humbled him, made him feel the most courageous of men. "I thank you, milady," he said for her ears alone. Taking her hand in his, he pressed a kiss upon it before gently turning her to face her brother.

The lad gazed at him in awe, for some reason—not the reaction Connor had intended, yet it couldn't hurt in these circumstances. Burying deep his pleasure at Moira's response—till he'd time to consider it at his leisure—he settled his expression. "Now then, Domnal O'Neill—are you ready to tell us what you were doing hiding behind that door?"

The lad looked from Connor to Moira and back again, uncertainty apparent in his demeanor, before looking down at the table in silence. Perhaps he didn't know what to say…. Or perhaps he didn't have any information to share, though Connor refused to believe that could be the case. O'Neill hadn't stumbled upon that passageway by accident.

Connor led Moira to the table and pulled out a chair for

her, then drew up a stool for himself once he'd seated her. She seemed hesitant in her brother's presence. Could it be that she couldn't decide if she should trust him? The look in her eyes when she gazed at Domnal appeared quite different from her reaction to Aidan. Connor thought he saw affection mixed with the indecision.

Perhaps once they discovered Domnal's purpose for coming here, she'd know how to respond.

Connor rested his elbows on the table and leaned toward O'Neill. "I suggest you tell us something, lad, else I'll be forced to lock you up in the guardroom like I did your brother. Unlike Aidan, however, I'll not set you free come the morning."

"You locked up Aidan?" Domnal asked, eyes round and amazement in his voice.

"I did."

The hint of a smile played around the lad's mouth and brightened his eyes. "He never said—"

"You couldn't expect Aidan to admit it," Moira interjected. "Our brother is naught but a bladder full of hot air, ready to burst forth with his own importance given the slightest opportunity."

Connor bit back a laugh, for she'd summed up Aidan exactly.

Domnal didn't bother to hide his amusement, chuckling merrily and slapping his hand on the table. "Oh, aye—when he returned from here a few days past, he was fit to explode." Once again he looked from one of them to the other, his gaze settling upon Connor this time. "You're nothing like he described you to Hugh and the others, milord. Not a bit." He shifted in his seat and his grin widened. "He said you were old and feeble, and wrapped tight about my sister's—" Connor caught his eye and he broke off, coughing. "Her thumb, milord."

"Did he indeed?" Anger filled Moira's voice, fired her eyes till they glowed a brilliant blue. "And what did Hugh have to say about that?"

Domnal glanced at his sister, then looked away. "I'd rather not say, Moira. It's not true, and it doesn't matter," he mumbled, his face flushed red.

Taking pity on the lad—and Moira, who looked fit to explode—Connor reached out and took her hand, giving it a squeeze, and sought to turn the conversation to a topic more important to them than Aidan's and Hugh's lies and insults. "Tell me, lad—why are you here?"

Domnal stared at them, so long that Connor imagined he could see the wheels turning in the lad's head, see him weighing what to say.

"You can tell Lord Connor, Domnal—tell him the truth," Moira said. "Say whatever you want. There's no way our brothers or the MacCarthys will know what you've told us. They need never know you were here, if you don't want them to." She slipped her hand free of Connor's grasp, reached out and took her brother's hands in hers. "You're safe here, Domnal, for as long as you wish to stay."

Moira held her breath and waited as Domnal gazed down at their joined hands. What would he do?

In her mind and heart, Domnal was still the lanky boy he'd been when she'd left home to marry Lord Brien. She'd seen him over the years, but always as a quiet youth lurking in their brothers' shadows. She didn't know him—not the young man he'd become. Could she trust him?

It felt as though they waited forever for Domnal to respond. 'Twas so hard not to hope that he'd brought the solution to their problems with him. She schooled herself to patience, though she tightened her clasp on his fingers—

for encouragement, she told herself, not to compel him to answer.

But he finally returned the pressure and looked up at them both. "I don't know everything about what they've been up to, but what they've done—what they're doing—is wrong, Moira, isn't it?"

"Aye, Domnal, it is."

Connor shifted in his seat. "They caused Lord Brien's death, lad, as well as many others. All to seize a place—and people—" he added, his glance shifting from Domnal to Moira, "they've no right to take."

Domnal slid his hands loose of her hold and shoved back his seat. "They want it all—the keep, your child and you, Moira!" He paced to the hearth and stared down into the flames. "I don't like Hugh," he blurted. He looked up, wearing the same petulant expression she'd seen too often upon her elder brothers' faces. Her heart sank. What if he'd turned out no better than they had? "He'll treat you just as bad as Aidan has—"

"Nay, lad, he'll treat her worse." Connor rose as well, striding to the window and leaning against the sill. "Your sister and her child need your help. *That* is how a man comports himself when his family needs him—by giving them your strength and aiding them, not by looking the other way or seeking how to benefit from their misfortune. Can you be a man Moira will be proud to call brother? Will you help me to protect her and the child?" he asked bluntly.

The change that came over Domnal as he listened to Connor was so unmistakable, Moira slumped back in her chair and breathed a silent sigh of relief. He stood straighter, his face firming into an expression of resolve. "I will help you, Moira—and you, milord." He returned to the table and leaned his hands on the polished surface.

''Hugh knows a way into Gerald's Keep,'' he said, his blue eyes full of concern.

''But Connor's men will guard the passageway where you came in,'' Moira told him. She turned to Connor. ''They cannot bring an army in through there, can they?''

Connor shook his head. ''Not now that we know about it.''

Domnal slapped his hand down on the table, making Moira jump and sending her pulse racing. ''There's another way,'' he cried. ''He's had sappers tunneling away beneath the walls. He's going to bring them down and take you away, Moira!''

Chapter Seventeen

Moira fairly leaped from her seat and grabbed Domnal's arm, her demands for more information drowned out by Connor's louder voice as he echoed her requests. Suddenly she noticed that Padrig, bearing a heavily loaded tray and accompanied by several servants laden with buckets of hot water, stood just inside the chamber. She quieted, though she didn't release her grip on her brother.

"Beg pardon, milord," the squire called. "I did knock."

Connor fell silent and glanced up at him. "Come in—just you," he added as the others, crowded about the doorway, jostled against each other. "And close the door behind you."

Padrig did so, then placed the tray on the table.

Connor raked his hand through his hair and stared off into the distance for a moment.

"Milord?" Padrig prompted.

Connor turned his attention to the youth. "Go to Will and d'Athée. Tell them to post guards to take their places, and to join us here." He nodded toward Domnal. "We might have a way out of our troubles, thanks to O'Neill."

Moira thought she saw a scowl pass fleetingly over Padrig's face, though she couldn't be sure. Of course, considering the way Aidan had acted, 'twould be a surprise if everyone here *didn't* suspect Domnal for his name alone.

"Aye, milord, at once," Padrig murmured. He bowed and hastened from the room.

Moira's stomach rumbled; a glance out the window confirmed that 'twas midafternoon. She'd missed dinner when Sir Will took her to the undercroft. "Sit. We might as well eat while we're waiting," she said. She laid out the food and drink, then realized that Domnal and Connor still wore a heavy coating of dust. "I'll be back soon—I'll find water so you can wash."

Not waiting for a reply, she left the chamber.

She'd hoped that the servants would have left the buckets of water in the corridor outside the room, but they had not; nor was there anyone in sight. Sighing, she headed down the stairs.

'Twas just as well she went down to the hall, for she was besieged at once by people with questions. She addressed what could not wait and put off as many as she could before dragging herself back up the stairs.

This wasn't quite what she'd intended when she'd headed for her chamber earlier. She'd get no rest now—nor later, either. No matter what Connor decided to do to stop the sappers, she didn't plan to sleep through his efforts to deal with the problem. Especially now, when it seemed the solution to their troubles could be at hand.

She would never have foreseen that her brother Domnal might bring them the information they needed. She was proud that he hadn't fallen in with Aidan's plans, proud that he had courage enough to overcome his obvious misgivings to do what was right. Not once in her life had she ever believed she could depend upon one of her siblings for help.

'Twas a heartening thing to know that Domnal was on

her side, but it didn't change the fact that she planned to remain a part of whatever Connor decided to do.

She'd been involved with defending her home for months now. She couldn't stop simply because help had arrived.

Hopefully, Connor wouldn't expect her to step aside.

If he did, he'd be in for a surprise.

''What does it matter if I cannot wield a sword or shoot a bow?'' Moira demanded. ''There's nothing wrong with my arms. I'm sure I could hit someone with a rock or a stick with no trouble.''

Slumped back against the wall of Moira's solar, Connor ran a hand through his hair, then rubbed at the back of his neck, though it did nothing to ease the strain tying him in knots. He'd thought that washing away the dust of the passageway and changing into clean clothes would have revived him, eased his tension, but it hadn't.

He wished now that he hadn't eaten, since the food sat like a stone in his roiling stomach. He let his gaze wander over the men gathered about the table—Domnal, Will and Sir Ivor—all three carefully avoiding his eyes. Clearly none of them intended to leap into the fray and help him.

Jesu, he hated confrontation!

Yet he could see no way to avoid it, not with this woman. ''Do you realize how close you'd have to be to do that?'' he asked, his voice rising despite his intention to remain calm.

''You think I'd endanger my babe, is that it?'' The outrage on her face matched that in her voice perfectly.

And made not a whit of difference in his decision.

''I wouldn't permit you to be there even if you were a virgin nun,'' he snarled. ''Jesu, Moira—there are trained men aplenty here to fight now. There's no reason for you to be defending the walls yourself.'' He sighed. ''There's a very good reason why you should not be out there, however. I want you as far away from MacCarthy's men as possible. What if they were to take you captive? Have you considered that?''

The color drained from her cheeks before his eyes, and he felt a brute for upsetting her. But he wanted her to realize the possible consequences if she ignored his orders. If that meant frightening her, so be it.

He'd do whatever he must to keep her, and the child she carried, safe.

When had his goal changed from handling the responsibilities Rannulf had laid upon him to protecting Moira? In some aspects, they were one and the same, but in his mind—in his heart—there was a huge difference between safeguarding the widow of Rannulf's vassal and protecting Lady Moira FitzGerald.

He risked a glance at her. Weariness lay heavily upon her, dulling the brightness of her blue eyes and etching shadows beneath them. She'd clearly slept no more than he had the night before, and most likely had done too much this morning as well. After their clash in his chamber, he'd seen her dealing with servants in the bailey, coming out of the kitchen shed, going into the stables.... Whenever he'd looked for her—and he'd looked often—he'd found her hard at work.

Then he'd dragged her down to the passageway and set her to work scraping at the wall as though she were the lowliest of servants. Add to that the emotional turmoil of finding her brother lurking about in the hidden passageway, his subsequent revelations... Connor drew in a calming breath. At least she hadn't insisted on going with them when Domnal had shown them the full extent of Hugh

MacCarthy's inroads into their defense. Even so, 'twas a wonder she hadn't collapsed by now.

Not Moira FitzGerald, the strongest and most stalwart woman he'd ever known.

But he feared for her—her and the babe both—if she didn't allow him to share the weighty load she'd carried upon her slender shoulders for far too long.

Will cleared his throat. "Now that we've decided that Lady Moira will not be joining us in battle, milord, what are your plans for the rest of us? I assume you've something special in mind for Sir Ivor and me, since I doubt you asked us here to finish off this lovely meal—" a sweep of his hand indicated the remnants of their dinner spread out over the table "—while watching the two of you argue." He sent a grin Moira's way. "No offense meant, milady. 'Tis just that I prefer something a bit sweeter after a meal."

Connor bit back a laugh, and he'd swear a glint of humor brightened Moira's eyes. 'Twas clear to him why Will's fellows at l'Eau Clair expected his japes and jests—he had a talent for knowing when they were needed most.

Pushing away from the wall, Connor returned to the seat at the table that he'd abandoned earlier, once they'd finished eating. He dragged the chair closer to the table and reached into the pouch on his belt for the scrap of parchment he'd used to map the areas where the sappers had plied their craft. "Aye, I've plans for you both," he said. He unfolded the sketch and weighted it down with his goblet. "Look here, they were able to work their way under the wall from the cliff. There's a tunnel here—" he indicated the spot with the tip of his dagger "—and here as well." He made a sound of disgust. "The guards on the tower walls couldn't see a thing."

"Why don't we just fill in their tunnels?" d'Athée asked.

"Now that we've men enough for a proper guard, they won't have a chance to dig them out again."

"Sapping a wall is a skill not possessed by everyone," Connor pointed out. "I'd rather eliminate them, then repair the damage they've caused." He glanced at Domnal. "Besides, from what O'Neill said, MacCarthy himself plans to lead the attack."

Moira reached out and turned the map to look at it. "If they've decided that tonight is the night to attack, and Hugh brings an army with him, will you be ready for them?"

"Moira, what are you about?" Domnal asked, his surprise plain. "Do you think to teach Lord Connor his business?"

"I suggest you abandon that idea at once, lad," Connor said. He didn't bother to hide his displeasure. Moira remained silent, but indignation at her brother's words was written plainly upon her lovely face.

Domnal shifted in his seat and glanced around the table, clearly weighing each person's reaction. "You don't mind, milord?" he asked once his gaze returned to Connor.

"'Tis very much your sister's business how we plan to rout her enemy. Hugh MacCarthy—and your brother Aidan—have caused her heartache and misery, have threatened all she holds dear." Connor didn't bother trying to hide his unyielding stance.

Domnal reached out and clasped Moira's hand. "I beg your pardon, Sister. I meant no insult. 'Tis habit, is all."

She gave him a faint smile. "You've been too long in Aidan's company. 'Tis past time for you to leave that arrogant fool and learn how other people live."

Connor watched them, so much alike in looks, but in personality... For Moira's sake, he hoped Domnal favored her, and not Aidan. If the fool caused her harm, or preyed upon her sisterly affection, Connor would see he paid dearly for it.

He closed his eyes and searched within the depths of his mind for patience. By Christ's bones, how had he believed himself ready to lead? How had Rannulf? This petty squabbling made him want to reply in kind, to snarl like a fractious child and lay about with his fists until he'd spent his anger. He'd no patience for it, even when it didn't directly involve him.

Was this how his father's temper had grown beyond his control?

Opening his eyes, Connor shoved aside that terrifying thought and stared hard at the sketch until his blood cooled. He eased his grip on the knife and scratched a mark on the map at the place where Domnal had shown them evidence of the invaders. "Will, I want you to wait here, hidden from view, with ten men. Sir Ivor will go with you, since he's more familiar with the area." He pricked the parchment again. "I'll lay in wait here." He straightened and looked at each man, weighing their readiness—and in the case of Sir Ivor, his willingness to obey orders. "I leave it to you both to choose the men we'll bring with us. The rest of our force will man the walls, and remain alert on the inside lest anyone makes it through."

Will nodded. "Aye, milord."

Connor turned to Domnal, pondering whether he should trust the lad. By the saints, he'd already decided to trust him; tonight's plans revolved around his belief that Domnal had been telling him the truth. Still, he didn't know how skilled he'd be in battle, nor did he wish to place the lad in a position where MacCarthy or Aidan could use him against Moira. "I depend upon you to guard your sister here in the keep. Go now with Sir Will. He'll see you settled.'' He nodded dismissal. ''I'll join you in the bailey soon to finalize our plans.''

Will and d'Athée bowed and, motioning for Domnal to join them, departed.

Leaving Connor alone with Moira.

Sheer will alone must have given her the strength to last through the meal and discussion. The instant the others left, her shoulders slumped and she propped her elbow on the table, her cheek on her hand. ''Forgive my rudeness,'' she mumbled, stifling a yawn.

''You could have left us to plot and plan on our own. I don't blame you for wanting to know what we're doing—even if you cannot come help us.'' He grinned. '''Tis our loss. I've no doubt you'd make a valiant warrior.'' He stuck his dagger in the sheath on his belt. ''I'd best keep watch over my sword, lest you wrest it from me and head off to battle without me.''

She smiled at his weak sally and yawned again. ''It's not the company that makes me sleepy. The babe does this to me most afternoons.'' Her eyes drifted closed.

He examined the map again, pondering the merits and drawbacks of their plan, before realizing that Moira hadn't moved since she'd closed her eyes. ''Moira? My lady,'' he murmured, to no avail.

She couldn't possibly be comfortable in that position. He whispered her name again; again, she made no response.

He lifted her from the chair, expecting some resistance or an argument, but she simply nuzzled her cheek against the soft wool of his tunic and gave a faint, pleasure-filled moan.

The sound, coupled with the feel of her in his arms, set fire to his blood. He opened the door to her bedchamber one-handed, hurried into the room and set her on the bed.

He should have left at once, but instead he stood at the

foot of the bed to watch her sleep. She stretched and nestled more deeply into the downy coverlet, but couldn't seem to find a comfortable position.

Perhaps she was cold. He tugged up the end of the coverlet and pulled it over her, kneeling on the mattress and leaning close to remove her veil and free her hair from beneath her. A hint of a smile touched her lips and she rubbed her cheek against his hand.

By the saints! 'Twas past time he left, but he couldn't resist lingering there, one knee on the bed and his hand cupping her face. If Brigit came in and discovered him in this position, the old maidservant would surely make him pay for his misjudgment.

Without warning, Moira's eyes opened. She stared up at him with terror, not recognition, in her gaze, and opened her mouth to scream.

Connor covered her mouth with his hand and sought to quiet her squirming without doing her harm. "Moira! It's all right, 'tis Connor." She flailed about with her arms, one fist striking perilously close to his groin.

He shifted away from her as much as possible while trying to hold her still, praying all the while that she'd not unman him before she realized who he was.

Of course, for all he knew, she might be as likely to do so if she knew 'twas him.

"Moira—dearling, hush. Hush."

Awareness returned to her eyes and he slipped his hand from her mouth. "Connor?" Tears streamed down her cheeks. "I'm so glad 'tis you!" She burrowed into his arms, her face pressed to his neck, muttering fiercely in Gaelic.

He could scarcely hear the mumbled words, let alone comprehend all they meant. The half-remembered Irish tales that his mother, in her native tongue, had secretly shared with her sons had not given him the vocabulary to decipher what Moira said.

Still, he could tell 'twas no childish tale she told. She told of a nightmare.... How much of it was true?

After a time her sobs eased and she rested quietly in his arms. He'd shifted till he could lean back on the bolsters at the head of the bed, with Moira cradled against him in his lap. Her gown had twisted around their legs, her hair lay in a tangle over them both and one tear-stained cheek had reddened where she'd rested her face on his wool tunic.

He gazed into her blue eyes, so full of hope, and found her beautiful.

It seemed the most natural act in the world to cup the mound of her belly in one hand, her cheek in the other, and kiss her.

He spread a line of kisses over her face till he reached her mouth. Stroking her lips with his tongue, he invited her to join him. She tasted of salt and sweetness, her lips soft and clinging to his. Her breath a sigh, she opened her mouth and gently nipped at his lower lip before drawing back slightly.

"Connor, why are you here?" Confusion clouded her eyes. She brought her hand up to trace the scar on his face, her touch as gentle as if the wound were new. She shifted away from him, though she didn't move his hand from her belly, and looked around the room. "How did we come to be in my bed?" she asked when she settled her gaze on his face.

He felt so guilty he almost leaped off the mattress like a lad found trysting with a maid. Awkward and uncertain, the old Connor returned full force.

But the "new" Connor would not behave thus, he reminded himself. He'd fought hard to imbue himself with strength and self-assurance. Rather than flee, he reached behind him and rearranged the pillows more comfortably. His hands about her waist, he helped her to settle onto them, and sat beside her on the edge of the bed. ''You fell asleep at the table,'' he said, watching to see if she'd remember. ''You wouldn't have been able to move had I left you sitting there for long, so I brought you in here.''

Moira heard the words, but her mind, still muzzy and overwhelmed, couldn't make clear sense of them. ''Why are you here?'' she challenged.

He hesitated, and she could tell from his expression that he hadn't decided what to say.

''Just tell me the truth, Connor, whatever it is,'' she said quietly. ''That answer should be the easiest to come by, don't you think?''

He gave a dry laugh. ''The easiest? Hardly.'' He slipped his hand off her stomach, the warmth of his touch lingering. ''The truth only sounds easy. 'Tis everything it means that is complicated.''

She sighed. ''I've heard the truth so seldom, milord, 'twould be a most welcome gift if you would share it with me. Let me decide if there are complications.''

He glanced away, then looked back, his dark gaze sweeping over her face. A tinge of red crept up from his throat to tint his cheeks. ''I stayed to watch you sleep,'' he said, his challenging tone matching his expression.

He was right, she decided, staring at him; the truth wasn't simple.

But she'd gain no answers from conjecture. She'd asked him for the truth; the least she could do was return the courtesy. 'Twould be interesting to see how he responded. ''Why?''

''I wanted to make certain you were all right,'' he said quietly.

The truth, perhaps—though not all of it? ''Was there

some reason you believed I was not? You could have called for Brigit to come sit by me, to help me, if that were the case. I would imagine she knows more about the maladies of women in my condition than you do, milord,'' she added. Another possibility occurred to her unawares, something especially chilling when she considered the closeness developing between them. 'Twas all she could do to force the words past the tightness in her throat. ''Or is that assumption wrong? Have you a lady wife—and children, perhaps—hidden away somewhere in England?''

The flush faded swiftly from Connor's face, leaving him pale, the area around his scar dead white. ''I asked *you* to marry me! That's scarcely the action of a man who is already wed,'' he growled. He rose and paced to the window, then spun to face her. ''How could you believe me so dishonorable?''

She pushed herself upright and squirmed to the edge of the mattress. ''Most men would avoid going anywhere near a woman like me, yet every time I turn around, there you are.'' Her hair had wound about her arm, the ends caught underneath her. Growling in frustration, she yanked at the tangled strands and climbed down off the bed, jerking her clothing into place. ''I cannot understand why that would be so.''

''What do you mean, a woman like you?'' Connor took a step closer to her, then halted when she glared at him.

''You know...'' Suddenly unwilling to face him, she turned her attention to gathering her hair together into a lopsided braid.

''No, I don't know what you mean. Tell me, Moira, what is there about you that could keep me away from you?''

She glanced up at him from beneath her lashes. Curiosity and temper warred in his face, and his dark eyes were heated, intense.

However, she doubted he felt any more heated than she at that moment. She'd grown tired of pondering her sins, weary of looking to her future and finding little but her child to brighten the rest of her life.

The child should be enough, she reminded herself, angrily blinking back tears. The fact that she had anything good to look forward to in her life at all was doubtless more than she deserved.

But knowing that didn't make her feel any better, not while standing face-to-face with a tantalizing glimpse of what might have been.

Except for her own misdeeds.

''Will you make me say it aloud, milord? Must I repeat the words already thundering through my head, the truth of them burrowed deep within my heart?'' She tossed her braid back over her shoulder and straightened her spine, the movement thrusting her belly into prominence. Holding her hands out at her sides, she cried, ''A woman tainted, who bears a child not her husband's.''

Connor's expression softened. ''Through no fault of your own, Moira. Doesn't the fact that you agreed to MacCarthy's offer to protect the others mean something? Does it not lessen the sin?''

''Going to Dermot's bed was not my sin, Connor.'' She forced herself to meet his questioning gaze, to remain calm and speak the truth when everything inside her cried out to be silent. ''But the fact that I went there willingly is.''

Chapter Eighteen

Eyes narrowed, Connor met Moira's challenging stare, weighing what she'd said and how she'd said it against everything he knew of her.

Moira FitzGerald—Moira O'Neill FitzGerald, he reminded himself—had lived her entire life as the pawn of men. Her brothers, and likely their father before them, had valued her only for what she could bring them. Indeed, to judge by Aidan's recent request, and what Domnal had told them of Aidan's involvement in MacCarthy's plans, 'twas clear they continued to look upon her as theirs to manipulate as would best suit them.

Especially now that she had no husband to deny their outrageous requests.

As for her husband… Lord Brien, by all accounts, had used her as well. He'd seen her as a broodmare, nothing more.

Still watching Moira, Connor dragged his fingers through his hair before settling his hands on his hips. "Well?" she demanded, her voice, her stance, challenging him to deny her claim.

"You expect me to believe that?" He shook his head, hoping 'twould jog some sense into it. He could see that what she'd revealed had upset her, so perhaps there was some truth in it—at least through her eyes.

"I expect you to say something," she said testily. "Though perhaps shock has struck you dumb."

"What should I say, Moira?" he asked wearily. "That 'tis your guilt talking, placing the blame for what happened on your own shoulders?" She certainly seemed angry, though at herself. "Or mayhap you could just as easily blame your husband for not protecting you or his people? For driving you into another man's embrace? If he'd kept Dermot MacCarthy away, none of this would have happened, would it?"

She sighed. "How can we know? Father Thomas says 'tis not for us to contradict God's will."

"You cannot believe all this was God's will!" Connor demanded. "If that were the case, you might just as well order the gates opened and walk outside into MacCarthy's hands. Now, before our men go tonight to defend this keep. Why should we risk our lives to keep your child away from them? Might it not be God's will for the MacCarthys to raise your babe, and not you?" he asked, his voice rising.

"No! It cannot be right for them to take away my child," she cried. "Nor to wrest it from our home."

By the saints, she'd drive him mad! But what did he know about women and how they thought? A lifetime's exposure to his mother, as she'd sought to avoid her husband and his temper even at the expense of her sons' well-being, had given him no inkling about other women.

He loved his mother despite all that had happened, but he could easily see that Moira's love for her child carried with it a protectiveness he doubted his mother had ever possessed.

Shame filled him. Moira hadn't asked to be placed in this situation, nor had she caused all her present woes. Including his advent into her life, with his questions and misplaced lust, he thought ruefully.

"You cannot have it both ways, Moira. If the priest is right and 'tis God's will for this to happen, why cannot the rest be the work of some greater power as well? You could just as easily say 'twas God's hand brought me here, that my presence here serves some purpose." He glanced at her, saw that she'd pressed one hand to her lower back, the other to her belly. Crossing to her in two strides, he edged her backward to the bed. "Sit," he ordered. Grasping her about the shoulders, he helped her obey his command. "My purpose here is either to protect you from all harm or to drive you into early labor. I know which choice I'd prefer." His mouth twisted into a rueful smile. "You're not—"

"Nay," she whispered. "'Tis naught but an aching back."

He stepped away from her and took up his previous position near the window. He trusted himself better when Moira wasn't within his reach. "Good. I've no wish to cause you harm, but I doubt we're through with this yet."

What she'd said before nagged at his mind, as did his own questions. He leaned back against the plaster-covered wall and folded his arms across his chest. "Why did you tell me?"

"About Dermot?" she asked, paying close attention to the knotted lacing at the end of her sleeve rather than meeting his curious gaze.

He drew in a steadying breath, glad she refused to look at him—and wishing he didn't want to know her answer so badly.

This was no business of his. If she'd desired another man, what did it matter to him? They scarce knew each other, and he hadn't lived a completely celibate life himself.

But he wanted to hear her answer, needed to know this facet of the woman he'd asked to be his bride.

Mayhap he simply wanted to torment himself, he thought with disgust. Had he had so little true enjoyment in life that he couldn't exist without finding some thorn to prick at any potential pleasure?

He unfolded his arms, straightened and turned to nudge aside the window shutter. "Aye, about Dermot." He stared out at the dark clouds scudding across the sky. Glancing back at her, he found her watching him, her eyes shadowed. "There's no reason I needed to know that bit of information, even if we wed." He shoved the shutter half-closed and faced her. "Especially if we wed," he added. "I'd just as soon not know if we were sharing our bed with a ghost."

"A ghost?"

"Dermot's ghost, his memory," he said, surprised she hadn't understood.

She laughed, the sound without humor. Using the bedpost for support, she rose. "I told you I had desired Dermot, 'tis true," Moira said. "He offered to give me pleasure, and I believed it might be the only chance I'd ever have to know a man in that way." Shaking her head, she gave Connor a sad smile. "I should have realized his proposal was naught but an empty boast from a cruel man looking for another way to strike out at his enemy. The memory of him is far more likely to give me nightmares—it already does—than to haunt me in that way."

Connor could not look away from the pain in her eyes. "He hurt you?"

"Aye, he did." She rubbed at her back again, her expression pensive. "It didn't take long before I realized he would." She paced around to the chest at the foot of the bed and picked up a small wooden box sitting atop it. "But

I managed to harm him as well, though he didn't realize it until 'twas too late."

"What did you do?" Connor couldn't imagine how she could have harmed a hardened warrior.

He'd be wise to find out, lest she ever thought to do the same to him.

Her eyes glowed blue in the fading light, and her smile held satisfaction. She undid the clasp on the coffer and opened the lid. "I plied him with a heady wine, in the hope 'twould render him unable to—" her cheeks flushed red and she glanced into the box "—to perform in bed." Her hand unsteady, she drew out a small pot and set the coffer aside. Dipping in a finger, she pulled it out stained with a dark, sticky powder. "I thought to help the wine along with this." She glanced up at him, all trace of pleasure gone from her face.

"I've heard of potions said to help a man 'perform,' but I didn't know there were ones with the opposite effect." It gave him a chill just to think of it.

"Why would I possess anything of that nature?" she asked, looking surprised. "This is made from the juice of the poppy. I mixed some of the powder into his wine to make him sleep—or at least to make him docile—but I didn't know how much to use, nor how long 'twould be before it had an effect on him." She frowned. "Or precisely what the effect would be."

"It took too long to spare you his attentions." The size of her belly confirmed that fact, assuming 'twas MacCarthy's babe. Besides, Moira had already admitted that Dermot had taken her to his bed.

"Aye, though it did make him sleep eventually. But the effects lasted even once he'd awakened—long enough to slow his reflexes the next day." Grimacing at the powder clinging to her finger, she grabbed a scrap of cloth from the sewing basket near the hearth and scrubbed her hand clean. ''I'm certain 'tis how my husband was able to overcome him, for though it took the better part of the night for the drug to work, once it did Dermot looked as though he'd been swilling wine for days. He could scarce walk down the stairs. The cold air outside revived him so that he appeared normal, but 'twas clear to me when they fought that he'd something wrong with him.''

''Strange that no one else noticed,'' Connor remarked.

''His men knew him for a drunkard.'' She covered the pot and stowed it away in the coffer. Raising her chin, she added, ''And I told them he'd drunk unwatered wine all the night long, till he was sick from it. They believed me readily enough.''

She crumpled the cloth in her hand, then looked around as if uncertain what to do with it. Connor took the rag from her and would have thrown it into coals smoldering in the hearth, but she caught his wrist to stop him. ''I've heard that even the smoke from it is potent,'' she warned. ''I know there's not much of it there, but I've no wish to expose you to its effects. I'll not send you off to fight drugged and unable to defend yourself.''

''That's encouraging news,'' he said. ''Of course, I'm fighting on your side. You need me battle ready.''

She frowned, doubtless at his flippant tone. ''Aye, we do need you, Connor.'' Releasing him, she took back the rag and tossed it into the chamber pot. Facing him again, her expression serious, she touched his arm lightly. ''Whether your coming to Gerald's Keep is God's will or not, I'm glad you're here—and not simply because you've come to protect us.'' She met his gaze. ''You're a good man, milord, and I'm honored to know you.''

He took her hand in his and bowed over it, letting go of it with unseemly haste. 'Twould be better for them both if he were to maintain some distance between them. "You honor me, milady. With your kind words, which I doubt I deserve—and with your secrets. I swear everything you've told me will go no further than the two of us."

"Thank you, milord." She sat down on the bed. "I fear I've kept you from your duties this afternoon."

"'Tis all right. The day isn't over yet." She stifled a yawn. "You should rest now, while 'tis quiet. I'm sure you'll not sleep tonight until I've given you my report after our foray beneath the walls."

"You're right about that." She leaned back against the pillows with a sigh. "The babe thinks the depths of night a perfect time to kick and squirm. Perhaps if I rest now, he will as well."

Connor glanced toward the window, where the sky had darkened further during the course of their conversation. "And now I must go see how Will and d'Athée—and your brother—have fared in their preparations. I'd hoped for a clear night, but the rain won't ruin my plans. It could even help us, for I doubt they'll expect us to set a trap if the weather is foul."

"Do you think Domnal is right, that they'll come tonight?"

"Given how close they are to breaking through, I'm sure of it. They'll not want to risk us discovering their plan." He grinned, anticipation raising his mood. "I look forward to spoiling their surprise."

Connor rubbed at his chin, which itched from the mixture of goose fat and soot smeared over his exposed skin, and cursed the weather. The rain had begun soon after he'd left Moira's chamber, swiftly turning the unpaved areas of the bailey to a morass of muck. By the time 'twas full dark, it had rained so hard that even the cobblestones felt slick beneath his thick-soled boots.

The MacCarthys would be fools if they didn't return tonight, in force. Did they realize Domnal had left them? he wondered. Or, God forfend, that the lad had come to aid his sister, to offer her the means to thwart MacCarthy's plans?

'Twas a miserable night to be out, but a perfect time for a furtive visit to the newly dug tunnels, better still for a full-scale attack. The guards on the walls couldn't see a thing beyond the dismal glow of the few torches the rain hadn't extinguished.

On top of that, the pounding of the rain against the castle walls and the howling wind could mask a multitude of sounds. Connor hoped the conditions would work to their advantage, however, for no one would be able to see or hear them, either.

And, he prayed, they had the element of surprise on their side.

They had restored the entrance to the tunnels under the keep to its former condition—in case MacCarthy tried to send anyone into the castle that way—but Connor had decided to concentrate his efforts on blanketing the vast empty area outside the castle walls with his men. According to what Domnal had overheard, that was where Aidan and Hugh would wait for the wall to come down, enabling them to enter Gerald's Keep through the gap.

The area near the gate was Will's province, while Connor led his men to the opposite side of the keep, near where the headland jutted out from the shore. They'd crept out the gate, through the usually dry, now rain-filled moat surrounding the wall. Will's party, unfortunately, had to wait there, in water nearly to their knees and rising. The spot Connor brought his group to remained above water level, but they had to contend with the wind lashing them hard as it whipped around the keep from the open sea, keeping them plastered against the wall to hold themselves upright.

He also hadn't realized that the thunder of the storm-tossed waves crashing against the rocky cliffs below would make it nigh impossible to hear each other speak.

Impossible, as well, for the reinforcements—waiting inside for a signal from a lookout in the tower—to hear if they came under attack.

How they'd fight in this, Connor couldn't imagine. This night's work could be a test of all he'd learned the past few years, not so much of his skill at hand-to-hand combat, but as a leader. Rannulf had warned him—as had Connor's mentor, Walter—that all his studying might prove of little use in real battle.

Connor wouldn't mind testing his mettle as a leader now, save for the fact that other's lives were at stake as well as his own.

Though he'd already found that the mere thought of the threat to Moira and the babe kindled a nearly overwhelming fire in his blood.

He peered through the murk, looking for a sign, any sign, that this venture wasn't a huge mistake.

'Twould be a simple matter for anyone to creep up and be upon them before they knew they were under attack.

But he saw, heard, felt nothing.

Their nerves stretched taut, Connor and his men huddled along the curtain wall near the more remote of the two tunnels and waited. Between his righteous anger that the MacCarthys dared threaten one of his family's holdings, and all they'd done to Moira, he yearned to come to blows with them.

Any MacCarthy would suffice, though he hoped for the chance to have Hugh at the sharp end of his sword. He wouldn't have minded finding Aidan O'Neill there, either, except that he'd just as soon not have Moira's brother's blood on his hands—despite all he'd done. But since Dermot MacCarthy lay beyond harm, his brother would make an adequate substitute, especially given Hugh's threats to Moira and her child.

Something—a change in the sound of the howling wind, perhaps—caught Connor's attention. His movements slow, silent, he signaled his men to remain where they were, then straightened and crept back along the wall toward where they believed the sappers' tunnel lay hidden.

He flattened himself against the rough stone wall. Despite the fact that 'twas black as pitch here, he kept his head down in case the rain had washed the greasy soot from his face. He heard it now, the rhythmic sound of digging, hushed but distinct from the higher-pitched noise of the wind.

Holding his sword away from the wall, he stole closer. His breath caught in his chest and he froze when he heard a faint wheezing coming from only a few yards away.

'Twas a wonder he noticed it at all over the sudden thundering of his heart.

Straining to see, he made out a man standing armed and alert near a shadowy area of the wall.

Connor shifted his sword to his right hand and covered the short distance to the dark figure in two long, silent strides. He closed his hand around the guard's throat and squeezed, lifting him off the ground and thumping him in the head with his sword hilt when he squirmed and flailed with his arms.

Connor eased his grip and caught the man as he crumpled. Pressing a hand to the guard's throat, he found a pulse, faint and erratic. He didn't want to chance the guard recovering and alerting anyone, so he tore a strip off the man's rough shirt and gagged him with it. Then, using two lengths of rope from the supply he'd tucked into his belt, Connor quickly bound him hand and foot. He took one last look around, rolled the body out of the way and inched closer to the wall.

The scraping sound grew louder the closer he got. He crept away and sat back against the wall, his sword out and ready, while he pondered what to do. Should they send men to attack the sappers, or perhaps seal them into the tunnel and entomb them there? A chill slithered down his spine at the thought, but 'twould resolve their problem.

Temporarily.

Besides, the sappers were not his quarry—not all of it. He wanted MacCarthy and as many of his men as he could take or eliminate, as soon as possible.

Nay, dealing with the sappers alone would do little to further his goal.

He pushed himself to his feet and proceeded farther along the curtain wall. He knew in his bones that Domnal had been correct. The sappers couldn't have come alone.

Nor had they, he discovered as he rounded the wall and neared the rough terrain near the cliffs beside the headland where Gerald's Keep perched. A low murmur of voices came to him on the shifting wind, voices speaking Gaelic.

The clouds parted then, allowing a brief, faint glow of moonlight to gild the land. Connor dropped down at once and lay flat on his stomach on the soggy ground. Cautiously he raised his head, eyes and ears straining for any hint of how many men were waiting to attack Gerald's Keep.

He'd guess near forty sat huddled together, though the clouds hid the moon again so quickly, he wasn't able to count them. He did see enough to tell from their dress and arms that they were Irish. Whether 'twas the MacCarthys or not, he didn't know, but who they were didn't matter.

Certainly they weren't sitting out in the open during a torrential downpour to make a civil visit come morning.

Keeping low to the ground, Connor hurried back to his men. The rain had eased to a heavy drizzle, but the wind continued to pound away. No one noticed his approach until he was nearly upon them.

"By the Virgin, you gave me a start, milord," Padrig gasped, his voice shifting from gruff to a squeak and back again.

His men gathered round and Connor shared what he'd learned. When he'd finished, he turned to his squire. "Padrig, go back to Will and Sir Ivor, tell them the situation here and find out if they've discovered anything. If they've nothing new to report, tell them to send word to the men guarding the undercroft to stay vigilant. I want Will to leave five men to guard the wall on their side and come back here with you. We cannot wait too long to move, lest the sappers finish their task." He clapped Padrig on the shoulder. "Hurry, lad—and be silent."

He awaited Padrig's return in a fever of impatience. His men grew restless and more miserable the longer they stood there motionless. He feared the cold rain would sap their strength, make them sluggish and unprepared once it was time to move.

The others soon arrived, Will at their head, Sir Ivor guarding their flank. Everyone gathered around and waited for Connor's command.

Will elbowed his way to Connor's side. "There is naught happening back there, milord," he whispered. "Save for a faint bit of thumping down in the hole. Do you think they'll collapse that bit of wall for a diversion only?"

"You saw no one else, heard nothing?" Connor murmured.

"Nay, milord. 'Tis quiet as the tomb, but for the wind howling like a banshee."

"Good. We'll liven things up here, though," he added, heartbeat racing in anticipation. "I hope you're all ready for a fight."

Connor could feel the men's excitement as they skirted the wall and crept toward the area where he'd found the Irish waiting. His troop fanned out, using the long, thick grass and occasional clumps of gorse for cover.

Despite the stiff wind, the moon remained cloaked and the sky dark. The wind helped as well, carrying the sounds of the Irish to them, while sweeping away any noise they themselves made.

Connor and Will reached the boulder Connor had chosen as a landmark. Shouting the FitzClifford battle cry, they rose, their men behind them, and ran toward the Irish interlopers.

Chapter Nineteen

Moira began the evening by remaining in the great hall after supper. She'd sent Domnal out to the guardhouse soon after Connor and the others had left, for his pacing increased her own agitation, until she thought she'd go mad with worry. He'd seemed glad enough to leave her to her quiet pursuits and move closer to where the excitement would be.

Her basket of sewing near to hand, she drew a stool toward the dying fire in the huge hearth, hoping to accomplish something while she waited for a report from Connor.

But once the tables had been cleared and the trestles dismantled and stacked against the wall, the servants who had finished the day's tasks began to drift back to the hall, dragging out their pallets. Though they didn't appear any more ready to settle for the night than she was, she couldn't bear to sit before them playing the calm and unaffected lady—a role she knew didn't suit her at all.

Her nerves were stretched taut, her stomach knotted, making her wish she'd skipped eating altogether tonight. Despite her best efforts to distract her thoughts, memories assailed her—frightening memories—and a wave of uncertainty that had her fidgeting and starting each time the door to the hall creaked open.

What would they do if Connor were taken? What if he were killed? She'd never concerned herself on her husband's behalf when he'd gone off to fight. However, not a moment had passed since Connor rose from the table and led his men out to ready themselves for the night's work that she hadn't worried—for his own safety and that of their men.

For the well-being of her people and her child, as well. What would happen to them if the MacCarthys took control of Gerald's Keep again? Would Hugh try to force her into another devil's bargain as his brother had? What did she have left to bargain *with,* except her child?

The more she mulled over the situation, the shakier she became, until she felt ill.

Too ill to sit up here on the dais, where her people could watch her worry and fret. 'Twas her duty to maintain a brave front, show her confidence in their overlord, in their men....

But such dissembling was beyond her ability—now, at least. All she could do was shake and fight back tears, she thought with disgust.

Since the beginning of her pregnancy her emotions had grown volatile and uncertain. She couldn't recall the last time she'd cried before that. These last months, however, it seemed she couldn't make it through an entire day without dissolving into tears. She found it mortifying and completely out of her control.

Connor must believe her a spineless ninny. Nigh every conversation she'd had with him had ended with her showing him yet another facet of her weakness.

That he'd asked her to marry him had been a shock; that

he hadn't rescinded his offer after continued exposure to her, nothing short of a miracle.

She simply could not make herself accept his offer.

Aye, it might resolve a number of her more pressing problems, but she couldn't permit him to put himself into such jeopardy for her sake.

She poked her finger with the needle yet again and dropped the piece of soft white linen into her lap lest she stain it with her blood. "By the Virgin," she muttered, shaking her head. "I can ruin even the simplest task!"

Unwilling to sit and stew over her shortcomings any longer, she wrapped a scrap of linen around her finger to keep from bleeding over everything, put her sewing into the basket and headed for the stairs and her chamber.

Halfway across the room, she realized she'd feel no better by hiding there. Indeed, she'd be better served to stay in the hall, where she might hear some news of how the confrontation—if there was any—progressed.

Moira looked around the hall to make certain Brigit wasn't there to stop her. Fortunately, the old woman was nowhere to be seen. Her basket of sewing clutched to her stomach, Moira slipped out the door.

Sword swinging, Connor raced up to the first Irish warrior he met and dove into the fight. In no time at all the exhilaration of battle drove everything from his mind but the sheer joy of action.

'Twas a challenge to take on an armed foe when he could barely see. By focusing all his senses, he could feel his opponent, guess how he'd strike next.

The clash of steel and the cries of men battling for their lives surrounded him, lent him strength. A final slash and stab, and his opponent crumpled to the ground. Connor moved forward in search of another.

The clouds parted, sending bright moonlight spilling over them. After the sheer darkness, the light was blinding till his eyes adjusted to it.

His men appeared to be holding their own, he noticed before an Irishman wielding a battle-ax charged at him. Connor had not faced such a weapon before. Nor had he ever faced the almost unholy zeal glowing in his opponent's eyes.

Each time their weapons clashed together, the man gave a shout of laughter mixed with what sounded to be Gaelic curses, and redoubled his efforts to slice Connor's head from his body.

Though this was not Connor's first battle, it was without a doubt the hardest he'd ever had to work to protect himself. He'd fought Normans and Welshmen, but the Irish seemed to best them all for sheer blood lust.

The ax blade slid down the right sleeve of his hauberk, slicing through the mail with surprising ease. The shock of white-hot pain shooting through his arm inspired him to finish this now, and he drew his dagger and held it clutched in his right hand, swinging his sword with his left.

Darting in and out with both blades, Connor danced around the Irishman, whose movements seemed somewhat limited by the way he wielded his weapon. He couldn't move in as close as Connor could if he wanted room to swing the ax, and Connor took advantage of that to harry him with the deadly dagger.

Suddenly the man tossed aside the ax, reached down and drew a long, thin knife from inside his boot. ''If 'tis steel you want, Norman, then take a taste of this,'' he snarled in rough French.

Now 'twas Connor who was hampered by the larger weapon, but he didn't want to be rid of his sword. He pivoted away and slid the blade into its sheath, springing at his opponent with his dagger as soon as he turned back to face him.

Over the uneven ground they moved, the grass slick beneath their feet, the drizzling rain dropping a kiss of blessed coolness upon Connor's sweat-streaked face.

He'd reason to be glad he wore a short mail hauberk, for anything more would have hampered his movements, and he needed every advantage if he were to beat this foe. The man fought without fear, clearly taking pleasure in every touch of their blades, his bearded face split by a gap-toothed grin.

Connor's arm began to throb, spurring him on to bring this meeting to an end. He was vaguely aware that the sounds of battle had died away, save for the cries of the injured. But he didn't dare shift his gaze from his opponent for a moment, for death would surely follow hot on the heels of such foolish distraction.

"Hugh!" someone called out.

Connor's opponent shifted his gaze for only an instant, but 'twas all the time Connor needed to slash with his dagger across the man's chest and upper arm. The Irishman staggered back, but did not fall. Shock lit his eyes as Connor raised his weapon to stab at him again.

The night went dark once more, so suddenly Connor could not see. He thrust where he thought the man stood, but his blade met nothing but air.

The thud of running feet told him their opponents were bolting.

"Damnation!" Connor muttered, waiting for his eyes to adjust to the darkness. The silence surrounding him convinced him the Irish had left the field. "Will, are you yet among the living?" he shouted.

"Aye, milord, so far as I can tell." Will's distinctive

laugh sounded from nearby. ''And yourself? Still got all your parts, I trust,'' he said, his voice coming closer.

''The important ones, at any rate,'' Connor told him. Steel hissed right beside him as a blade slid into its scabbard, and he glanced over at Will, surprised to see a frown on the other man's face.

Just then the clouds parted, revealing most of their men on their feet and relatively unharmed. The rest lay scattered over the ground—some moving, attempting to rise, while others would clearly never move again.

Connor glared at the moon, glowing fat and bright above them now that the enemy had fled. ''Much good you did us,'' he muttered. He turned to offer a hand to a man who'd pulled himself to his knees, supporting him until one of the foot soldiers came to lead him toward the keep. ''Just as I thought we'd prevail—''

''Didn't we win, milord?'' Will asked. He looked out over the field, squinting at the Irish bodies scattered among their own. ''Seems we're still here, and most of us still breathing.'' He crossed himself. ''More of us than not.''

''But did we accomplish anything by this?'' Connor asked, indicating the field with a sweep of his hand.

Will turned to peer back at Gerald's Keep. ''The wall's still standing,'' he said. ''And look there, milord.'' He pointed toward the tower near the tunnel where Connor had attacked the guard. A group of men carrying lanterns and swords escorted four strangers onto the wall walk. ''Lord Connor, I do believe we've caught ourselves some live Irishmen,'' he said with a satisfied grin.

Sir Ivor approached them then, nudging along a battered and bloodied Irishman with the tip of his sword. ''We've caught more than that, milord,'' he said, the smile on his face changing his entire appearance. He gave the man a poke, his smile widening as his scowling captive cursed him. "This is Kieran, Hugh MacCarthy's kinsman."

The bailey stood empty when Moira left the hall and paused beneath the small overhang. She'd forgotten about the rain, but she could scarce ignore it now. It poured over the roof and spilled down in front of her, a shimmering cascade in the torchlight. As she'd done as a child, she cupped her hand and filled it, bring the water to her lips.

The water tasted sweet. Usually she'd view it as a treat from God, but not tonight....

Not when it might increase the danger to Connor and the others.

She didn't want to go back inside, not even for a cloak, so she rooted in her sewing basket until she found a man's shirt, one of Lord Brien's she planned to cut down into clothing for the babe. Draping it over her head and shoulders like a hood, she tucked the basket under her arm and crept down the stairs.

'Twas eerie to see the bailey completely empty. Between the men Connor had taken outside the walls with him and those he'd left behind, stationed at intervals along the length of the battlements and in the towers, almost all the men save the servants were gone. In this weather, she'd not expect anyone else to be roaming about, but it did give her a turn.

A chill roamed her spine, not entirely caused by the rain. What was happening?

Head down, she hastened across the courtyard to the gatehouse.

She understood Connor's objections to her being involved in tonight's activities. And she had no desire to endanger her child or herself.

But she had to know what was happening.

She could no longer remain cloistered away while the men dealt with events that could shape her life.

Her ignorance had cost dearly, and not only she had paid the price. She'd not allow herself to fall into that trap again.

Besides, a good many of the men who'd gone out to fight, Connor included, didn't know the MacCarthys or their men.

Or precisely what they were capable of.

Treading with care over the slippery cobblestones, Moira crossed the last few yards to the tower door. It swung open before she reached it. ''Milady!'' the guard cried. He raced out into the rain and, catching her by the arm, helped her the rest of the way.

The man, one who'd come from England with Connor, released her at once and shut the door against the blowing rain. ''Beggin' your pardon for grabbing you, milady,'' he said quickly, bowing. ''Looked like you needed help.''

She waved aside his apology. ''I thank you for it. 'Tis foul weather to be out in.'' Her brief enchantment with the beauty of the rain had disappeared now that her feet were cold and wet and her gown liberally spattered with water.

''Is there somethin' wrong, to bring you here?'' he asked.

Moira slipped the shirt off her head and held it at arm's length while she looked for somewhere to put it. Since she'd likely need it for the trip back to the keep, she tossed it, dripping, over a rack of pikes.

She set aside her basket. ''Where is the captain of the guard?'' she asked, starting up the stairs.

''Out with Lord Connor, milady.'' The man followed her up the stairs. ''Cedric is taking his place tonight.''

''Is my brother Domnal up here?''

''Nay, milady. He's with the guards in the other tower.''

An unforeseen blessing! She'd hoped he wouldn't be,

since she didn't know how he'd react to her presence here. Despite what he'd told her this afternoon, she couldn't help but wonder whether he could completely escape the effects of Aidan's influence.

If—or when—he reverted back to what she considered the usual O'Neill behavior, she'd rather not have to deal with it before witnesses.

They entered the room at the top of the gatehouse. A man—Cedric, presumably—stood at the window peering out through the half-opened shutters. He glanced back over his shoulder at them, then spun and bowed to Moira so swiftly he bobbled on his feet, banging into the shutter and slamming it closed.

She hoped he had better balance in battle, else he'd not last long. Perhaps that was why he'd been left behind.

Cedric straightened. "Lady Moira! Have you come to see how Lord Connor's plans proceed?"

Moira barely hid her shock. Neither man seemed surprised to see her, nor that she'd want to know about the defense of the place.

Until Lord Brien's death, which had forced her to assume command of Gerald's Keep, she hadn't ever been inside the gatehouse. And it had been a difficult adjustment for the remaining garrison to accept her involvement in military concerns. Some of them had never accepted it, she thought, Sir Ivor springing to mind.

But if these men expected it of her…

"Aye." She crossed to the window and tugged open the shutter. "Have you anything to report?" she asked, peering out into the murky darkness.

Her belly prevented her from leaning far; she could see nothing, and rain spattered on her head. She drew back and watched as the two men exchanged a look she couldn't interpret. "Well? Surely something's happened by now."

"I couldn't see much, milady," Cedric said. "Every once in a while the clouds part and the moon breaks through, but it's stayed dark, mostly, since they left. Too noisy to hear much, either, with the wind and all. But it looked to me like something must have happened, since no one's come back. Sir Ivor, Sir Will and the others are to wait for orders from Lord Connor—"

"Unless somethin' happens on this side," the other guard interrupted. "Then we're to send 'em help, if necessary. Got men ready to go, but it doesn't look to me like they'll be needed," he added, sounding disappointed.

"We'd better keep a close watch, then." Moira glanced out the window again, motioning for Cedric to join her there. "You'll need to know if 'tis time to send out the others."

She hoped he would, since she didn't want to display her ignorance, nor ruin Connor's plan by making a wrong decision.

The guard who had let her in went downstairs to his post, leaving Moira and Cedric to keep watch. Cedric extinguished the lanterns in the room save for the one at the head of the stairs, which he turned away. "Don't want to show ourselves in the window," he told her. "Besides, we'll be able to see better without 'em."

Once she'd stared out into the darkness for a time, she could see more clearly. She noticed a sudden burst of motion near where the curtain wall curved away, not having realized the dark mass there was men until they moved. "Cedric," she whispered, nudging his arm and pointing. "What are they doing?"

"Going back to join Lord Connor, most like," he said. Squinting, he leaned out into the rain. Just as she thought she'd have to grab him by the belt to keep him from falling, he popped back in. "I'd better go tell Jean to make certain the men are ready to go,'' he said, shaking his head like a dog and spraying water everywhere.

Grimacing, Moira stepped away from him. ''What's happened?'' she asked urgently. She looked out again.

The moon showed through the clouds suddenly, exposing a small group of men huddled against the wall. ''What if the MacCarthys come while Sir Ivor and the others are gone?'' she asked, unable to keep her growing sense of urgency out of her voice. ''There aren't enough men there to guard the gate. And what about those who are supposed to guard the tunnel?'' she asked. She straightened and moved back from the window. ''If something is happening, perhaps we should send more men to the undercroft, as well.''

Would these men obey her orders? she wondered. She could only try, see how they reacted. ''How many men are waiting below?''

''Twenty, milady,'' Cedric said. ''Most of them aren't soldiers, though, just men who can handle a pike and look fierce.''

That would be useful in the dark, Moira thought wryly. Still, mayhap there'd be strength in numbers. ''Tell Jean to send out half the men as reinforcements,'' she told him. ''And tell the others to remain near the entrance to the undercroft, in case they're needed there.''

''Aye, milady,'' he replied with nary a bit of hesitation.

He raced down the stairs, leaving Moira to her solitary vigil. She didn't understand why these men had obeyed her so readily, but she was grateful for it.

Grateful, too, that Connor had left Cedric, and not a member of her garrison, in charge of the gatehouse. Despite the months she'd been in command, she doubted her men would follow her orders now that Connor was here.

A quiet creak from below told her the door beside the

huge gate had opened, and soon she saw men slipping along the narrow verge at the base of the wall.

Cedric ran back up the stairs, his face alight with excitement. "Jean says that the guards Lord Connor posted near where the tunnels are—in the undercroft—thought they heard the sappers getting ready to collapse the tunnels. Our men are going to see if they can roust them out before they get a chance to do it."

"Is that what Lord Connor wanted?"

"I don't know, milady," he said. "But we cannot let them go that far, can we? Even if we stop the Irishmen now, who's to say they won't be back once the wall's down?" He came to the window and gazed out, then turned to face her, his expression worried. "I've seen it before, milady. We cannot let that happen here."

She understood what he was saying, but if Connor had not ordered it…

Uncertain, she returned her attention outside. Despite the moon's glow there was little to see, but she thought she could hear something. "Listen, Cedric!"

They opened the shutters wide and Cedric hung out over the edge as he had before. "I hear battle cries, milady!" He wriggled in. "They're fighting."

Moira's stomach clenched with fear, and the babe began to kick and squirm, perhaps in reaction to her tension. Taking several deep breaths, she willed herself to be calm and consider what they should do.

"If we can hear the battle, so might the men in the tunnel, yes?" she asked.

"I can't say for certain, but they might, milady."

'Twas clear to her now what they must do. "Tell Jean to send word to our men to capture the sappers. This could be a diversion so that they can fire the tunnels."

"At once, milady," Cedric replied, already at the head of the stairs.

The sounds carried on the wind had intensified. Moira stroked her stomach to soothe the babe—and distract herself—and tried not to imagine what could be happening to Connor and the others.

What if the MacCarthys had arrived in force? Or if they'd lain in wait for the castle garrison to venture outside the walls? They might have been gathered out there every night for some time, waiting for a chance to attack. 'Twas entirely possible that Domnal didn't know all of Hugh's plans.

Of course, if that were the case, they probably wouldn't have expected a force of the size and skill that Gerald's Keep possessed since Connor's arrival.

Nay, she reminded herself, the MacCarthys knew the FitzCliffords had sent reinforcements. Aidan had said as much the night he'd come, and he'd also had the opportunity to gauge the size of their garrison, since he'd stood in the hall and seen how much larger their company had become.

By the Virgin, they should never have allowed Aidan into Gerald's Keep....

Or having made that mistake, they assuredly shouldn't have permitted him to leave, carrying information to his ally.

To her enemy.

She watched as Jean's messenger slipped past her, lantern in hand, and joined the others. They moved beyond her sight around the curve of the wall, and all she could do was wait.

The sounds of battle faded away, and the clouds thickened again, obscuring the moon and draping the night in darkness.

Moira stood there and prayed, hoping that a sinner's prayers had some value in God's eyes if 'twas a just cause she prayed for.

Eyes closed, she repeated a paternoster and crossed herself. She thought she heard voices carried on the wind and opened her eyes.

Out of the night shone a lantern, then another, lighting the way for the men who approached, walking single file along the narrow band of earth between the base of the wall and the moat.

Praise the Virgin, they'd survived! She reached up to close the shutters, intending to meet them in the bailey.

She saw Connor then, at the end of the line of men. He paused just below her and glanced up. His face, pale and grim in the flickering light, became positively glacial when he spotted her. Silent and stern, he took a lantern from the man standing outside the door and disappeared into the building.

Heart racing, Moira stepped back from the window and headed for the stairs, bracing her hand on the wall for support.

Men crowded the guardroom, and she paused at the foot of the stairs. She couldn't see Connor in the crush of large, armed warriors, and she didn't dare venture among them. She moved up a step, hoping she'd be able to see better from the higher perch.

Suddenly the men fell silent, and a path opened across the middle of the room. She could see Connor now, though once she caught a glimpse of his expression, she wished she'd stayed upstairs.

"By the saints, woman—what the hell do you think you're doing here?"

Chapter Twenty

Though she was dearly tempted to run back up the stairs, Moira held her ground and raised her head high as Connor crossed the guardroom and halted in front of her. Because she stood two steps above the floor, she had a clear view of him. His hair hung, dripping wet, to his shoulders, and fine beads of moisture clung to his skin. A flush of color rode his cheekbones, and the scar on his cheek shone stark white in contrast. His eyes glowed with anger. She could not meet that intent stare for long. She lowered her gaze, gasping at what she saw.

A dark stain ran the length of his right arm, the blood glistening bright against the dull iron of his mail sleeve and smeared along the side of his green surcoat.

She descended the last two steps and reached for his right hand. It was icy, damp with rain and blood. ''My lord, let me take care of this.''

He shrugged free of her loose hold. ''I asked you a question, milady.'' His voice sounded calmer now, but 'twas as cold as the expression on his face.

She realized no one had moved nor said a word since Connor had spoken. Glancing past him, she saw that they were the focus of everyone's attention.

She spied Dermot's cousin standing behind Sir Ivor, watching them with mocking intensity. Raising her chin, she met him stare for stare and ignored his leering smile.

Anger fired her blood. Did Connor think to take her to task here, in full view of their men?

In view of a MacCarthy?

How dare he?

She stepped past him into the middle of the room. Connor swung around to keep her in view. "I'll answer your question when I'm ready, milord, and I tell you now, it will not be here." She tossed her hair back over her shoulder. "Nor before witnesses."

A murmur of laughter filled the room, bringing a surge of color to her cheeks. Connor's expression changed, shifting from angry to thoughtful, curious.

Had she confused him?

She hoped so! No more of the tearful widow, she vowed. 'Twas past time she showed Connor FitzClifford the strong woman she wanted to be.

Starting now.

She cast a sweeping glance around the room. "I wouldn't dream of taking you away from your duties." Dropping into a respectful curtsy, she added, "Perhaps you'll join me afterward to tell me how we fared."

Connor bowed. "Perhaps I shall," he said, one eyebrow quirked upward—a taunt, she decided.

Or a challenge?

She traversed the path that had opened for her and paused by the door. As soon as Jean opened it for her she nodded to the room at large and swept out—before her courage escaped her completely.

Connor watched Moira leave, wondering as she made her impressive exit if she'd forgotten that the weather was miserable and she hadn't so much as a cloak to protect her from it. He nearly chased after her, but hadn't the heart to spoil her accomplishment.

After he'd been such a fool.

He deserved every bit of her scorn for the way he'd spoken to her, he thought as he set about questioning his men. Once he realized that she'd been up in the gatehouse tower during the attack—that she'd been actively involved in commanding some of the garrison—his heart had clenched with fear for her.

Now that his temper had eased and the surge of battle lust flown from him, he regretted snarling at her—especially before their men. She'd been as safe there as anywhere else within the castle, and he'd been wrong to chide her as he had.

As the men reported what they'd seen and done during the battle, he knew Moira's decision to send more men to help both inside and outside the castle had been wise. The sappers could have easily fired the tunnel while the battle raged, or fled to the cliffs. Connor had left her reinforcements outside on patrol, lest the MacCarthys return.

They'd been lucky that Domnal had come to them and shown him what MacCarthy planned. Gerald's Keep remained intact and in their hands.

And he had a MacCarthy as hostage.

Connor ordered Sir Ivor—with Will's help, in case d'Athée experienced a sudden return of his earlier behavior—to lock up their prisoners in the vaulted cells below the great hall. Placed under heavy guard, the Irishmen could stew there for a bit. Perhaps 'twould make them more amenable to talk—or to compromise.

His duties to his men carried out, Connor found the time had come for him to seek out Moira. Anticipation sang in his blood, sharp and tantalizing. Though he regretted what he'd said to her in the gatehouse, he couldn't be sorry for her reaction.

Her beauty could not be denied, no matter what her mood, but as she'd been tonight—blue eyes flashing, her posture straight and proud—she'd been magnificent.

The hour was late—past midnight, he'd guess. Far too late to pay a visit to a lady. But she'd said she wanted to see him, and far be it from him to refuse a beautiful woman, he thought with a smile.

He passed through the hall, silent but for the occasional snores and coughs of the servants sleeping there. He ran lightly up the stairs and rapped on the door to her solar.

There was no answer. Either she'd fallen asleep while waiting for him, or she hadn't waited for him at all, but had sought her bed straightaway.

He eased open the door, his gaze sweeping the room. The one candle gave light enough to show that she wasn't there.

Taking care to be quiet, he crossed the floor and nudged open the unlatched door to her bedchamber. The only illumination came from the low-burning fire in the hearth, but he could see that the bed was empty. "Moira?" he said softly, but heard no reply.

Where could she be? he wondered as he stepped out into the corridor and closed the door behind him. By the saints, 'twas the middle of the night—where else should she be but in her bed?

He crept past the sleeping servants once more and left the hall, pausing at the top of the outside stairs. The rain had stopped while he'd been in the guardhouse, and the sky had cleared in the short time he'd been in the keep itself.

Will came out of the gatehouse and headed for the door to the barracks built against the wall opposite the keep. Connor hurried down the steps to catch up with him.

"Milord," Will called quietly. He stopped in the middle of the bailey and waited for Connor. "I thought you'd have retired by now."

Connor shook his head. "I went looking for Lady Moira, but she's nowhere to be found."

"Did you look in the barracks?"

"The barracks? What would she be doing there?"

"Hiding from you among her new champions?" Will suggested with a cheeky grin. Connor frowned. "'Tis naught but a jest, milord," he added. "We all know you'd never harm a woman—and I've no doubt the lady knows it, as well."

He'd just as soon ignore that topic altogether. Connor rubbed at his right shoulder, where a dull throbbing had settled, and grimaced when the motion jarred his injured arm. "Why would she be in the barracks?"

"She and the old woman, Brigit, went there to care for the wounded, soon after she left the gatehouse. Though no one was hurt bad, perhaps she's still there." Will nodded toward Connor's arm, wrapped about with a scrap of his surcoat. "Looks to me like you could use a bit of her help—if she's forgiven you for shouting at her," he added with a laugh. "Otherwise, I don't believe I'd want her sticking a needle into me."

"She may have at me with a needle if she wishes, after the way I spoke to her," Connor said ruefully. "Though I'd rather it happens without the audience we had earlier. I suppose I should be grateful she wasn't armed."

They resumed walking, heading to the barracks. "Aye. No telling what she might be capable of if she were," Will agreed. "According to Cedric, Lady Moira proved herself Lady Gillian's equal tonight. 'Commands nigh as well as our lady,' he said."

"Lofty praise indeed," Connor acknowledged, knowing

how highly the men of l'Eau Clair regarded their mistress's ability to lead.

He mulled over Cedric's words. "I wondered why Cedric and Jean obeyed Moira so easily, without reservation. I didn't stop to think that they're used to a woman giving them orders."

"It's not that Gillian orders them about, as a rule," Will said. "But they know that any command Sir Henry gives might well come from Gillian." He stopped before the door to the barracks, eyeing Connor with a measuring gaze. "She was a fine leader, back before your brother took command of l'Eau Clair."

"And will be so again, when my brother must be away," Connor said. "I found no fault with Rannulf's choice of wife, Will. Gillian is dear to me, a woman—and wife—to be proud of. My brother is a fortunate man."

"May you be as fortunate, milord," Will said, his expression serious, though his eyes were bright with humor. "You very well might be, if you've the sense to recognize a prize when you see it."

Connor frowned. "What do you mean by that?" he demanded, though he believed he knew what Will meant.

"Lord Connor, you're not a stupid man," Will chided.

"Faint praise—"

"But if you don't take advantage of the opportunity the good Lord placed right beneath your nose, I might need to alter my opinion." He jabbed Connor with his elbow—on his left side, saints be praised. "A comely Irishwoman, fertile—" he waggled his eyebrows "—with the courage to face down an ill-tempered, scar-faced Norman. If you're fool enough to let her get away from you, milord, *I* just might have to try my luck with Lady Moira."

Connor found it amazing that Will had the mettle to say to his face what he knew others said behind his back. But far from being offended, he respected Will all the more for his honesty.

That didn't mean he intended to step aside, however. "I wouldn't if I were you," Connor said dryly. "Besides, I've already asked her."

"Milord! You sly dog." Will grinned. "I take it she hasn't given you an answer yet, else we'd have heard the happy news."

"Let's say I've yet to bring her around to my way of thinking. But I'm hopeful she'll—" A roar of laughter sounded from inside the barracks. Connor reached for the latch. "They're a merry lot."

"Been celebrating our victory, I imagine." Will motioned for him to go ahead. "We should be in there doing the same."

"'Tis no place for Moira, then, if they've been drinking," Connor said, a sudden urgency filling him. They were decent men, but rough. No telling how they might treat her once the ale flowed freely.

"Sit you down here, Padrig," Moira directed, pointing to the bench beside the one she occupied. She resisted the urge to rub her lower back, for she knew if Brigit caught her at it again, she'd nag at her to leave off stitching and bandaging the injured men, and make her return to the keep to seek her bed.

Not that the thought didn't hold a certain appeal... A very strong appeal, if truth be told, for her body ached with weariness. But she didn't want to leave the barracks, not now that the men—hers and Connor's—had joined in a bond forged in the heat of battle.

A bond that included her, for some reason.

Whether from the fact that she'd given a command to some of them—which they'd surprisingly obeyed—or that she'd been willing to come into the barracks to tend their hurts, they'd decided to include her in their post-battle revels. Every man had a tale to tell, some straightforward, others embellished. Especially once the ale began to flow.

She motioned Padrig closer and smiled at something Cedric said. They'd never know how much their easy acceptance and camaraderie meant to her.

By the rood, even Brigit had joined in their celebration once she'd determined that Moira had the better skill at stitching up cuts. She'd claimed the one crude chair in the place, accepted a foaming tankard of ale—much depleted already—and sat there smiling widely as the stories flew.

Moira reached for the hem of Padrig's shirt, intending to tug it up and over his head as she would a child's, to examine his bruised ribs, but he scooted back from her and pulled the shirt down about his waist, clutching the worn linen in both hands.

"Lad, are you daft?" one of the men asked, his voice loud and slurred with ale. "Never refuse a lass when she wants to help ye take off yer clothes." He grunted when the man next to him gave him a poke in the gut. "Beggin' yer pardon, milady."

A roar of laughter greeted his comment, and Padrig's face went from milk-pale to cherry-red in an instant.

Before she could try to ease his humiliation, the door flew open and Connor stepped inside, Will behind him.

Moira placed a hand on Padrig's shoulder—for support and to hold her balance—and rose.

She didn't know how to interpret Connor's expression, but to her eyes, he didn't appear best pleased. *Don't let him spoil this for them,* she prayed.

He glanced about the crowded room, his gaze lingering the barest moment on Brigit, then on Moira, before he grinned and turned to Will. "Why weren't we invited here sooner?'' he asked. ''Do you think they feared we'd guzzle all their ale?''

The men roared at that, as enthusiastically as they had earlier, and the man tending the ale keg held out brimming mugs to Connor and Will.

Relief took the strength from Moira's knees and she dropped down onto the bench. ''Are you all right, milady?'' Padrig asked, concern replacing embarrassment on his face. ''Do you need Brigit?''

She peered over at the maid, slumped back in the chair, her wrinkled cheeks pink, her veil askew, and shook her head. ''Nay—and 'tis a blessing I don't, for I doubt she's able to stand, let alone do much else.'' Meeting Padrig's eyes, she added, ''I believe she's been drinking something stronger than ale. How shall we get her back to the keep?''

He gave a mischievous smile. ''Mayhap Lord Connor will carry her to her bed.''

''You honor me, lad, but you greatly overstate my strength,'' Connor said from behind Padrig. He stepped over the bench and sat down facing Moira, giving her a nod of greeting.

Despite her boldness earlier—or perhaps because of it—she felt shy of him. But it would not do to let it show, lest she destroy any progress she'd made in keeping the weak and tearful Moira hidden away. So she met his dark, intent gaze. ''Have you finally come to let me tend your injury, milord?''

''Later, perhaps,'' he said. He turned to Padrig. ''How fare you, lad? You took no serious hurt tonight?''

''Nay, milord, I'm fine.'' Padrig looked at her as he said it, as though daring her to refute his claim.

What to do? she wondered, holding Padrig's pleading gaze. She dared not send him off without seeing to his ribs, yet she knew he didn't wish to appear weak before his master. "He's a tough fellow, milord, for he took little hurt, save for someone thumping him smartly in the ribs."

Though Connor's expression remained serious, she saw a spark in his eyes that told her he knew precisely what she was about. "Excellent, Padrig!" For a moment, she thought Connor meant to give his squire a congratulatory slap on the back, but he merely clasped Padrig's shoulder briefly. "Has Lady Moira finished with you, then?"

Before Padrig could make some excuse and escape, Moira held up a long strip of linen. "I was just about to begin, milord." She met the squire's resigned look with a faint smile. "Will you indulge my motherly concern, Padrig, and let me wrap your ribs? I know 'tis naught but a woman's foolishness, but I'll worry that you'll end up with a rib stuck through your lungs by morning if I don't bind them up. Just for tonight," she added.

"Excellent advice," Connor said. "You cannot be too careful." He stood. "We all must heal quickly, to be ready to fight again if necessary."

"Aye, milord, milady," Padrig said. He tugged his shirt up over his head and emerged with his brown hair sticking out in every direction. "Do what you must," he told Moira, his voice and face resigned.

"I'll leave you to your work," Connor said, turning away. He took two steps, paused and glanced back at her. "Are you nearly through here?"

"Aye." She placed the end of the linen beneath Padrig's arm and nudged him to his feet. "This is my last patient." She reached around his slender middle and pulled the wrap tight. "Except for you, milord," she added, loudly enough to mask the squire's grunt of discomfort.

Connor nodded, took a swallow of ale. "I'll escort you back once you've finished here. Padrig can help me get this off—'' he indicated his hauberk ''—before he seeks his pallet.''

Padrig shifted on his feet until Moira gave another tug on the bindings wrapped about him. ''But what will you do with Brigit, milord?''

Brigit, Moira noted without surprise, had nodded off where she sat, her head tilted back, a gentle snore emanating from her open mouth. ''I'd suggest you leave her here, milord.'' She chuckled. ''But the men might not get much rest if you do. Once she's had a bit of ale, she can snore fit to wake the dead.''

''Are you certain you want her in the keep?'' Connor asked. ''She sleeps in your chamber, doesn't she?''

Moira nodded, resigning herself to a restless night.

He smiled. ''Don't worry. Two of the burliest men-at-arms will carry her over when you're ready to go. I'll find a place for her where she won't disturb you.''

Something about his voice, the promise in his smile, made a shiver of…something unrecognizable tremble along her spine.

Whatever the sensation was, it made her breath catch, her heart race, her skin feel more sensitive. The brush of Connor's gaze over her felt as solid and real as the touch of his hand might.

Her weariness seemed to melt away. Sitting up straight on the bench, she met his smile with a tentative one of her own.

His smile deepened. ''Just let me know when you're ready.''

Chapter Twenty-One

Connor and Moira followed along as their motley troop returned to the keep. Two men supported Brigit, her bulk slumped between them. Padrig carried Moira's basket of bandages and Connor the wooden box of simples. Moira, her mind still distracted by Connor, let him lead her through the silent, torchlit bailey, a supportive hand beneath her elbow.

Somehow they stole through the hall full of servants without waking anyone. Once they reached the top of the stairs, however, they paused in the dimly lit corridor to decide where to put Brigit.

"There's that empty room at the end of the hall," Connor suggested.

"The bed's not made up," Moira told him, a shudder passing through her at the mere thought of going in there.

"She sleeps on a pallet anyway," Connor pointed out. "'Tis the easiest solution. The room has a door stout enough to quiet her snores, yet she'll be close if you should need her."

He took the basket from Padrig and strode to Moira's solar. He returned carrying a lighted candle in one hand and Brigit's pallet rolled up under his other arm.

While Moira stood watching from the corridor—feeling a fool for refusing to enter the room, but still not willing to do so—Connor and the others settled Brigit for the night.

Once he'd sent the two soldiers back to the barracks, he turned to his squire. "Make up the fire for Lady Moira."

Padrig nodded, his eyes drooping with fatigue, and headed into Moira's bedchamber.

Connor took her by the arm, his touch making her senses spring to life once again. "Solar or bedchamber?" he asked. His eyes met hers, searching them for something.

She took a step toward her solar, but realized there was no water there to wash away the blood from his wound. But the pitcher in her chamber should be nearly full.... Did she want Connor in her chamber now? 'Twas past midnight....

Padrig returned and bowed. "Go to bed, lad," Connor told him. "Don't bother waiting for me." The squire nodded and crept past them to the stairs.

Moira tugged free of Connor's hold. "Come into my room. I'll see to your arm there."

Not waiting for a reply, she entered the solar and lit a candle from the banked fire, then went into the next room and lit the two branches of candles there.

The metal ewer held water—cold now, but not unbearably so. Still, she placed it on the hearth and knelt to feed more fuel to the growing blaze.

The door from the corridor opened and Connor slipped into the room. "Let me do that." He carried a pitcher—from his chamber?—which he set on the table beside the bed.

"I need no help to lay peat upon the fire," she said tartly. "I'm not some helpless idiot! I know I've not done much to prove otherwise since you came here, but I'm usually competent enough to get by without a keeper."

"Nonetheless, you need not do everything yourself," he chided. He joined her by the hearth, reaching down and clasping her about the shoulders.

Even with his support, it seemed a formidable task to stand. She wavered on her feet, and Connor wrapped her in his arms.

It felt so good, with his warmth and strength surrounding her, that Moira knew she must break away from him at once. But he refused to release her, instead cradling her to his chest. "Don't run away," he whispered into her hair. "Rest here a moment, till you've caught your balance."

"That's not likely to happen if I remain where I am," she said, too tired to hide her regret.

He drew back to look at her. "What do you mean?" he asked, watching her with a hawk's all-seeing stare. "I wish only to keep you from harm, Moira, nothing more than that." He smoothed her hair away from her face, his fingers caressing her cheek. "For tonight, at any rate."

She remained in his arms for a time, savoring the closeness and giving silent thanks that he'd returned from battle relatively unharmed. But the rough weave of his hauberk against her face, felt even through the light padding of his surcoat, reminded her that he had yet to remove the signs of combat from himself.

Easing away, she raised her hand to cup his whiskery cheek. "Come, 'tis late, past time to take care of you."

She retrieved the pitcher he'd brought, setting it on the hearth with the other one. When she turned back to him, he'd unbuckled his sword belt and hung it over the back of the chair. Moving gingerly, he tugged at his surcoat, trying to pull it up over his head one-handed. "Here, let me," she offered.

Together they drew it off. He yawned as he emerged from the garment, and she urged him toward the chair. She folded the surcoat and set it on the chest at the foot of the bed, then gave a cry of dismay when she saw him still standing there, trying to remove his hauberk by himself. "Should I wake Padrig?"

"There's no need." He untied the material bound round his upper arm and handed it to her. Then, leaning forward from the waist, he let the heavy mail tunic slide down over his head to land in a pile at his feet. "I never had a squire till I left for Ireland," he said, picking up the hauberk and setting it by the door. "You see, I'm self-sufficient as well," he added with a tired laugh. "I'm used to managing on my own."

He drew the chair close to the chest and pointed to it. "You sit there. 'Twill be more comfortable for you."

She scowled at him and stood her ground, waiting for him to sit in the chair as she had planned.

"Did you think I wouldn't notice how you've been rubbing your back?" He took her by the shoulders and turned her, then walked her backward until her legs bumped the chair seat. "As your overlord's representative, Lady Moira, I command you to sit down." He pressed on her shoulders until she obeyed.

"Do you think to suddenly become a tyrant, milord, now that you've discovered I have a backbone?" she asked while he moved the candle stands closer.

He went into the solar and returned with her bandages and simples. Placing them within her reach, he sat on the chest and faced her. "I've always known you have backbone, Moira. Only a strong woman could have held Gerald's Keep and kept it out of Hugh MacCarthy's hands these many months until help arrived." He took her hand and held it loosely clasped in both of his. "Despite the odds against you, your people are safe, the keep is still standing and you've even managed to plant some of the fields.

You've provided for your people—ofttimes, I imagine, at your own expense. It cannot have been easy to do all that, and to care for a dying man as well.''

She blinked back tears; she'd done all she could, but she'd wondered—wondered still—if she'd done enough.

She was so tired—not simply the physical weariness, but emotionally. She'd had no one to share that burden with.

Could she share it with Connor?

He gave her hand a squeeze and set it in her lap, reaching up to rub his right shoulder above his bloodstained sleeve. Perhaps they'd find the time to speak of those things later, but for now, she'd ignored his injury for too long already.

She sat forward to peer at his arm. So much blood had soaked into the sleeve, it clung to his arm from below his shoulder all the way to the wrist. ''Is it stuck to the wound?'' She gave the linen at his wrist a tug. It didn't move.

''Aye, it's clotted over.'' He endured her gentle probing as she worked her way up his arm. ''Just needs a bandage over it, most like—'' His breath hissed between his teeth when she touched a spot just above the crook of his elbow.

''I hope you've more shirts, milord, for this one's life is over.'' She stood and removed her eating knife from the sheath on her belt, then caught hold of the loose fabric at his throat.

''The shirt's life, or mine?'' he asked, the faint smile in his eyes telling her 'twas a jest.

She tightened her grip on the shirt and pulled him closer. ''You *do* trust me, milord?''

''You know I do,'' he murmured.

Ignoring the tide of warmth that flooded through her at his words, she poked the blade into the material and sliced it open.

Despite the steady throb in his arm, Connor felt quite

well enough to savor Moira's closeness. Her sweet scent of flowers and spice surrounded him; he turned his head, brushing against a strand of her hair where it had escaped her veil. He was tempted to ease closer, to brush against the softness of her cheek, to make her shift her obviously averted gaze to his face.

But he didn't. He didn't wish to force himself on her in any way, whether it be his presence, his ardor, his body....

He'd better abandon that line of thought soon, else she'd know precisely what thoughts had taken over his errant mind.

"Turn around," she told him. He did so, and she slid the blade into the back of his shirt, then tore at the fabric until the sleeve hung free. She moved to stand before him. "Do you want to take off the rest of the shirt before I begin?"

"I might as well." If she didn't mind him sitting there half-dressed, *he* certainly didn't.

She'd seen his scars already, heard him admit who had caused them. If she mentioned them again, he would tell her more—tell her all, if she wished to hear the tale. He had asked *her* to trust him with her life and that of her child; surely he could trust her with the story of his own.

He reached up, tugged the remains of the shirt over his head and let the material drop into his lap. For the moment, it appeared her attention remained focused on his latest scar-in-the-making.

As was his own, he thought when he glanced up. She placed a needle and stout thread on the chest, alongside some strips of white fabric and a small pot of unguent.

Moira moved about the room, gathering together a basin, a dish of soft soap and a towel. Setting the basin on the chair, she filled it from a ewer on the hearth. Straightening, she rubbed her lower back, the arching movement emphasizing the mound of her belly.

"Moira, your back is hurting." He reached out and moved the basin from the chair to his lap. "Sit down, please."

"It's never ached so much," she told him. "But it's been a long day, and I've spent the last few hours trying to bend." She glanced down at her belly. "Something I cannot do right now."

"Would it help if I rub your back?"

She shook her head and, grabbing hold of the chair's arms, eased down into it. "I don't dare relax until I'm through with your wound." Laughing, she added, "You wouldn't want me to fall onto the floor in the middle of stitching it up, would you?"

"I'd catch you, I swear," he said, chuckling as well.

"It strikes me that we're both too jolly, considering the situation." She picked up a towel and dunked it in the basin. "Which tells me we're both too weary and should be abed by now." She wrung out the cloth and laid it over the cut, holding it in place to loosen the sleeve.

"I guarantee I'll not fall asleep while you're doing this."

"It might be better if you did." Catching hold of the top of the sleeve, she began to gently pull it free.

It stung, but he'd felt worse—for a far less worthy cause.

Other than the sheen of sweat that broke out on his brow, Connor sat silent, motionless, expressionless while Moira bathed away the blood from his arm and set stitches along a cut the length of his hand. Her face had paled, but he couldn't be sure if 'twas what she was doing, or sheer exhaustion that caused it.

"There," she said, laying aside the needle and the knife she'd used to cut the thread. Sitting back in the chair, she sighed. "You were lucky, for it's not deep, and 'tis a clean, straight wound. It should heal well."

She spread a creamy, sweet-smelling ointment over the cut and wrapped a long strip of linen loosely around his arm, tying it securely near his armpit.

He rolled his shoulder, hoping to loosen the tension, and wriggled his fingers. "Everything works fine." It certainly felt better, now that she'd finished. There must have been something in the ointment to draw away the pain, as well, for some of the ache had disappeared already. He took her hand and brought it to his lips. "Thank you, milady."

"I'd hoped you'd tell me everything that happened tonight, but I'm so tired, I doubt my brain could understand it."

Connor rubbed his hand over his face. "I doubt whether what I'd say would make sense, either. We'd best wait until tomorrow." He stood and began to gather up the items she'd used, intending to put them away.

"You needn't do that."

"You've done enough yourself. It's late—"

"I'll leave it for Maeve to take care of in the morning."

He didn't believe her, so he finished the task, ignoring her frown. "You see, it took but a moment," he told her, snuffing all but one of the candles.

She'd grasped the arms of the chair once he released her, getting ready to lever herself up. She hadn't moved, however, so he caught her about the waist before she could do so. "You've toiled long and hard today—and yesterday, as well," he added. "For 'tis a new day already." He swung her up into his arms and carried her to the bed. "You've earned your rest."

He tried to settle her onto the coverlet, but she clung to him hard—harder than necessary to hang on. "That may be true, Connor, but I don't believe I'll get the chance to rest for a while longer."

He shifted her beneath the blankets and would have straightened, but still she wouldn't release him. "What do you mean?" he asked, though he feared he knew the answer.

She nestled against his throat. "I mean, milord, that I think my child has decided to be born."

Connor settled next to Moira and pried loose her hands. "Please tell me this is false labor again," he begged.

Her eyes closed and she shook her head. "I don't think it is," she murmured. "The pains feel stronger, and there's an ache low in my belly that hasn't gone away." She opened her eyes and grimaced. "Add to that the dull pain in my back—"

"I believe you," he interrupted, unwilling to hear more. "I'll get Brigit. She'll know better than I what to do." He tried to rise, but Moira clung to him. "You'll have to let go, dearling, unless you'd rather I carry you into that room with me."

She let go of him at once, as he'd suspected she would. He crawled over the mattress, grabbed a candle from the stand, lighting it quickly, and quit the room, leaving the door wide in case she called out.

He heard Brigit's snores before he opened the door. "Not a good sign," he muttered. He went to the pallet where he'd left the old woman, but the pile of bedding lay empty. She wasn't on the bed, either, though she had to be nearby. He got down on his knees, the candle flame wavering in a draft, and dug through a mound that looked to be the bed curtains.

Brigit lay under the dusty pile of fabric, her mouth open wide, her gown askew. "Brigit!" When he shook her, she caught hold of him and tried to pull him onto the makeshift pallet with her.

He scrambled back and dropped the candle, which by some miracle didn't go out. Snatching it up before he set himself aflame, he grabbed the bedpost for support and pulled himself to his feet.

Leaving the maid where she lay, he raced up the stairs to his chamber and shook Padrig awake. "Lad, I need your help," he said, loudly enough that Moira could likely hear him in the room below. It couldn't be helped—his squire slept like the dead and was nigh impossible to awaken.

"Padrig!" Connor shouted when his first attempt met with no reaction. "To arms, lad!"

Padrig sprang up from his pallet and stood beside it, eyes wild. "What, milord, what is it?" he gasped. His gaze focused on Connor, standing half-dressed, candle in hand, and he stilled. "We aren't going to battle?"

"Nay, lad." Connor's laugh held a touch of desperation. "Not as we usually do." He headed for the door. "Come with me."

They hurried to Moira's room. "Wait here," he told Padrig, and entered her chamber alone.

The bed was empty. "Moira?" Frantically scanning the room, he found her on the far side of the bed, struggling with her tunic. "By the Virgin, what are you doing?"

"This is wet. I need to take it off." She picked at the knotted lace at the throat of the gown.

He scooped her up and deposited her back on the bed.

"No! I told you, 'tis wet," she scolded, trying to climb off. "Connor—"

"All right, I'll help you," he said. "Come on."

"*You* cannot help me." She pulled away from him and stood propped against the bedpost. "Where is Brigit?"

Feeling desperate and completely out of his element,

Connor left her and went to the door, wrenching it open just far enough to talk to Padrig. "Go downstairs and find the maid—what the hell is her name? Maude? Nay, 'tis Maeve. Do you know her?"

Padrig looked at him as though he were a madman.

Perhaps he was; he certainly felt like one at the moment.

"Is something wrong with Lady Moira?" Padrig asked, concern lacing his voice. He tried to peer into the room.

Connor held his ground. "'Tis her time," he snapped, his attention distracted by the sound of Moira moving about.

Padrig stared at him blankly.

"Her babe, it's about to be born. She'll be fine, I'm sure, once I find someone to help her." He glanced over his shoulder; Moira knelt by the fire, giving it a stir with the poker. "Damnation, Moira, put that down," he snarled, then had to hold on to the door so that Padrig couldn't push past him.

"Milord—"

"Padrig, go and fetch Maeve now." He started to close the door in the lad's face, then whipped it open. "And send someone up to wake Brigit. They've my permission to do whatever necessary, but I want her awake and in Lady Moira's chamber as soon as may be." Padrig stared. "Do you understand?" Connor roared.

"Aye, m-milord, at once," the squire stammered before racing down the stairs.

Connor turned and hurried to the hearth. "Dearling, you cannot be doing these things. Come back to bed." He helped her up off the floor. Mistrusting the look in her eyes as she glanced from him to the poker in her hand, he took it from her and let it clatter to the hearthstones.

Moira shrugged free of Connor's gentle grip and faced him. She would have caught him by the front of his shirt had he been wearing one, but since his chest was bare, he should count himself fortunate that she didn't grab hold of his chest hair to catch his attention. ''Connor, stop it,'' she shouted.

''What?'' He looked so wild-eyed, he might have frightened a weaker woman. As it was, she merely found him exasperating.

At least she'd finally captured his notice.

''Connor, where is Brigit?'' Moira didn't know how long till the next pain; she must do what she could in the interim. That included bringing some semblance of calm to Connor, and finding the help she and the babe would need soon.

He raked both hands through his hair. ''Drunk.'' He drew in a deep breath. ''She's completely beyond help—or helping you. I couldn't wake her. When I went to get her, she tried to haul me into bed with her!''

In spite of the situation, Moira laughed, as much at the outrage coloring his cheeks and his voice as at the image his words brought to her mind. ''She does find you a fine figure of a man. A bit thin, she said, but tolerable.''

''Have you gone mad?'' he demanded. He tried to herd her toward the bed again.

''Nay, though I might ask you the same, milord.'' She bent to pick up her wet gown from the floor and caught at her belly as another paroxysm twisted through her.

He came up behind her and wrapped her in his arms, not flinching though she dug her fingers into his forearms. ''Shh, dearling, relax.''

A moan escaped her. She bit down on her lower lip, feeling as though her insides were being torn from her body.

''We'll think of something else, Moira—we'll go somewhere else, where there's nothing but happiness and pleasure and beauty. You and me together, in our minds.'' He slid one hand down to cup her belly, the warmth and strength of his touch a soothing balm to ease the cramping ache, even as his voice and words helped to calm her fears. "Where shall we go?" He nuzzled aside her hair and pressed a gentle kiss to her cheek. "Tell me where we are."

Pain washed over her, filling her and leaving little room for anything else. Did he expect her to think, to talk…?

"Moira?" He shifted her weight against him, then backed up. He carried her along with him, lowering himself into the chair and cuddling her in his lap. "Don't tell me the babe has robbed you of speech—I cannot believe 'tis possible," he teased.

The spasm eased and she shifted so she could see his face. "I need you to help me," she said, her voice scratchy from suppressing the urge to screech and moan. "Now, before the next pain comes." She lifted his hands from about her middle and wriggled forward to climb off his legs.

He clamped his hands back in place, holding her on his lap. "Help you?" he asked suspiciously. "You should be in bed."

"And so I shall be, eventually. But there's plenty to do beforehand, especially if Brigit can't help me." That thought was enough to nearly freeze the blood in her veins. Moira hoped Connor couldn't tell how frightened she was at the prospect of enduring this without Brigit's knowledge to guide her.

"You'll have to help me," she said, and took advantage of his momentary shock to wriggle away from him. Her legs felt a bit unsteady, but they'd do.

"What do you mean?" He stood as well and approached her, his intent—to grab her again—quite clear.

She tugged at the lid of her clothes coffer. "My gown and shift are wet, and I need to change them," she said, rooting among the folded garments until she found what she needed. ''You must help me change the bed, but we need new sheets—''

Connor caught her by the shoulders and drew her away from the chest. ''I've sent Padrig for Maeve, and to get someone to wake Brigit, if it's possible,'' he added darkly. ''Until then, I'll help you.'' Releasing her, he took the clothing from her hands. ''Though I'd rather someone else helped you to undress.''

Still muttering to himself, he strode past her and closed the door, then nudged her to sit in the chair. ''You need to take this off?'' He plucked at the loose folds draped over her belly, his hands visibly unsteady.

''Aye, I've tangled the laces into a knot.'' She raised her arm to show him.

He set to work loosening the strings. ''Once I untie these, you can do the rest yourself?'' he asked, his expression hopeful.

''If I cannot, I'll need your help.'' Moira glanced at his face, so close to hers as he knelt beside the chair and bent to the task. His hair, dry now, was more wavy than usual, the springy strands shining in the firelight's glow. She had no difficulty understanding why Brigit had tried to drag him into her bed....

A flush rose to Moira's cheeks, and it was all she could do to keep from burying her face in her hands. What kind of woman had she become, practically lusting over Connor while she was about to give birth to another man's child?

Instead she sought to distract herself from her shameless yearning, and Connor from his nervousness.

''I cannot believe you're hesitant to remove a woman's clothes,'' she said, forcing a tart edge into her voice. Mayhap that would catch his notice—and disguise the fact that she was nervous, frightened and mortified that he would see her like this. "Or is it that you'd rather not see me that way?" she mused. "In my present condition—"

"By the saints, Moira," he muttered. "What are you trying to do to me?" He glanced at her face, his own awash in red, and his expression grew thoughtful.

"I'm doing nothing save pointing out that you're a handsome man. I'm sure you've helped many a woman out of her—" Connor's hand on her mouth cut off the rest of her foolish babble.

"Stop," he said softly. His gaze holding hers, he slipped his hand away. "You're as skittish about all this as I am, aren't you?"

Uncertain her voice would work, since her throat seemed to have closed up, Moira nodded.

"I can understand that," he added. "You've an important new experience ahead of you, and a child waiting for you at the end of it." He picked up her hand and laced his fingers with hers. "And I'm not the person you expected to face it with. How could we have known that Brigit would indulge so freely?"

"Or that the babe would choose tonight to arrive." The pressure in Moira's belly began to build. She squeezed his hand. "Here comes another one," she whispered.

Releasing his hold on her, Connor splayed his hands over her stomach again, leaning close, murmuring sweet-sounding nonsense as they rode out the spasm together. He rested his forehead against hers when it was over, reaching up to smooth her hair away from her face.

"Thank you," she said quietly.

He sat back on his heels. "'Tis quite a battle, bringing a babe into the world. I hadn't realized—" He broke off as the sound of running feet reached them.

Someone pounded on the door, then shoved it open. "It took me a while to find Maeve, milord," Padrig gasped, rushing into the room. ''She was—'' Someone grabbed his arm, and he clapped his mouth shut.

The maid, her hair curling wildly and her clothing untidy, walked past the squire, throwing him a menacing glare. ''I wasn't where you expected me to be, is all.'' She gave her gown a tug to straighten it and dropped into a curtsy, her expression shifting from annoyance to concern. ''I beg yer pardon, milady, for the delay. The boy said yer time's come?'' She moved closer.

''Aye, Maeve,'' Moira said with a weak smile. ''I'm sorry you've been dragged from your bed—'' she ignored the derisive sound Padrig made ''—but Brigit can't help me now. Can you?''

''I'll do whatever you want, milady. But I've not brought a child into the world by myself. We might need someone else besides you and me.''

''Should I go for another servant, milady?'' Padrig asked. He looked eager to be away.

Connor, who had remained kneeling by Moira's chair, stood up. ''For now, I want you to find someone to help you rouse Brigit and sober her up. I'll stay here.''

Moira caught Connor's hand in hers and tugged him down. ''You need not do this! I know 'tis not comfortable for you—''

''It seemed you found some comfort when I held you,'' he whispered. ''If you're not uncomfortable having me stay?''

''I don't mind now,'' she told him. ''If you're willing, I'd be pleased to have you here. Though later on, I might tell you to go.'' She had no notion how long she could endure—how long she would have to endure—before the babe arrived.

Nor did she know if she had the strength to make it

through everything yet to come without becoming a screaming madwoman.

"Then I'll stay as long as you wish me to," he said. He straightened. "Padrig, go do as I told you. Maeve, I'll leave for a moment so you can help your mistress." He gave Moira's hand a squeeze. "I'll be back as quickly as I can. If you need me before then, just send Maeve after me. I'll go to see if I can wake Brigit now." He grabbed the water pitcher from the hearth and left, Padrig trailing along behind him.

Connor hastened from Moira's chamber to his own, grabbed a shirt from his clothes chest and pulled it over his head as he rushed back down the stairs. Padrig, with a branch of candles in one hand, the pitcher of water in the other, waited for him outside the room where Brigit still lay snoring. Motioning for the squire to come with him, Connor took the water and stomped into the chamber.

When Padrig caught a glimpse of Brigit still snoring away in her nest of bed curtains, he set the candle stand down with a thump and edged toward the door again. "I'll go for more help."

Connor grabbed him by the back of his tunic and spun him around. "Lady Moira's need is great, lad. I believe we can take care of this ourselves. If we can't, *then* you can get a pair of men-at-arms up here to drag her out and toss her in a puddle." He took up the pitcher and used his foot to nudge Brigit off the makeshift pallet. "Preferably a muddy one."

"Aye, milord."

"'Tis time to get up, my lovely," Connor shouted, laughing in spite of himself. "Come, Brigit, Moira needs you now." Brigit's snores ceased and she shifted on the floor, but she merely caught hold of the bedpost and curled up around it, mumbling a variety of Gaelic curses.

''What did she say?'' Padrig asked, moving closer.

''You don't want to know.'' Connor bent and shook her by the shoulders, to no avail. ''You had your chance,'' he muttered, and tossed the contents of the pitcher in the old woman's face.

As the maid sat up, sputtering and swearing, thundering footsteps sounded from the stairs. Connor spun about as Sir Ivor bolted into the room. By the saints, now what?

''Come quickly, milord,'' d'Athée gasped. ''We caught Domnal O'Neill trying to break into Kieran MacCarthy's cell.''

Chapter Twenty-Two

Moira watched Connor leave with mixed emotions. She could feel the strength drain out of her with every step he took away from her. 'Twas unfair of her to expect him to stay—especially when the child was not his own.

Nay, she'd see how she did on her own while he was gone. If it seemed she could get by with only Maeve to help her, she would do so.

Maeve set to work, adding yet more peat to the fire and opening the bed curtains wide to let the heat from the fire warm the bed. "Now then, milady, what do ye need done first?" She gathered Moira's wet gown from the floor, then nodded. "Lord Connor said ye needed help with somethin'. Yer gown's wet—did yer water break?"

Her legs feeling surprisingly boneless, Moira pulled herself to her feet. She'd better dig deep within herself for a reserve of strength, else she'd be a spineless mass upon the bed by the time she was through. "Aye, it did—while I was in the bed, of course. I managed to take off my gown, but there's a knot in the lacing of my underdress—"

Maeve picked up Moira's knife from the table where Connor had placed it and sliced through the string. "There," she said with a decisive nod. "What does a bit o' string matter when there's more important things to think of?''

Moira dressed in a dry shift with Maeve's help, and had just settled into the chair to wait while the maid changed the bed when a roar of noise sounded from the corridor.

She half rose from her seat. Maeve rushed to her side and urged her to sit again.

''Let me go see what's wrong, milady,'' the maid stated. ''I have to go find some dry bedding, so I'll see what's wrong, then fetch some sheets. If that's all right?''

''Aye,'' Moira said. ''But don't be gone too long.''

The maid bobbed a curtsy and slipped out into the corridor.

The door had scarcely closed behind her when the next pain struck. Moira rose from the chair and crumpled to the floor.

She curled into a ball and bit back a scream at the severity of this pain. It seemed she'd have a chance to test her newfound resolve already—and completely alone.

Connor muttered a curse that made Brigit's words seem mild in comparison, and dragged his hand through his hair. ''Where are they?'' he demanded of Sir Ivor.

''Will's bringing O'Neill to the hall, milord.''

His mind awhirl, Connor quickly gauged the situation and found no easy way to approach it. Everything must happen at once, so it seemed.

He couldn't abandon Moira now, not after he'd promised her he'd stay with her. ''Double the guards on MacCarthy, and in the undercroft, and tell Will to bring Domnal here, to this room.''

Sir Ivor gaped at him. ''What?''

''Lady Moira's babe is about to arrive, and I cannot leave her.'' He glanced down at Brigit, who had rolled over, sputtering and cursing. Using the bedpost as a crutch, she pulled herself up to sit leaning against it, her head lolling to the side. "As you can see, her maid is in no condition to help.

"Padrig, go to the gatehouse and tell Cedric to keep a close watch." The squire nodded and left at once. "I hope O'Neill hasn't been misleading us to help his brothers and the MacCarthys," he said to d'Athée.

Sir Ivor shrugged. "I'll bring them at once, milord." He turned and followed Padrig down the stairs.

Connor shifted his attention to the maid, hoping to resolve this problem before the next arrived on its heels. "It's about time you woke up, you old besom," he growled.

Brigit opened her eyes, moaning loudly. Squeezing them shut, she turned her face toward the post and pressed her forehead against the carved word. "Move the candles away, there's a good lad," she mumbled, waving one hand behind her as though 'twould make the light disappear.

"Milord?" Maeve stood in the doorway.

"What's wrong?" Connor asked wearily.

"My lady is fine, sir—as fine as she can be right now, at any rate. I came to see what the ruckus is out here, milord."

"Another problem, 'tis all," he said. "Naught for you to concern yourself with. Right now, 'tis more important that we get Brigit sober so she can help your mistress."

"Aye, milord." Maeve entered the room and stared at the other maid. "What should we do?"

"Damned if I know," he admitted. He picked up the stand of candles and held it so the light shone on Brigit's face. "Come, open your eyes, Brigit. You've no more time to lounge about on the floor. Moira needs you."

"Moira?" She could scarce hold herself steady, but she raised her head and opened one eye to stare at him.

He hunkered down beside her. "The babe is coming,"

he told her, speaking slowly and clearly. ''We've brought Maeve—''

''Maeve?'' Brigit's other eye popped open and she sat up straight. ''A good lass, she is, but she knows nothin' about birthin' a babe.'' She sounded less muddled with every word.

''Leastways I know better 'n to drink myself blind,'' Maeve muttered.

Brigit stared up at her, a frown crossing her still-slack face. ''Why aren't you with my lady?'' she demanded. Moaning, she managed to get her legs under her. Connor caught her about the middle and helped her to her feet.

''Sweet Mary save me, but that ale must o' been potent,'' she cried. Still clinging to his arm, she turned to meet his gaze. Her faded eyes held guilt, but were more alert than he'd expected.

''Can you walk?'' he asked. It felt as though his support alone kept her on her feet.

''If I can't, you'll carry me to her, milord?''

He nodded.

''Padrig? Did I see the boy here?'' She scanned the room.

''He left,'' Connor said, surprised she'd been aware of the squire's presence.

''Maeve, then—go down and rouse the cook, tell him I need his potion to settle my stomach and put my head back together. He'll know,'' she added, waving her hand weakly. ''Go on.''

At Connor's nod of permission, Maeve hurried from the room.

If anyone in the keep still slept after all the racket they'd been making, it had to be a miracle, he thought wryly.

Brigit slumped against him as soon as the maid left.

"Beg pardon, milord. Don't think my legs'll work quite yet."

He'd suspected as much. He swung the old woman into his arms and shouldered the door wide to carry her through.

"My luck always was bad," she muttered. "Strong young buck to carry me, and I'm too sick to enjoy it."

But not too ill to give him a poke in the arm—fortunately not the injured one. All he needed now was to drop the old besom on her head!

Still, she'd made him laugh, even as he felt his face heat. "I heard you thought I was too thin," he teased.

She clutched his upper arm. "Some parts o' you aren't," she said with a chuckle that turned to a cough. "Put me down here," she ordered. "Don't want my lady to see me like this."

He set her on her feet outside the door, just as a loud shriek sounded from Moira's chamber.

He left the maid standing in the corridor and rushed into the room. Moira sat curled up in the chair, her arms wrapped about her belly, her eyes clamped shut and her lower lip caught between her teeth.

"By the Virgin, we shouldn't have left you alone." He dropped down beside her. "Moira, hush," he said as he tried to loosen her arms. "Remember what we did before? Come, think of someplace else," he said, gently helping her sit up. As soon as she did, he caught her in his arms and sat down atop the chest, laying her across his lap.

"My lady," Brigit said. Connor glanced over Moira's head and saw the old woman had made it inside the room. She closed the door and made her way to them, clinging to anything she could hold on to as she went.

Connor felt the instant the spasm holding Moira in its grip eased, for her entire body relaxed against his. "Brigit?" she called, raising her head.

The maid stood before them, eyes downcast. "I'm sorry, milady. I ne'er should have touched the ale, not with you so near your time."

Moira swung her legs around, slipped off Connor's lap and sat beside him on the chest. "There's naught to forgive, for I'm fine," she said, her smile as weak as her voice.

That Brigit noticed, he didn't doubt. She glanced around the room, a frown adding more wrinkles to her face. "I hope Maeve hurries," she mumbled, looking near the end of her endurance as well.

"She went to fetch clean bedding," Moira told them. "She'll be back soon, I'm sure." She gestured toward her clothing. "You see, she helped me already."

Since she wasn't wearing the same gown she'd had on before Connor left, it appeared Maeve had been of some use, after all.

Brigit, recovering swiftly from the ale, it seemed, went out the door and began shouting down the stairs.

Connor glanced at Moira, still seated next to him. "Now that Brigit is here, do you want me to stay away?"

"I should tell you to go," Moira said quietly. "But the truth is, I'd rather you did not." She looked away. "Though I don't understand why you want to be here."

He reached over and caught her chin in his hand. "I have to leave for a little while, but I'll come back and stay if you want me to—because I wish to. I know how hard it can be to face pain, to bear it, alone."

She met his gaze, held it, seemed to weigh his words before coming to a decision. "Then I thank you for your generosity, Connor. But know that you may leave whenever you wish."

He nodded. "Whenever *you* want me to go, I will." He stood and paced to the window, where he could see the palest streaks of light showing through the slats. A new day—a day when he must decide what to do next, to hopefully bring an end to this feud with the MacCarthys.

With the men who wanted Moira's child.

"My lady," he said formally. He should turn to face her, but he didn't dare, lest he lose his nerve.

"Connor, what is it?"

"My lady, I asked you a question before, and you refused me." He forced himself to abandon the window, to face her. "My offer stands, Moira, and I beg you to accept it—for the child's sake, if not for your own."

"Connor, no..." She held her hand out as though to ward off the words.

"Just listen," he said, rejoining her on the chest. "If we wed before the babe is born, I can claim it as my child."

"But anyone who knows you knows you've not been here till recently. Who would believe it?"

"I challenge anyone to tell *me* differently," he said, his voice as cold as ice.

"If 'tis a son, you cannot want another man's child to be your heir!"

"I am a second son, Moira. It doesn't matter to me, at any rate." He took her hand. "If you will marry me, I'll be proud to call your child my own," he said urgently. "Son or daughter, it matters not. 'Twill be *our* child."

"You cannot mean it, Connor." She began to rub at her belly, and he quickly gathered her into his arms again.

Brigit entered the room then, nodding her approval when she saw the way he held Moira. "'Tis a brave man, milady, who will do for you what Lord Connor is doing right now. If you're wise, you'll not let him get away," she added.

Moira glared at the maid and focused her gaze on Connor's face. "Did you tell her to say that?" she muttered, her eyes fierce.

He rubbed her belly, amazed at how hard it had become,

and realized for the first time just how little she wore—and how intimate their positions were. Though there was nothing sexual about this, there was a closeness he'd never felt with anyone before.

They rode out the pain together, Moira pressing her face against his throat. 'Twas as though they were connected somehow, for he knew before she sat up that the spasm had eased.

"How long does this go on?" he asked Brigit, who appeared to be feeling better, if the fact that she was humming a merry tune as she bustled about the room was any indication. They hadn't slept, but it felt as though hours had passed since Moira had told him her labor had begun.

It seemed that she awaited the old woman's answer as eagerly as he. Brigit ambled over to them, her wrinkled face creased in a wide grin. "Getting impatient already, are ye?" Her laugh sounded dry as old bones splintering. "You've scarce begun, milady." Hands on her hips, she added, "I don't expect that babe to make its appearance till after midday, at least." She snorted. "And judging by the time Maeve's been gone, 'twill be nigh that long before I get you settled in that bed."

She stomped to the door and yanked it open, calling out for Maeve at the top of her lungs.

"She must be feeling better," Moira said dryly.

She made to ease away from him, but Connor kept his arms looped loosely around her and refused let her go. "It appears we've much work ahead of us."

She turned to look at him, her cross expression no surprise. "What do you mean, us?"

He leaned down to whisper, "I told you I would stay with you, and I will." A thought occurred to him then, a snippet at the edge of his memory. "My brother stayed with his wife when their daughter was born," he told her. "In fact, if I remember correctly, he said that Gillian withstood the labor better once he was there with her.''

Moira's eyes held disbelief. ''Are you certain he wasn't bragging about something he had no hand in?''

''Nay, 'tis true—would you call Rannulf a braggart? Gillian's labor was—'' Perhaps he'd best not describe the long, hellish labor his sister by marriage had endured.

''Was what?'' Moira snapped. ''Easy? Difficult? You cannot leave a statement such as that unfinished.''

Brigit and Maeve entered the room then, and Connor felt he'd been given a welcome reprieve. Moira's usually sweet nature had apparently disappeared, leaving her short-tempered and testy.

The women swiftly stripped the bed, turned the mattress and made it up again. ''Come along, then, mistress—climb in,'' Brigit directed. '''Tis time I stop acting the maid and start being the midwife.''

Connor helped Moira up and led her to the bed.

Brigit motioned him away. ''You'll need to leave for a bit, milord, while I see how things are comin' along. We'll call for you once 'tis safe to return.''

That would work out well for him, since he'd plans aplenty to set in motion before the child finally arrived. ''Will you be able to manage awhile without me? Will should be back anytime—''

Moira caught him by the arm. ''Will? Back from where?'' She leaned against him, tightening the invisible bonds binding him to her. ''Connor?''

He sighed. She'd not be put off with lies, but how much to tell her? He didn't want her worrying, not now. And he had to leave her, to go discover for himself what was happening. '''Tis just that something has occurred that needs my attention.''

''Go, then—do what you must.'' She tightened her clasp

on his arm and surprised him by tugging him closer and pressing a soft kiss on his cheek. "We'll manage fine," she said, casting a stern glance at the maids. "Go," she urged. "You'll not be easy until you do."

She was right. He stepped back, aware of a surprising reluctance to break contact with her, despite his need to discover what was going on. "I'll be back as soon as I'm able," he assured her. He took her hand and brought it to his lips. "While I'm away, I want you to reconsider my offer to you." Her gaze rose to meet his, filled with a warmth he hoped meant his feelings for her were returned. Settling his hand on the mound of her belly, he added, "You haven't much longer to decide."

She placed her hand atop his. "I know," she murmured. She released him and gave him a smile. "Be careful, Connor—and hurry back."

He couldn't have timed his departure better, for he left Moira's chamber just as Will and the others came up the stairs. Connor hastened into the other room, kicking aside Brigit's pallet and snatching the empty pitcher off the floor, and set about lighting the candles scattered about the spacious room.

Will and Sir Ivor came in, followed by two guards leading Domnal O'Neill. The lad, hands tied behind his back, looked weary but defiant. He stood straight under Connor's measuring stare, but 'twas clear that was naught but bravado. Domnal looked scared, more than anything—as well he should. The position he'd put himself in appeared suspicious, to say the least.

Add to that the level of tension the occupants of Gerald's Keep had lived under for months, and 'twas a miracle the lad hadn't suffered worse than the bruise he sported high on his cheek.

Yet Connor didn't see treachery when he looked at Moira's brother, he saw a young man overwhelmed by the situation he found himself in.

Connor bit back a sigh. 'Twas a state he recognized—and understood—too well.

He crossed his arms and leaned back against the bedpost. "Shut the door," he ordered. Will, who had stationed himself beside the doorway, swung the heavy panel closed with a resounding thud. "Now, then, O'Neill, I understand you were discovered lurking outside Kieran MacCarthy's cell. What were you doing there?"

Sir Ivor stepped forward. "He was—"

Connor held up a hand and cut him off. "I asked O'Neill, not you." Sir Ivor only shrugged, his mild reaction a surprise, and moved back to take up a position on the other side of the door from Will. "Domnal?" Connor prompted.

Domnal took a deep breath, as though preparing to spew out a burst of defiance, then shook his head and sighed. "When I heard you'd captured Kieran, I thought to see if I could talk him into coming round to our side, milord."

"Indeed?" An unexpected response, but promising.

The lad nodded. "We've talked before about how stupid his cousins' plans were. As if we could wrest a fortress such as this from the Normans and keep possession of it," he scoffed. "His kin and my brothers are well-matched, milord, in their arrogance and foolish pride. 'Twas great sport at first, I admit, to plot and scheme about how we'd take the castle and lord it over everyone." He shuffled his feet, glancing away for a moment. When he met Connor's gaze again, his eyes were dark and filled with pain. "But I never wanted Moira to get hurt—nor her child, either. They spoke of her as though she were nothing but a pawn in their hands to use however they would, not our blood." He blinked away tears. "When Hugh spoke of taking her to his bed as soon as her babe was born, I knew none of them cared what happened to her at all. They only wanted to use her. She's my sister, milord, her babe my kin as well! I couldn't allow them to prevail."

Connor unfolded his arms and pushed away from the bed, moving to stand directly in front of Domnal. "And you believe Kieran agrees with you?" he asked, watching the lad closely.

"Aye, milord, I do."

"Do Hugh and Aidan know how he feels?" Connor fought down a rising sense of excitement, of anticipation, as a scheme began to take shape in his mind. But he didn't dare hope—not yet.

Domnal shook his head and looked at him as though he were daft. "They never saw us together, milord, I'm sure of it."

"How can you know?" Will scoffed.

"They'd not have brought him here with them if they doubted him. Hugh's justice is swift and final—Kieran would be dead if they had any suspicion that he wasn't behind them completely."

"Do you think that Kieran knows enough about Hugh's plans for the information to be useful?" Connor asked.

Domnal nodded eagerly. "Aye, milord. Hugh makes little secret of his plots, not within the circle of his family and mine."

"Would he be willing to share what he knows with us, do you think?"

"I cannot speak for him, but I believe he might—especially if you don't harm him." Domnal shrugged. "If you tell him you'll protect him from Hugh's wrath, he'll likely tell you anything. He's lived with his cousins most of his life, and they haven't treated him well."

His thoughts racing, Connor nodded. "We'll question

him now.'' Drawing his knife, he turned Domnal and sliced through the rope binding his wrists. ''All of you, come with me.''

After Connor left, the maids busied themselves with their preparations for the child's arrival, leaving Moira with nothing to do but think in the long intervals between contractions. While curiosity about why Connor had had to leave nagged at her mind, his parting words—the generosity of his offer—haunted her. He'd left her with much to consider.

And scant time to do so, she realized as another pain swept through her.

Though it might seem as though 'twould take forever before the babe finally made its appearance, in truth she knew she'd hold her child in her arms before the day was through.

Certainty filled her. The best gift she could give her child would be a father who would protect the babe, who would honor his responsibilities—and honor her.

That Connor was such a man she had no doubt.

What of his own past? she wondered yet again. Her mind had brimmed with conjecture ever since she'd realized the source of Connor's scars. He'd made veiled comments about his parents and his family before, though she hadn't considered precisely what he meant. Should she wed him if he wouldn't tell her about it, or was it unimportant, save as a tale to show her how he'd become the man she knew?

Both he and his brother seemed bold warriors, exceptionally considerate—decent, caring men. Connor FitzClifford had treated her better than anyone ever had in her life! She'd no qualms over entrusting her child's safety—or her own—to him.

As always, it was his own security that concerned her.

But he was a man full grown, a man who presumably knew what he wanted. She'd been honest with him. More honest than ever before. He knew her situation, her past, yet he was still willing to marry her.

How could she deny what she knew was right?

Aye, she wanted him, with a desire that should have shamed her, she thought with a wry laugh. She also liked him—his character, his humor, his strength. She couldn't have found a man more to her taste if she'd conjured him up with a witch's spell.

Another pain filled her body. Following Connor's advice, she imagined herself elsewhere, in a place she wanted to be. With a smile on her lips despite her discomfort, she closed her eyes and envisioned herself in Connor's arms.

Chapter Twenty-Three

A smile on his face, Connor passed through the bailey in the predawn mist and considered everything he'd learned from his talk with Kieran MacCarthy and Domnal. With Will and Sir Ivor present, he'd questioned the two Irishmen at length, assuring himself that they spoke the truth—both about Hugh MacCarthy's plans and their own opinions about those schemes.

It had been an interesting discussion in many ways, for in the course of the conversation he'd also discovered the cause of d'Athée's change in attitude toward Moira.

Sir Ivor had drawn him aside before he could leave the barracks. "I wish to explain to you, milord, and to apologize for my manner toward you—and Lady Moira—when you first arrived."

Despite his impatience to return to Moira, Connor nodded and followed d'Athée out into the bailey. "Be brief," he cautioned, "for I've a vow to keep."

Sir Ivor drew in a deep breath, visibly gathering himself. "'Twas foolishness on my part, milord. I admit it freely. Lord Brien was mentor and friend to me, and I resented Lady Moira...." He met Connor's gaze and held it. "I feared if she gave her husband the son he desired, he'd have no further use for me. He was not my father by blood, milord, but in every other way that matters.'' He glanced away. ''Once I got in the habit of insulting her, I could not stop. But observing you and Will has shown me another way, milord. I thank you for it.''

''I'm glad to hear that you've changed your mind, Sir Ivor. But you're apologizing to the wrong person.'' Connor gave a weary sigh and waited. As he'd hoped, d'Athée glanced at him again. ''My anger was on Lady Moira's behalf, not my own,'' Connor said firmly. ''There's no reason to treat anyone as you did her. I hope that once her child is born, you will tell her what you've told me, for I know 'twill ease her mind.''

Sir Ivor bowed. ''Aye, milord. Thank you.''

Connor cast a look at the brightening sky, took him by the arm and urged him toward the barracks. ''A new day is about to dawn, and we're not finished with the last one yet,'' he said wryly. ''You've work still before you, and so do I. We'd best get to it.''

His heart as light as his stride, Connor hurried back to the keep. He'd letters to pen and yet more orders to give before he could return to Moira's side; he hoped the babe hadn't arrived in his absence.

But it couldn't be helped. So much had happened in so short a time to perhaps—nay, he'd not consider failure—to bring this entire situation to a swift end. He had to set everything into motion at once. Only then could he move on to the next step in his rapidly forming plan.

Giving scant attention to the servants stirring in the hall, he raced up the stairs to his chamber and dug through his coffer of clothing to find his writing materials. He was no scribe, he feared, nor did his mind always work in a clear and logical fashion. But 'twas essential that these missives present his stance plainly, in a straightforward manner without equivocation. The futures of everyone at Gerald's Keep—especially Moira's and the babe's—depended upon it.

Padrig rushed into the chamber as Connor sprinkled sand over the last of the letters and shook it to make certain the ink was dry. "Well met," he told the gasping squire. "Are the couriers ready?"

Padrig nodded. "As you ordered, milord."

"Good. Get these to the men and tell them to be on their way." He folded the last parchment and, taking a candle from the stand on the table, poured a trail of wax along the seam. "Here, lad." He thrust the letters toward Padrig. "See that you return at once. I may have need of you again soon."

He followed him out of the room, grinning at the clatter of the lad's boots against the stone steps. If anyone had slept this past night, 'twould be a miracle.

Connor paused outside Moira's door and stared at his hands. They were steady, praise God, though none too clean. He'd spattered his fingers with ink in his haste to get the letters finished.

No matter. At least he hadn't blood on his hands, as did the other man who wanted to make Moira his bride.

Next Connor went in search of the priest, Father Thomas. The reclusive cleric seldom ventured beyond the bounds of his chapel and home in a quiet corner of the bailey, generally preferring to focus his attention on the study of a treatise of some sort.

The sun had scarcely cleared the horizon, and within the castle walls, the dusky light of morning lent a mystical softness to everything it touched.

Connor found Father Thomas in the candlelit chapel, preparing for Mass. "May I speak with you a moment, Father?'' he called as he walked across the open floor of the empty church.

The priest smiled and hurried toward him. ''Of course, milord, of course.'' He motioned Connor toward a narrow bench set along the back wall. ''Please, sit.''

Connor shook his head. ''I haven't much time to spare, Father. But please, you go ahead. Sit down.''

Once the priest had settled onto the bench, gazing up at him expectantly, Connor hardly knew where to start. Staring at the crucifix over the altar, he tried to marshal his thoughts. He'd never imagined taking this step until he'd met Moira, learned of her particular circumstances. The idea was so new to him, it made him uncomfortable.

But Father Thomas knew Moira, knew most of what had happened before Connor's arrival here. Perhaps that would make this conversation easier.

There was only one way to find out. That, and the knowledge that the longer he delayed, the longer he'd be away from Moira when she needed him, gave Connor the strength to begin.

Taking a deep breath, he forced his gaze back to Father Thomas, who waited with a patient smile on his round face.

''There's no hurry,'' the priest said. ''Take your time.''

''But there is, Father. Moira is about to give birth—her labor has already begun.''

''So soon?'' He looked thoughtful. ''Perhaps 'twill turn out to be Lord Brien's child, after all. Do you think the MacCarthys will leave her alone?''

''Nay, Father, they will not. Even if the child is the image of Lord Brien, the MacCarthys will never accept the fact, for 'twould destroy their plans to gain Gerald's Keep.''

''Indeed, milord, I fear you've the truth of it.'' He frowned. ''I hadn't wanted to accept that their greed might outweigh their compassion—or their honesty,'' he added sadly. He jumped up from the bench. ''Did you come for me to attend her or the babe? Nay, you'd have told me at once....''

''Moira was well when I left her a short time ago,'' Connor reassured him. ''Be at ease, Father.'' Once the priest sat down again, he raised the subject he'd come here to discuss. ''I've asked Lady Moira to marry me, Father—several times, the last just before I left the keep. She has refused me, despite the fact that I've sworn to her that I honor her, that I will raise her child as my own—''

Father Thomas held up a hand to silence him. ''Slowly, my son. Perhaps you should wait until some time has passed after the child is born. Perhaps then Lady Moira will be better able to see the value of your very generous offer. You *do* realize that sometimes women in her condition develop strange ideas?''

''She must see that this is the best course. If we wed now, the child will be legitimate—''

''Technically, yes, that could be considered true. However, while 'tis common knowledge that the child's parentage is in question, 'tis also obvious that you could not possibly be the father of the babe.''

''If I say the child is mine, Father, who other than the MacCarthys will say otherwise?''

Why did no one believe him? He'd be a good and true father to the child—and a true husband to Moira, if she'd let him.

''Father Thomas, I didn't come here to discuss this with you. I've already set plans in motion that will help to protect them, to resolve the problem with the MacCarthys for good. I came to ask you to go back with me, to convince Moira that marrying me would be in her best interests—

and her child's.'' He paced the width of the small chapel, halting in front of the priest. ''Will you do that, Father?''

The cleric rose to his feet, his eyes fixed upon the statue of the Blessed Virgin nearby. Connor followed his gaze, studied the way the Holy Mother cradled her child, gazing down upon Him with love and devotion. In just that way would Connor expect Moira to look at her babe....

He knew she would.

And by protecting them both, he would make certain that she could do so.

He said a prayer of thanks to the Virgin for making him see that his decision was right and sound. Impatient to return, he halted near Father Thomas while the priest bent his head in prayer.

Finally he crossed himself and turned to Connor. ''I believe you've the right of it, milord. 'Tis certain that you're well able to protect her, and you're more of an age with her, so perhaps the two of you will...'' He shook his head. ''No need to travel down that road again,'' he muttered. ''I will plead your case, milord, should it prove necessary.'' He headed for the altar. ''And I'm willing to wed you now, before the child is born, if you'll permit me a moment to collect what I'll need.'' He disappeared behind the altar for a moment, then reappeared carrying a polished wooden case.

''You might want to say another prayer before we leave, Father.'' Connor genuflected and crossed himself. ''I suspect I'll need all the help I can get.''

It seemed to Moira, in those brief moments when she could think clearly, that climbing into her bed had somehow caused her labor to speed up.

And now that Connor wasn't here, she had to face the pain and fear alone. She'd submitted to allowing Brigit to examine her—an embarrassment, though nothing compared to what came later, she knew. Brigit told her 'twould be a long while before the babe finally arrived, and to cease her whining, to conserve her strength for when she'd truly need it....

For later, when the spasms were worse.

Worse later? 'Twas all she could manage to face *now.*

The moment Brigit stepped away from the bed, Moira let the hated tears drip down her cheeks. Children were born every day—women did this all the time, did they not? Why, then, did she find it so difficult?

She dashed the moisture from her cheeks with the back of her hand, then used the edge of the sheet to blot her cheeks dry. By the Virgin, she wanted this babe! She'd suffered for it already—what did the pain matter, when she'd be able to hold her child in her arms at the end of it?

Much heartened, she obeyed Brigit's order and settled back against the pillows to rest until the next spasm came. Weariness vied with anticipation, but with the soft bolsters nestling her in their warmth, and the hypnotic dance of flames in the fireplace visible to her through the open curtains at the foot of the bed, Moira's thoughts drifted even as her eyelids slipped closed.

She dozed briefly, between contractions. Time had no meaning—indeed, it seemed she had been awake for days—though she heard the sounds of the keep coming to life. They were more subdued than usual, perhaps because not everyone had recovered from the past night's battle and the drinking that had followed. Whatever the reason, she wished for more noise, so that her cries or screams, should she prove as cowardly as she feared, might be disguised by the sounds of day-to-day life.

She started awake when another spasm, more intense

than the others, rolled through her body and settled, hot and painful, low in her belly. Catching hold of the leather straps Brigit had tied to the headboard, Moira pulled herself up and concentrated on willing herself somewhere else in her mind, as Connor had taught her, until the worst of it eased.

But there'd be no wishing this one away, that much became clear to her at once. Muttering curses she hadn't realized she knew, she gritted her teeth and tried to breathe as Brigit had suggested.

"I hate this!" she shrieked, seizing the straps so hard her nails bit into them. "Brigit, I need you right now!" she screamed as loudly as she could, since the maid had left the chamber.

Silence met her plea.

As soon as the pain began to fade, Moira crawled to the edge of the mattress and, clutching the bedpost for support, dragged herself to her feet. Her shift had twisted around her waist, leaving her legs exposed to midthigh, and the sheet had wrapped about one ankle, tethering her in place and throwing her off balance. "Everyone promises to stay, to help me, but where are they when I need them?" she grumbled. "Probably off swilling ale and telling lies." Since she couldn't seem to loosen the sheet from around her ankle, she jerked it free of the mattress and sent herself flying.

She landed hard on her backside on the floor. "By the Virgin, when I get my hands on Connor FitzClifford," she screeched, "I'll—"

Strong arms grabbed her from behind, and a hand clamped over her mouth to stifle her in midscream. "You'll do what?" Connor asked, his voice amused.

Moira caught him by the wrist and jerked his hand away. "Where have you been?" she gasped.

His arms about her waist, he helped her to her feet and turned her to face him.

And Father Thomas.

A wave of shame washed over her, making her tremble and flush.

"I've brought the priest," Connor said, his tone wry. "To convince you to be my bride."

Face still flaming, Moira tugged the end of the sheet off the bed and dragged the material up in front of her. She caught hold of Connor's shirt with her other hand and pulled him closer, leaning toward him. "Could we discuss this alone?" she whispered.

Connor glanced at her, then back at Father Thomas—whose face looked nigh as red as hers felt—and nodded. He gently detached her hand from his shirt. "Will you excuse us, Father?" he asked, going to the door and opening it.

"Of course. I'll wait in the corridor, milord," the priest said, and left, closing the door quietly.

Connor scooped her up and laid her in the bed. "What are you doing wandering around?" he scolded. She drew the sheet, still clutched tightly in her hand, up to her chin and settled back against the bolsters. He scanned the chamber and frowned. "Where is Brigit?"

"I don't know," Moira muttered. "I fell asleep, and when I woke, everyone had left." To her shame, she felt like pouting. The sensation of pain building within her wiped that thought from her mind in no time, replacing it with panic. She grabbed Connor by the arm and tugged until he climbed up onto the bed with her. "It's happening again," she whimpered. "And the last one has scarce faded away."

He cuddled her against him, rubbing her belly and whispering to her until the pain began to fade. Then he tried to move away from her, but she held him fast.

"I need to call for Brigit," he told her, bending to press a kiss on her brow.

"Aye, we need her," she agreed. She met his gaze, looked deep into the warm brown depths and saw nothing but good in him. "But you'd better bring Father Thomas back as well. I don't believe we have much time to wed before the babe arrives."

Connor stared at Moira's face, her eyes, and gave a sigh of relief. "You *will* marry me."

She nodded. "You were right—about so many things." He tried once again to slip off the bed, but again she held him back. "I want you to know, Connor, that..." She lowered her gaze for a moment. When she glanced at up at him again, her eyes held so much emotion he could not mistake it. "I am marrying you because I want to be wed to you—not because of the babe, or Hugh, or anything else. Only for you, Connor."

His heart thundering in his chest, Connor held her close, savoring her words, her nearness—so much more than he'd ever hoped to have in his life. But he couldn't accept the truth of her words until she knew the truth about him.

He raised his head and turned her face toward him. "I should tell you about—"

She covered his mouth with her hand. "You need not tell me anything unless you wish to, but you might as well wait till later. Whatever you have to say—save that you don't want me—doesn't matter right now. Tell me later, once we're wed, once the babe is born—when we've more time to talk." She slid her hand up, running her fingers over his stubble-covered cheek. "I wish to marry *you,* Connor FitzClifford—the man I've come to know. Our lives begin now. The past doesn't exist unless we want it to. Do you still wish to marry me?"

He laughed. "You know I do."

She nudged him toward the side of the bed. "Then what are you waiting for?" She clutched at her belly. "You'd better bring Father Thomas back at once."

Chapter Twenty-Four

Father Thomas no sooner declared Moira and Connor man and wife than Brigit banished him—along with Domnal, Sir Ivor and Sir Will, the witnesses—to the hall. "Go on, swill some ale and stay out of the way," she directed. "You'll need to drink enough for his lordship, since he's decided to stay with my lady."

Moira accepted their hastily offered good wishes and tried not to cry out until the door closed behind them. 'Twas a near thing. As soon as they were gone, however, Connor clambered onto the mattress and leaned back against the headboard, gathering her into his arms. He held her through the endless pain, his cheek nestled against hers, and didn't flinch as she dug her fingers into the brawny strength of his forearms. Panting, she slumped back once the spasm eased. "Thank you, Husband," she whispered, savoring the word.

"Thank *you,* milady, for making me the happiest of men." He laced his fingers with hers and brought her hand to his lips. "Scarce a husband, and already a father," he said with a laugh, cradling his hand over her belly. "You're giving me so much, Moira. I swear I'll protect you and our child—our children, for I doubt this will be our only one,'' he added, chuckling again. ''Always.''

She held his words in her heart as the pains came one atop the other, till she wondered how she'd bear them. But Connor held her through each one, sharing his strength, his humor, as she pushed their babe into the world.

''You have a daughter, milady, milord,'' Brigit cried as she eased the child onto a blanket. After wiping the babe clean, she placed her in Moira's outstretched arms. ''She's a beauty, milady!''

Her dark blue eyes staring, unfocused, at them, their daughter began to howl, her tiny fingers clenched into fists. They looked her over, marveling at her fingers and toes, at the mass of dark curls clustered on her head.

Tears welled in Moira's eyes and spilled down her cheeks. Despite all the times she'd imagined this moment, used it to sustain her through the long, difficult months, she hadn't realized how deeply she would feel its intensity—nor that Connor would be there to share it with her.

''So quiet—just like her mother,'' Connor teased as the babe continued to wail. He leaned over Moira's shoulder and traced his finger across one soft pink cheek. ''I can see I'll be busy once she's grown, chasing away an army of suitors. What will you name her?'' he asked, tucking the blanket up around the babe's shoulders.

''I thought to call her Brenna. 'Twas my mother's name,'' Moira added. ''What do you think?''

''I think that Lady Brenna FitzClifford is a fine name,'' he said. He shifted, until he met her gaze. His dark eyes suspiciously damp, he took her mouth in a heartbreakingly tender kiss. ''Our daughter is lovely. You've done well, milady,'' he murmured after he broke away.

Once she caught her breath, she stroked her hand through

Connor's disordered hair and gazed down at their child. "Aye, milord—that we have."

The next two days flew by in a daze for Moira, as she sought to regain her strength, care for Brenna and convince her stubborn husband that she should be included in whatever plans he had to deal with Hugh MacCarthy and her brother Aidan.

It took her a solid day's coaxing before Connor would tell her what he had in mind—and even then, she'd had to resort to wheedling information out of Sir Will. When the knight discovered she'd misled him—or tricked him, as he would have it—about her knowledge of Connor's scheme, he'd become so angry he refused to tell her anything else at all.

It amazed her that she could feel such love for Connor—for such was the depth of her feelings for him, it could not be anything else but love—and wish to throttle him at the same time. How could one man be so devastatingly tender one moment and so pigheaded the next?

But she'd not endured the long months between Lord Brien's death and Connor's arrival without learning something about stubbornness herself. Her husband would learn soon enough that he could not ignore his wife's will, she vowed.

When he did finally agree, she continued to rant for a bit before his words sank into her brain. A tide of heat rose to her cheeks when she realized what she'd done; if not for the fact that Connor sat next to her on the bed, trapping her in place, she'd have tried to escape him and his sharp gaze.

As well as his knowing grin. "Go on," he coaxed. "I'd like to hear what other arguments you planned to use to convince me." He reached out and toyed with the end of her braid. "Such foreknowledge might be the only way I'll have a chance to marshal my own arguments the next time." Giving the ribbon tied round her braid a tug and sliding it loose, he added, "Not that I expect I'll win then, either."

She poked him in the stomach, not that it made any impression upon him. "So, Husband, since you've decided I may know your plans, do you intend to tell me now?"

He gave a huge sigh. "If I must." He caught her hands in his. "Who knows what you might do to me otherwise?"

Thus it was that Connor found himself escorting his wife, along with his troops and those of Sir Robert de Montfort, to a meeting with Hugh MacCarthy and Aidan O'Neill. They'd agreed to meet in a large open area not far from Gerald's Keep for the proposed purpose of coming to terms over the release of Connor's "prisoners"—Kieran MacCarthy and Domnal O'Neill.

The promise of an alliance with Connor, as well as Lord Rannulf FitzClifford, had been enough to sway Sir Robert into lending his aid. After the way the MacCarthys had wreaked havoc in the vicinity, Connor had no doubt that de Montfort would be happy to thwart Hugh MacCarthy any way he could.

Kieran and Domnal seemed glad to be involved in stopping the madness that Dermot MacCarthy had set in motion and his brother seemed determined to bring to fruition. In fact, the two young men had contributed a great deal to the scheme.

As their party crested the last hill before the meeting place, Connor glanced behind him at Moira. Mounted pillion behind Will, she looked tired, but he couldn't miss the trace of exhilaration in her bright blue eyes. He wished he dared allow her to ride with him, but he didn't know exactly how the meeting might unfold. MacCarthy might come after him, and Connor didn't want to endanger her more.

Nor would it be wise for both Brenna's parents to be together, lest they make one easy target.

MacCarthy's troops streamed over the opposite hillside and onto the plain, spreading out in a line facing Connor's party. Will kept Moira behind them, surrounded by a well-armed group of fighters—the best warriors from Gerald's Keep, any one of whom would gladly lay down his life for their valiant lady. Domnal and Kiernan were equally well guarded, encircled by the best of the men Connor had brought from l'Eau Clair.

Connor urged his mount forward, Sir Ivor and Sir Robert on either side of him, the line his men had formed closing up behind them. He singled out the bearded Irishman he'd battled outside Gerald's Keep, for he knew in his bones the man must be Hugh MacCarthy—had known since they'd fought. The fact that he rode flanked by Aidan and a man who was obviously Aidan's brother Finan simply confirmed his assumption.

"So you're Connor FitzClifford," MacCarthy shouted. "If I'd known that the other night, I'd have made certain you left the field in a shroud."

Connor gave a wry laugh. The posturing fool! "You had your chance, MacCarthy, but you're not up to the task. If you could have done so, you would have," he said bluntly.

MacCarthy waved away Connor's comment. "I've come for my kin, Norman, mine and the O'Neills'. The babe and its mother, and our kinsmen you took captive." MacCarthy looked past Connor. "Moira! Show yourself, lass," he bellowed. "Come—you've no need to hide behind them now that your own kinsmen have come for you."

Connor held his breath and prayed. He'd warned Moira

that MacCarthy might try to speak with her, had cautioned her to choose her words with care should she decide to reply. But he really didn't know what she'd say.

"I'm already with my kinsmen, Hugh—the only ones who matter to me," she cried. "Can you not give up this senseless scheme of Dermot's and leave us be?"

MacCarthy's face reddened and his eyes grew cold. "'Tis my duty to carry out my brother's wishes. And 'tis *your* brothers' decision for you to join us, to give over yourself and the child—and Gerald's Keep—into our hands. Once you do, all will be as it should be." He urged his mount forward, fixing his gaze upon Connor, and spat on the ground. "And these damned Normans can go back where they belong."

Connor slid his dagger from his boot and held it loosely in his hand, his elbow resting upon the saddlebow. "We *are* where we belong," he said in an even voice. "This land is my brother's. It was my mother's and my grandfather's before that. We will not give it up," he said flatly. "Nor will I give over to you my wife and daughter."

"Your wife?" MacCarthy roared. "Daughter? You've wed her, and the child has been born? By Christ's eyeballs—" Aidan reached over and grabbed MacCarthy by the back of the tunic when he lunged toward Connor "—she could be a widow in a trice, Norman."

Connor remained at his ease, merely glancing over his shoulder at his force—more numerous and far better armed than MacCarthy's. "She will not. I intend to be a good and faithful husband to Moira for many years to come. I'll see to it," he vowed.

MacCarthy sank back into his saddle, his face still contorted with rage. "Then show the child to me, that I may judge for myself whether 'tis my brother's daughter," he demanded.

"She is *my* daughter, MacCarthy. And Moira is my wife. My family remains with me." Connor didn't bother to hide his disdain. "Admit it—you've lost it all, not that you ever had it. Gerald's Keep is not Moira's to give to you, nor would she do so in any case. Did you truly believe you could abuse her and her people, cause them to live in a state of siege for months, then expect her, without hesitation, to give her entire world into your hands at your bidding?"

"Not likely, Hugh," Moira called. "'Tis nigh impossible, in fact. I suggest you give up now, for my daughter shall never be yours, no matter who fathered her."

MacCarthy growled. "I simply want to see Gerald's Keep returned to my family, my blood."

Connor shook his head. "I've heard many things about you, Hugh MacCarthy, but I'd not heard you were a stupid man." He leaned forward, investing his expression, his voice, with the steely determination that had brought him from weakling to warrior in a few short years. "I know your plans, MacCarthy—all of them. I also know you haven't the men to carry them out, now that you've lost the element of surprise. And lest it escape your notice, I have the support of the FitzCliffords and of the earl of Pembroke behind me. If you take Gerald's Keep, they'll harry you until you'll be glad to hand it back to them. You cannot win," he stated. "'Tis up to you to decide what you want to lose."

"Gerald's Keep was ours once," MacCarthy blustered. "I—"

"If Brenna is indeed of your blood, you'll be glad to know that one day Gerald's Keep will be hers. 'Tis the only way anyone with a drop of MacCarthy blood will ever rule there again." Connor settled back in the saddle and rammed his dagger into its sheath. "One other thing—what

I have, I keep. Remember that fact. This topic is no longer open for discussion.''

Pinning MacCarthy with his gaze, Connor sat and waited. 'Twas clear that Hugh's force hadn't the power to overcome his own—else they'd already have tried, he had no doubt. Would MacCarthy even recall the other reason for this meeting? he wondered. Or had his ''concern'' for Kieran and Domnal merely been an excuse for him to agree to this encounter?

MacCarthy edged his horse closer to Aidan's and bent to confer with him. Their discussion, while too quiet to hear, was obviously heated, for both men gestured wildly, their expressions fierce.

Finally Aidan moved away from MacCarthy and prodded his mount forward. ''The O'Neills accept you into the family, milord,'' he said, his voice tinged with a mocking tone.

Connor stifled a wry laugh. Moira had told him that her brothers always chose the side that would benefit them most, he recalled. It appeared that hadn't changed. ''I'm sure my wife will be pleased that her brothers no longer want me dead.''

Scowling, Aidan shifted in the saddle. ''Indeed. That being so, we'd be grateful if you would return Domnal to us.''

''Domnal?'' Connor called. The jingle of harness heralded Domnal riding forward to join him. Connor glanced over at his young brother by marriage, noting that he appeared completely at his ease.

''Aye, milord?'' he asked, smiling.

''Do you wish to return to your brothers?''

''Nay, milord. If I'd wanted to stay with them, I never would have run away in the first place.''

Hard-pressed not to grin himself, Connor nodded. ''It

looks to me as though Domnal doesn't wish to go with you, Aidan. He's welcome to stay with us, of course.''

''Thank you, milord.'' Domnal nodded, turned his mount and joined the others behind Connor's wall of soldiers.

MacCarthy looked fit to burst, he noted with amusement. Before he could say anything else—before he knew what to say next—Hugh grunted. ''I suppose you want to stay with the Normans as well, Kieran?'' He sneered. ''At least I know *you* didn't go running off to join them when things didn't go your way,'' he added, casting a scorn-filled glare at Aidan and Finan.

Kieran rode up to the wall of men, but no closer. ''Nay, Cousin, I don't wish to stay with them. But I don't know that I care to return to serve with you, either, not if you continue this foolishness that Dermot started. It's done with, Hugh. You didn't win everything you wanted, but you haven't lost, either.'' He straightened and stared across the expanse at his kinsmen. ''Did you honestly want to marry Moira? No offense meant, milady,'' he said to Moira. ''She's far too strong-willed for you, Hugh. By the saints, you'd kill each other in a month! And a child as well? 'Tis not your way, Hugh, not now. 'Twas Dermot's dream, not yours. Accept what Lord Connor has offered so we can go home.''

Connor watched in silence as Hugh MacCarthy pondered his cousin's words. Perhaps Kieran's plea made more of an impression than his own—or added weight to his own words, more like.

Whatever the reason, he knew the instant MacCarthy decided. ''I'll leave you be, Norman. And perhaps some day—once she's a bit older—you might see fit to let me meet my niece. I'll never do the lass any harm, my word on it.'' He stared hard past Connor; looking back, Connor saw that Will had brought Moira up to the line of men.

MacCarthy bowed to her, surprising Connor—and Moira, to judge by her expression. Then, giving a wild cry, the Irishman wheeled his mount and led his men away over the hillside.

Kieran spurred his horse and rode after them, leaving Connor's forces on the plain.

Will rode up beside Connor's mount. "Here, milord—take your wife before she drives me mad," he said, grinning all the while. "I vow, you've wed a fighter, milord. I'd never have guessed she just gave birth, the way she kept trying to wrest the reins out of my hands and take control!"

Moira poked him in the ribs, then soothed the sting by giving him a smacking kiss on the cheek. Will's face grew red, and though his mouth moved, no words escaped. "I thought that might silence you," she said. Laughing gaily, she held out her arms for Connor to take her.

He did, gladly. "We won, Husband," she murmured, nestling into his lap.

He pressed his lips to hers and kissed her deeply. "Aye, Wife, we did." He caught her veil as it slid off her hair, the wind sending the fragrant mass streaming about them. Her cheeks alive with color, her eyes bright, Moira smiled at him and sent his heart soaring. "I've won it all."

Epilogue

"Come here, Brenna." Hands outstretched, Connor coaxed his daughter to her feet. Moira, seated nearby on a blanket, held her breath as the child wavered, gifting him with a grin Moira knew would melt her father's heart, as it always did her own.

"Papa!" Hands waving wildly, she set out toward him over the smooth grass, managing three steps before her legs gave out and she landed on her backside.

Her lips quivering, she glanced from her father to her mother. Evidently she decided 'twasn't worth the bother to cry, for she gave a trill of laughter and set off on hands and knees toward her mother.

Connor rose up on his knees and scooped Brenna into his arms, then dropped down beside Moira and settled their child upon his chest.

The child she carried beneath her heart chose that moment to kick her hard, bringing a smile to her lips and her hands to her rounded belly.

Connor shifted and sat up, cradling Brenna upon his shoulder. "Do you need help with this one, too?" he asked, his hand already settling over the babe.

The soothing motion of his palm worked its magic for

this child, as it had done for Brenna. ''Aye, I need you, Husband—always,'' Moira murmured, reaching to draw him close. ''I love you.''

His gentle smile wrapped itself about her heart. ''And I love you, dearling.'' He brushed his lips over hers, then gathered her to his side. ''All of you.''

Moira glanced out over the sun-swept headland and the sea. After years of darkness, how had she found this light, this joy? Her present—her future—were right beside her, within her. She shifted her gaze to Connor, the man who had given her love and contentment, passion and pleasure. Smiling, she held her joy close and savored the life they'd made together.

* * * * *